BY SARAH GRAVES

THE GIRLS SHE LEFT BEHIND

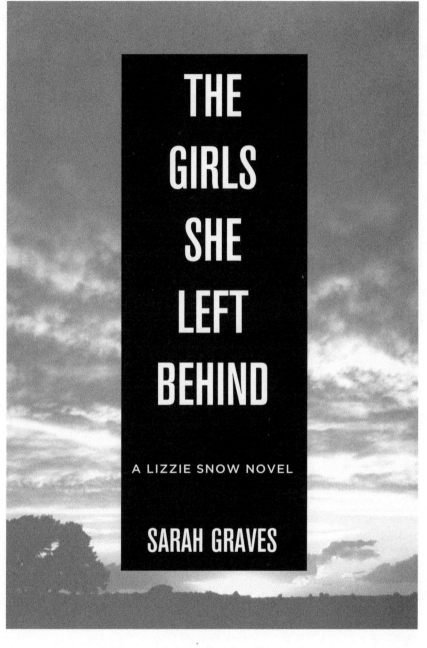

THE
GIRLS
SHE
LEFT
BEHIND

A LIZZIE SNOW NOVEL

SARAH GRAVES

BANTAM BOOKS • NEW YORK

Published in the United States by Bantam Books, an imprint of Random House, a division of Penguin Random House LLC, New York.

BANTAM BOOKS and the HOUSE colophon are registered trademarks of Penguin Random House LLC.

Library of Congress Cataloging-in-Publication Data
Graves, Sarah
The girls she left behind : a Lizzie Snow novel / Sarah Graves.
pages ; cm
ISBN 978-0-553-39043-8
eBook ISBN 978-0-553-39044-5
I. Title.
PS3557.R2897G57 2016
813'.54—dc23   2015029898

Printed in the United States of America on acid-free paper

randomhousebooks.com

987654321

First Edition

Book design by Jo Anne Metsch
Title page art: © FreeImages.com/Layne Turner

This book is for George and Penny

PROLOGUE

It wasn't even my idea. Nothing ever was, when my cousin Cam was around.

Come on, she mouthed impatiently at me, rolling her heavily made-up eyes from the doorway of St. Anselm's basement meeting room in New Haven, Connecticut. Under the room's buzzing fluorescent lights, I sat on a hard metal folding chair pulled up to a long table with a dozen other teenage girls, all of us knitting industriously.

Cam spread her hands wide, making a face at me: *Well? Are you coming or not?*

We'd just turned fifteen that summer and were often mistaken for sisters, both of us slim and fox-faced with wavy dark hair, brown eyes, and the kind of smooth, faintly olive-complected skin that never got pimples. Our mothers, who really were sisters, had looked alike too when they were young and, like us, had been raised to be sure that their necklines were modest, their skirts weren't too tight, and their hems always touched the floor when they knelt.

Not that Cam ever knelt much. That was the difference between us. I was the good girl, always agonizing over my sins, half dying with anxious guilt while I waited outside the gloomy confessional on Saturday mornings and floaty-feeling with relief afterward, only to feel the sly pinch of renewed temptation moments later, as if the devil liked a clean slate. I did all my homework and practiced my piano lessons religiously, too, the mocking image of unreachable perfection always spoiling any pleasure I might have taken in any of it, and for fun I read the gory parts of Butler's *Lives of the Saints.*

Cam smoked stolen cigarettes and put on eyeliner and mascara the minute she left her house each day, and walked like she was dancing to the beat of some music I couldn't hear. Made up to look older, she snuck us both into a popular downtown club one Friday night by whispering something filthy to the guy checking IDs at the door. When somebody there reported us as underage she ran out the back exit laughing, dragging me along.

She was always getting the two of us into things like that, and though I loved her extravagantly I was a little scared of her, too: what she might do, what I might end up doing with her. Cam was very good at persuading me to try things I'd have never dared otherwise, and the night I lost her was no exception.

I'll go without you, she warned me from the damp-smelling basement hallway, her dark eyes sparkling with mischief. *I mean it. Last chance.*

I glanced nervously around at the other girls, all of us knitting with scratchy, mismatched yarn while our bottoms chilled on the metal folding chairs. Even in July it was cold down there, the old stone walls of the church sweating icy droplets that trickled down and puddled on the poured-concrete floor.

Hurry up, Cam threatened, narrow-eyed, her lips tightening to a thin, mean line and her chin thrust out warningly in the same way that our mothers' did when they got mad at us.

I looked around again, shrugging. *I can't.* We were making warm hats for the little pagan babies in Africa; it was an article of our faith that pagan babies required clumsily knitted headgear, no matter the climate.

Cam sighed elaborately—*All right then, be that way, see if I care*—before she turned away and vanished back into the hall's musty gloom.

Quietly I placed my knitting needles on the table in front of me and got up. Most of the other girls had completed their hats and were working on the tassels, but I had done only four rows on account of having to rip out so many mistakes.

I wasn't friends with any of these girls, particularly, and I hadn't done anything to make anyone want to tell on me. So no one was watching me, and our group leader, Mrs. Hart, was leaning back in her chair with her chin on her chest, snoring. Probably they'd think I was just going to use the restroom, if they noticed me leaving at all.

Smelling of cigarettes, Cam grabbed me as soon as I reached the hall. "Cripes, what are you waiting for, d'you want Creepers to catch us?"

Creepers was what she called Father Crepinski, the pastor of St. Anselm's. And sure enough, just as she said it we both heard the heavy old wooden church door upstairs groan open and his dragging step—he'd had a leg permanently paralyzed by polio as a young child—start unevenly across the tiled vestibule and down the stairs toward us. *Ka-thump.* Pause. *Ka-thump.*

"Come *on*," Cam whispered urgently as she scurried toward the other stairwell. If I didn't want to get caught with her—Cam had already been banned permanently from parish youth activities for being a bad influence—I had to follow.

Five minutes later the two of us were hustling along Whalley Avenue as fast as we could. "What if someone notices I'm gone?" I worried.

"Oh, please," Cam retorted, her voice full of scorn. "They'll just think you're upstairs in the chapel praying or something."

At her words I cringed inwardly. It was the kind of soft, warm early evening when everything good seems possible; typical of me to be worrying about something bad, her tone said.

Besides, she was right about me and the chapel.

She lit another smoke, cupping the flame expertly. "Anyway, you actually think they'll miss you? One great thing about being boring like you," she added, "is that no one notices if you're not around."

She spewed an acrid gray plume from her lipsticked mouth. "Besides, they've got the Creepster down there with them now, probably he brought along his guitar and they'll all sing folk songs together. I mean if he's not too senile to remember them."

I giggled reflexively, feeling a pang of sympathy for poor old Father Crepinski. Only the previous Sunday he'd confusedly begun saying the start of Mass in Latin the way he'd learned it in the seminary a hundred years or so ago, instead of in English.

Kyrie eleison, Christe eleison ... well, Greek for that part, actually, don't ask me why. Lord, have mercy, it meant, which I knew because I liked the old languages much better. They sounded mysterious to me, as it seemed that all things related to religion should, while the English version was more like someone trying to write poetry with a dull crayon, gripping it in a clumsy fist.

But I didn't say so to Cam. She didn't care about things like that. As far as she was concerned if you couldn't eat it, drink it, wear it, smoke it, dance to it, or (briefly, and only to tease the guy) make out with it, it didn't exist.

So instead: "Where did you tell them we were going?" I asked. When we went out like this, Cam handled the alibis.

She laughed carelessly, eyeing a cute guy in a convertible as he drove by us. "Well, first I told my mom that I was going over to your house for a sleepover, and then I went there and told your mom that I was picking you up at the church hall and taking you home to my house for the night."

So no one would be waiting up for us, she meant. It was the other thing that Cam could do really well: make you believe her.

Around us the standard Whalley Avenue crush of early-Friday-evening traffic filled the oncoming night: cars full of kids our age or a little older, thumping with the bass notes of the music blaring inside. Exhaust fumes and oily restaurant aromas mingled with the cigarette smoke Cam exhaled, and above it all the stars were just now coming out one by one in the deepening blue sky.

She turned happily to me. "So we are free, free, free," she sang, her dark eyes gleaming wickedly as she nudged me a little too hard with her elbow. "Come on, Janie, can't you smile even a little?"

I tried, but it couldn't have been very convincing. It was glorious to be out here at night on my own with no one telling me what to do or how to do it, I would admit that much. When I went out with my mother in the evening she was always terrified of everything, and every other word out of her mouth was about how I should be careful—did she really think that at my age I would get kidnapped, or hit by a car?—or that something I liked was an occasion of sin.

But by that summer I was starting to realize that you didn't just shrug off your whole upbringing so easily. It took work and dedication to be as free as Cam was, and I wasn't sure I was up to it. So I just trotted along silently with her until we reached the walkway leading into Edgewood Park.

Away from the street, the smells were of freshly cut grass, damp earth, and chlorine from the public swimming pool, closed now for the night. Along the white concrete path curving in among the trees the old-fashioned streetlights glowed hazily, making the park look magical. In the nearby shadows fireflies bobbed like tiny lanterns flickering.

There was a public dance being held at the tennis courts that night, and in the distance I heard the band tuning up; it all made my heart race happily but a little nervously, too, like something wonderful was about to happen.

Wonderful but scary. "Somebody got raped down there last week," said Cam as we hurried along the path toward the music. She pointed into a secluded glade at the foot of a small hill, densely leafy and dark where the lights didn't reach.

"She was walking here all alone, late," Cam added. "And I mean, really. I'm sorry for what happened to her and all, but can you imagine?"

Doing anything so stupid, she meant. It had already occurred to me that this was why Cam brought me along with her to places where guys might hit on her, so she wouldn't be alone. I could get help for her if she needed it, or she could use me for a handy excuse if somebody was a pest: She had to take care of her cousin.

I looked up into the night sky full of stars, feeling the air like warm lotion on my skin. "I don't know. I'll bet it's really nice being out here all alone late at night."

Cam made a scornful sound. "Yeah, right. If you want to get *attacked* by some *pervert.* And as if that wouldn't be bad enough, d'you know what they *do* to you if you get raped? After, I mean?"

Silhouetted by the headlights of cars heading down to the parking lot by the tennis courts, clusters of laughing young people flocked toward the music. "No, what?"

From her tone I could already tell she was about to drop some R-rated bombshell on me, something I probably didn't want to hear about and wouldn't like at all when I did; it might even give me night-mares.

But I was still curious. "Come on, Cam, what?"

She gave me a dark look. "They take you to the hospital and tie you to a bed and cut your clothes off. *All*," she emphasized, "your clothes."

I stared at her, horrified. "Why would they do that?"

"So they can *examine* you," she replied, sounding gratified by my reaction. "With *instruments*."

She shuddered theatrically, and as we approached the tennis courts where the band was now playing she provided more details: the personal questions they asked, worse than anything I'd ever encountered in the confessional, and the restraints they used.

"Strapped in," she emphasized, "they *strap* you into them."

How she might possibly have learned such a thing didn't even occur to me, much less that it might not be true. Cam was my go-to source for adult information, the certainty in her voice always making up for any small deficiencies in her actual knowledge.

"You know what I'd do to the guy, though, if I could? The guy who did it? I'd . . ."

She went on to tell me at length and in terrible detail what awful punishments she would inflict on the attacker.

"Anyway," she finished authoritatively, "take my advice, you little dope, and just don't go to any dark places alone, and what happened to that girl won't ever happen to you."

Now that she'd terrified me sufficiently to be sure I was hanging on her every word, she spun away from me, eager to join the throngs inside the tennis court fence. But I hung back.

"What's wrong?" she demanded, half turning to me again. From the tennis courts came the first twanging of a guitar solo, and it was as if her whole body was already in the grip of the music, the summer evening's unspoiled promise, her own innocence.

Despite her self-assured manner she had been brought up the same way I had: If you liked something, it must be wrong, and if you did it anyway something bad would happen to you because of it. But Cam had rejected all that, not stopping to wonder if any part of it might be true—that what you wanted could hurt you, whether or not it was a sin. So she was defenseless.

I just didn't realize it yet.

"Come on, Janie, don't be such a baby," she said. "It's just a dance, for pete's sake. What do you think, there's going to be a rapist waiting for you in there, too, or something?"

Which was what I did think, actually, because the people around us looked friendly enough now, didn't they? All happy and laughing . . .

But I didn't know any of them, those dark shrubberies were very near, and—as my mother always liked to say—you never could tell what that stranger might be thinking.

"Come on, Jane," Cam coaxed again. She might act impatient, but she was used to my being a chicken about everything at first. "We'll just go in for a little while, and if there's anything weird about it or if you don't think it's any fun then we'll both go home. Okay?"

She smiled into my face, so funny and pretty and most of all brave that I couldn't resist her. Cam would do anything, take any dare; once she'd climbed with some boys from school to the top of the water tower at East Rock and spray-painted her name up there, then took a picture of herself with the disposable camera she'd gotten for her twelfth birthday to prove it.

Later when school started a girl in her class called the photograph a fake. A few weeks after that, on a rainy day, the girl somehow ended up being pushed into the mud. All the way in. And when she was asked who did it, the girl wouldn't say.

Because she was scared to.

"Okay," I replied at last, and Cam smiled, satisfied.

Like I said, I couldn't resist.

Somebody had a cooler full of beer poured into Coke bottles, though the dance had been billed as alcohol-free. Cops cruised the tennis courts' perimeter where, beyond the bushes landscaped along the fence, the sounds of couples giggling together mingled with the smell of marijuana. But from the officers' casual attitudes it was clear they were on the scene only to make sure nobody got hurt.

And at first no one did.

Cam danced like crazy, flinging her arms around and stomping her feet opposite one guy after another, not letting any of them bird-dog her, as she called it whenever some boy tried acting romantic.

I stood by the fence alone, trying to look as if I preferred it that way, that I didn't care. No one wanted to dance with me because even though Cam and I looked very alike, it was obvious to everyone which one of us was the firecracker and which the dud.

Once in a while Cam came over and told me impatiently to get out there, for God's sake—a little fun wouldn't kill me.

But in my own way I was having fun, sort of. I found out about the beer by taking a swig and then another, the stuff going down my parched throat scouringly cold. The night all around me was warm and wonderfully strange, filled with faces I didn't know and vibrant with the loud music.

I was, I told myself wistfully, simply the sort of person who enjoyed watching. After a while Cam seemed to tire of it all, too, returning to me with her mascara smeared, her eyes bright, and her face reddened with heat.

She grabbed the beer out of my hand and chugged it. "Okay. I'm done, let's get out of here."

She dragged her arm across her sweaty forehead theatrically. "Look at you, though, silly. Did you even dance once?"

By then the scene had gotten rowdy, the band drunk and just goofing around onstage. A fight started at one end of the crowd and a girl wept wretchedly at the other, her friends all crowded around her glaring accusingly at a boy who looked miserable and defensive, unable to get near.

"Sure, I danced," I lied, but Cam just smirked knowingly at me.

"Right," she drawled, "sure you did." She finished my beer and tossed the bottle away carelessly. "Come on, baby, let's get going. It's way past your bedtime."

We skirted around the thick bushes lining the tennis court fence and made our way toward the parking lot, the shortest route in the direction of home. But when we got near the rows of cars lined up in the lot, Cam stopped suddenly.

"Hey, who's that?" She was eyeing a guy who sat in a gray van at the lot's far end, watching us.

He was cute, kind of, and pretty harmless looking, with wavy blond hair and a sly, knowing smile that he flashed at us while gnawing a fried chicken leg. He seemed sleepy, as if he'd just woken up, and mildly amused by the scene: the park, the summer night with the kids out in it.

But I still didn't like the looks of him. Maybe it was just because he seemed too old—in his thirties at least—to be leering at girls our age. Or maybe it was like the nuns at St. Anselm's always said: that my guardian angel was warning me.

The guy jerked his head lazily, beckoning us over. "Hey."

I took a cautious step back. Cam, though, had drunk enough beer to make her feisty; apparently my bottle hadn't been her first.

Feistier than usual, even. "Hey, what?" she demanded right back at him, her chin jutting out and her voice sounding snotty. "What do you want?"

Loser, her tone added clearly as she stalked toward the van. Even on her best behavior, Cam took no nonsense from anyone.

And now she was drunk. Fists bunched, she stomped over to the open driver's-side window and stuck her face belligerently up at the guy, who was still gnawing the chicken leg.

"What're you, a pervert? Some kind of weirdo, sitting here jerking off while all the young girls go by 'cause you can't get one of your own?"

His grin widened sleepily and he put the chicken leg down. "Aw, come on, honey, what's the problem? Don't be that way." But that only made her madder.

"Don't be that way," she mimicked nastily while I watched in growing alarm though I wasn't sure why, my mouth suddenly dry and my heart thudding.

"Cam," I said. "Cam, we should . . ."

The bushes growing thickly between the parking lot and the tennis courts blocked the view, and right now everyone was on the other side of them, the lot full of cars but empty, just at that moment, of people.

And he'd parked, I noticed now, way down at the end, in the one place where the streetlights didn't reach, so the van was in shadow. It was as if he'd stationed himself there deliberately.

Cam thumped her fists hard against the driver's-side door and spun away. "Freak," she muttered loud enough for him to hear, which was when I really knew we were in trouble, because although his face didn't change at all, his eyes did.

Then he got out, still with that lazy grin, moving toward us slowly but confidently like some big cat that knows it doesn't have to do very much before it leaps.

"Cam, come *on*," I yelled, starting to run, but I'd gone only a few panicked steps before her muffled scream stopped me in my tracks.

When I turned back, he had the van's rear door open and was muscling her roughly in. "Jane!" she managed to cry.

That's when he hit her. The punch snapped her head sideways, and I saw her face go blank. As she sagged in his grip he finished loading her into the cargo compartment, slammed the door shut, then strolled casually back up to the driver's door and got behind the wheel again.

I tried screaming, I really did. But I was so frozen in fear and disbelief that I couldn't even speak. I stood paralyzed. My mouth moved but no sound came from it as he reversed out of his parking space. He pulled the van up alongside me, then past.

But as he started to drive away, suddenly the spell broke. "No! Stop! Help! Someone . . ."

A howl of electronic feedback from the guitar amplifiers at the dance drowned my cries, and I knew that in another moment he would be gone. So I did the only thing I could think of: I hurled myself at the van, running straight at the driver's-side door.

I hit the van's door panel hard with my whole body, grabbed the side mirror, and clung on desperately, hooking the fingers of my right hand over the window opening and hauling myself up until my elbow was inside, shouting into his face.

"I saw your license plate, I'll tell the police!"

I hadn't seen it. But it was the only threat that I could think of that might possibly stop him. And it did.

Slowly his head turned toward me. I clung there sobbing and kicking the door panel as hard as I could while the van still crept forward. Finally, with a look of disgust he hit the brake, pushed my elbow out of the window so I dangled from the mirror and fell, then got out and stood over me.

The next thing I knew he had gathered me up in his arms. I was crying so hard I couldn't breathe, kicking weakly and trying to get away from him, but it was no use. He was strong, pinning my arms to my sides, and still no one had come into the parking lot to save me.

To save us. He held me so tightly that I couldn't get enough breath in to scream as he dragged me around the front of the van, yanked the passenger-side door open, shoved me in, and slammed it. Scrabbling for the door handle I found that there was none, only a ragged hole in the panel where it had been removed, and as I leapt for the one on the driver's side I met him getting in.

I shrank back against the door, and I will never in my life forget the look he gave me then, not saying anything, just . . . looking. Like he was inspecting me to see if I was worth keeping or not, and if I wasn't—

There was an open bottle of kiwi juice in the van console's beverage holder; he grabbed it and shoved it at me. "Drink."

His eyes were the deep, marine blue of Long Island Sound on a clear day. There was no question of defying him; I took the juice bottle with both trembling hands, unable to look away from him as I lifted it shakily to my lips.

But I must not have done it fast enough for him. "Drink the juice, honey," he said softly, starting the van rolling slowly forward again. "Or I'll slit your throat open for you and pour it down your gullet."

I obeyed, trying to control my gasping sobs long enough to swallow. The lukewarm juice had something gritty and bitter in it, like Kool-Aid with some of the powder still undissolved.

He pulled out of the park, looking both ways before hitting the gas. I wiped my arm across my snot-smeared face. "Wh-what do you w-want?"

Like I didn't already know. This was it, the thing that my mother had always warned me about: If you let a strange man get near you—or God forbid one of them should ever get you into his car— then it was all over. He would rape you and murder you and bury you in a shallow grave somewhere, guaranteed.

Or so she'd insisted, shaking a finger at me to drive the message home. And now here was the proof: A heavy metal grille divided the van's passenger compartment from the rear cargo area. I heard Cam taking labored breaths back there, the sound like air slowly bubbling through thick muck. Once in a while she moaned.

"I have some money," I tried again tremblingly, even though I didn't. By now we were pulling onto I-95 at the on-ramp before the bridge, headed east.

No one knew where we were. Because of Cam's lie, for a while no one would even know we were missing—not until tomorrow. And by the time anyone figured out what had happened . . .

Although if my mother was right, no one would ever know for sure. DISAPPEARED, the headlines would say. HAVE YOU SEEN ME? the MISSING posters on light poles and in store windows would read.

But only for a little while. After that, some other kid would vanish and we'd mostly be forgotten, pushed off the charts by a newer runaway teen or snatched toddler.

It happened all the time. "It's a lot of money," I lied. "If you'd just let us go, I could go home and get it and—"

"Shut up." His face intent, he stared straight ahead, hitting the gas hard. "Just shut up and do what I say. It'll go easier for you."

Which I didn't like the sound of one bit. Headlights glared, then broke into wild, multicolored spinning pinwheels. I thought about my chances if I grabbed the steering wheel and yanked it, got us into an accident. But then suddenly I felt sick, too dizzy and sick to do anything.

Anything at all. My ears rang like gongs. *That juice,* I thought woozily. My eyelids slammed shut with a bang that echoed through my brain and my head felt swimmy. And then . . .

Then I was gone.

Fifteen years later I still had nightmares about it: long, bloodily insistent shockers that ended with a hand flattening itself to the glass of a dark window, then clawing its way down. Awake, I walked around with a slide show running in my head, girls' faces screaming and pleading. And then, after all that time . . .

THREE SAVED FROM BASEMENT PRISON, said the breaking-news crawl on the TV, and HOMEOWNER QUESTIONED IN WOMEN'S CAPTIVITY.

Both my parents and my grandparents had passed on by then, leaving me their house. Sitting in the same threadbare living-room recliner that I'd been using ever since I had graduated from my high chair, I stared at the TV screen, barely believing. But it was true:

Earlier that day a young woman had managed to get out of a house in a run-down neighborhood—only a few miles from where I now sat—and flag down a squad car. On the TV screen she and another girl were being helped into a police van while my long-ago kidnapper, still slim, even-featured, and yellow-haired just as I recalled him, stood talking with a policeman.

He looked cordial but cautious, as if while he chatted he was trying to come up with some innocent reason for having two girls locked in his basement. Each time he glanced at the policeman you could see he was gauging the cop's response.

The officer didn't smile. Then a third girl came out. *Cam . . .*

Thinner than I remembered but with the same narrow face and large, dark eyes, she cast an unreadable look at the man who had grabbed us, then allowed herself to be guided into the police van with the first two young women.

Cam is alive . . .

More officers approached. As the van left with Cam and the other two girls, the cops surrounded Henry Gemerle, who'd begun ruining my life fifteen years earlier in that park and had just now finished the job.

Because of course I was happy and relieved that, somehow, my cousin Cam had survived. But now that she had, she could tell people what I'd done, couldn't she? That on that night all those years ago I'd left her behind and never said anything about it.

No one would ever understand my side of it: that I'd been terrified, traumatized, drugged. That I'd been not much more than a child, that I'd thought for sure Cam was already dead when I got out of his house, and that I'd kept silent because I hadn't dared tell anyone what had happened or what he'd done.

That I'd been afraid to. But now if people found out, I'd lose my job, probably, or be forced to leave it on account of the terrible publicity. I'd lose what few acquaintances I had and even my home, since I would never be able to stay where anyone knew me. I might—the awful thought closed my throat in terror—I might even go to jail.

All of which meant that somehow, fifteen years after I'd left my cousin Cam in the hands of a monster and then kept silent about it, I had to fix things so she wouldn't tell on me.

Or so she couldn't.

THE GIRLS SHE LEFT BEHIND

ONE

Sleet needles lanced through the January night, gleaming slantwise in the headlights of the cars making their hesitant way along the street outside. Splattering against the big plate-glass front window of Aroostook County sheriff's deputy Lizzie Snow's storefront office, the wet ice bits made a sound like tiny fists weakly hammering to get in.

Just another fine evening in Bearkill, Maine, Lizzie thought glumly, peering through the streaming glass as Dylan Hudson's familiar figure came striding into view. Galoshes splashing in the slush, the tall plainclothes detective's shoulders hunched sharply under his topcoat and black-and-white-striped scarf, ice-melt trickling in a shining stream off the brim of his hat.

At the sight of him she let the familiar lurch of feeling go through her, then set it firmly aside. Emotions were one thing but actions were entirely another, she told herself sternly.

"Hi." He swung in, shedding showers of icy droplets as he crossed the sparsely furnished office. Except for the half dozen WANTED posters on the bulletin board and the police scanner on a shelf, the white-painted walls and gray industrial carpet made the place look like an insurance agency's not-very-successful branch office.

Dylan deposited the large white paper shopping bag he carried on her desk. Delicious aromas floated from the bag.

"Hi, yourself." She should not have let him come, but the miserable night made his driving the ninety miles back to Bangor unwise even for a Maine state cop, and his promise of Thai food delivered to her office had sealed the deal.

"So, anything shakin'?" He pulled out the familiar white cardboard cartons, pushing aside the flotsam on her desk to make two places amid the clutter.

"Couple things." Last from the bag were a pair of Tsingtaos, the cold brown bottles dripping condensation, and a bottle opener.

"Fire crews're still out," she added with a glance at the scanner on the shelf above her desk. "But wrapping it up."

Despite the wintry mix pelting outside now, northern Maine was in the grip of a serious long-term dry spell; a rash of brush fires around Bearkill had made chatter on the police band lively all day. But since the sky had opened up late this afternoon the radio spat only routine local dispatches.

The cash register slip in the shopping bag said the food had come from Bangor. "Dylan, how'd you keep this stuff hot? And the beer so—"

Well, but it was no problem keeping things cold in this kind of weather, was it? On a night like tonight, back in Boston that cop scanner would be hopping with more minor vehicle mishaps than you could shake a tow truck at.

Here in Bearkill, if you slid into a ditch most likely your neighbor pulled you out. "Microwave," Dylan explained.

He gestured toward the combination convenience store and gas station down the block. It and a dozen other small businesses made up the bulk of downtown Bearkill's commercial activity.

If you could call it activity. Situated in the very rooftop of Maine at the edge of the Great North Woods, Bearkill had once been the thriving center of a booming lumber industry. But the boom had gone bust, and now drab storefront tenants like the Cut-n-Run hair salon, the Paper Chase office and party supply store (BALLOON BOUQUETS OUR

SPECIALTY!), a tae kwon do studio, and the New to You used-clothing exchange dominated what remained.

"There's a few pretty beat-looking forest service guys and gals in that convenience store right now," Dylan added, sounding sympathetic.

The combination gas station and snack vendor was called—really, a less appetizing name could not have been found, Lizzie thought—the Go-Mart. "What I heard, they've been out trenching in the fields and forests for nearly twenty-four hours," he said.

By this time in a normal year, the fire danger in the area would be long over. But it had not been a normal year.

Dylan shook his head ruefully. "Digging firebreaks, that's no-kidding hard labor. Remind me of that the next time you hear me bitching about my job, will you?"

"Um. Yeah." On the shelf with the scanner was a framed commendation from the Boston PD, where until two months earlier Lizzie had been a member of the elite Homicide/Violent Crimes Investigation Unit. Beside those items, a Lucite stand held a snapshot of a little blond girl.

The little blond girl was the reason that Lizzie was no longer in Boston, and no longer a homicide cop. "They're catching a break now, though," she added, waving out at the sleet.

She debated telling Dylan about the other thing she'd been working today. If she did, she'd have a much harder time getting rid of him after dinner.

On the other hand, a second opinion might not be such a bad idea. "Listen, I've got a local teenager gone missing."

Just weeks earlier she'd been hired to be the eyes and ears of the Aroostook County Sheriff's Department here in Bearkill. And why an ex–Boston homicide cop had turned out to be exactly the right person for the job was a whole other story.

But it was not the one preoccupying her now. "Fourteen-year-old—you know the type, she thinks she's twenty."

Northern Maine, with thousands of square miles of forests, mountains, and farm fields sparsely dotted by tiny, struggling towns much like Bearkill, was so different from Boston that it might as well have been on some other planet. But teenagers were the same just about everywhere, she was coming to realize.

"I'm hitting a wall on it," she admitted.

Dylan was a murder cop, too. So he knew all about missing girls; the found ones, and the ones who never got found.

Especially them.

Lean and sharp-featured, with pale skin, dark, hooded eyes, and dark, wavy hair that she happened to know curled into tight, Botticelli-angel-type ringlets when he was in the shower . . .

Stop that, she told herself firmly. *Stop it this minute.*

He popped the tops off both beer bottles. "Yeah, well, why don't you fill me in on the case while you eat. Dig in."

She didn't have to be invited twice. One of the first things a cop learned as a rookie was to eat whatever, whenever; regular mealtimes were for civilians.

"Any reason you think she isn't just a runaway?" he asked, shoveling shrimp in red curry onto hot noodles.

"Yeah, there is. Couple of them, actually." She chewed, swallowed, drank beer. A stickler for the rules would've said no drinking, her being on the job and all. But then a stickler probably wouldn't have been stuck in a sleet storm way out here at the ass end of the earth.

Hell, if she'd been a fourteen-year-old girl in this nowhere little berg, she'd have probably done a runner herself.

At the same time another thought niggled persistently at her, something she was forgetting. But it remained elusive.

"Tara's taken off several times before and she's always come back," Lizzie said. "Everyone goes nuts looking for her for a few days, then she waltzes in like nothing happened. Even though her mother's frantic, she thinks that's probably how it'll all end up this time, too. But . . ."

She let her voice trail off, trying to put into words what a bad hit she got off the situation. Some things looked worrisome at first but ended up fine; others stank from the get-go.

Like this thing now. Dylan eyed the dark front window, still hissing with sleet. "Yeah. But," he repeated. "How long?"

"No one's seen her since yesterday morning. It was a school holiday," Lizzie replied reluctantly.

It was now Tuesday night. "She's never skipped a whole day of school before," Lizzie added.

Dylan's eyebrows went up and down once in reply. *Bad sign,* they signaled.

But she knew that, too. "I mean, I guess she could be just a runaway. Which is what most everyone around here is assuming."

Everyone but me. A shred of broccoli clung distractingly to his lower lip.

"And like I say, the girl's done it before. Maybe decided to push it a little further this time. But the other difference is that the earlier times she's always phoned home to let her mom know she's okay."

Lizzie ate a shrimp. "Not right away, maybe, but she's always done it. This time, though, not a peep. And none of her friends knows where she is, either."

The friends had been the usual gaggle of teen girls, diffuse and dreamy with the occasional speculative glance at Lizzie's weapon. Overall it had been like talking to a basket of kittens.

"You believe them?" asked Dylan. "And is there a boyfriend?"

Standard questions. The broccoli shred was gone. "Yeah, and he's missing, too, along with his motorcycle. So duh, right?"

The boy was an eighteen-year-old local kid with nothing on his record but a couple of misdemeanors; one was a pot bust but even that was only for possession, and the rest were just for underage drinking. So no real red flags had gone up from Aaron DeWilde, who was no Boy Scout but merely the kind of sullen, doe-eyed misfit that girls like Tara had been finding the sensitive side of since time began.

"No Amber Alert," added Lizzie. Tara Wylie had already been the subject of two of these; each time the girl had showed up on her own, demanding to know what all the fuss was about.

"Not yet, anyway. Mom's put up a few homemade posters in case someone around here saw something but that's all. Hey, not my decision," she added at his look of surprise. "Maybe if I knew the girl better, I'd feel better about that, too."

"Cell phone?" Dylan scraped a slice of mushroom from one of the cartons and ate it.

She shook her head. "She's got one, but it's a hand-me-down, just a cheap little burner." No GPS tracking software in it. "And either it's turned off or the battery's dead."

Outside, the sleet stopped suddenly as if a switch had been thrown. "Damn," Lizzie said.

Since her arrival here in Bearkill, the weather had featured a single blizzard that met all her expectations for a take-no-prisoners northern Maine winter event. But the snow had melted swiftly, leaving the rural terrain looking oddly like the "after" pictures on a global-warming-alert website: cracked soil, spring-fed ponds dried to muck-holes, withered winter wheat.

Tonight's sleet, in fact, was only the second measurable precipitation since Labor Day, all moisture instantly inhaled by the fiery breath of a summer that, but for the one brief wintry interlude, just wouldn't quit. And the weather now, while impressive to look at, was giving little relief to the desperately parched earth.

"All the fire teams'll be right back out there tomorrow," predicted Dylan, eyeing the streaming front window skeptically.

Chewing, she nodded agreement. The danger had been critical for weeks, everyone in the county on high alert for the smell of smoke; in the grand scheme of things tonight meant nothing.

"What's that sticking out of your shirt?" A corner of some thinly woven silvery material peeked from above his loosened tie.

Dylan rolled his eyes. "New vest. Testing it out for a little while. I guess the brass in Augusta decided I wasn't bulletproof enough."

"Yeah, well, I don't blame them. You must be killing them in workers' comp alone, not to mention their safety stats."

She touched her napkin to her lips, then wadded it. "You've been nailed three times, right? Or four? It's a wonder you don't have lead poisoning by now."

He nodded, grimacing. Dylan liked to pretend it was no big deal, getting shot. But she noticed he wasn't complaining about the new vest.

"It's been comfy enough so far. Not heavy or bulky, and they tell me it's chock-full of bullet-stopping space-age polymers," he said. "For what that's worth." Then:

"Little bird called me today," he remarked.

She swallowed. So that's why he was here. "About . . . ?"

But she knew. *Nicki.* She looked up again at the blond child in the framed photo. Nine years old, eight years missing . . .

If she was still alive she was Lizzie's only surviving kin, the daughter of Lizzie's murdered sister, Cecily, whose body had been found nearly a decade earlier on the Maine coast.

Oh, Sissy, I'm so sorry . . . After Sissy's death there'd been a murder investigation with all the right bells and whistles. But no culprit, or any possible motives, had ever been found, and her baby wasn't found, either. And now there were rumors that a little girl very like what Nicki would've grown up into had been spotted here in Aroostook County.

More than rumors, actually. It was why Lizzie was here. She looked away from the photo.

"Yeah," said Dylan. "Guy I talked to says it might be Nicki, anyway. But don't get your hopes up," he added unnecessarily.

The food was gone. She gathered the cartons and napkins and the plastic cutlery together to stuff into the trash. Later she would haul the bag to the dumpster behind the building. It was a far cry from what she'd gotten used to in the Boston PD where, to a decorated homicide cop like herself, handling the trash meant snapping a set of cuffs onto it.

In Bearkill, in fact, everything was a far cry from Boston. But she'd been here only a few weeks, she reminded herself. She couldn't very well give up on looking for Nicki when she'd barely settled in.

"So what else did your guy say?" she asked when Dylan came back from rinsing the beer bottles in the washroom.

Recycling bottles and cans was huge around here, not so much for the environment as for the nickels, northern Maine not being a high-income territory unless you were a lumber company manager or farm-equipment distributor.

Or a methamphetamine cook. Just in the time she'd been here the

MDEA had busted a trio of operations, small teams making the lethally attractive drug in mobile homes or at remote, unlikely-to-be-stumbled-upon campsites.

"Says he saw a kid." Dylan put a hand companionably on her arm as he passed, let it rest there for a more-than-companionable moment. "With a couple. Transient. Living out of a car, he said."

"Oh, great." From what she could tell so far, poverty in Maine boiled down, as it had anywhere she'd ever been, to people just doing what they could to keep a roof over their heads. Like those meth cooks, even; it was a filthy, dangerous, and basically depraved way to make a living, but there weren't many jobs around here and people had expenses to cover.

The warmth of Dylan's touch faded; another pang of longing pierced her before she banished that, too. *Dammit,* she thought, *why am I still so vulnerable to him?*

But when she looked up incautiously into the full force of his crooked smile, she knew why and cursed herself for it. She'd said she would leave him; swore it, in fact, from the moment she'd learned that he was married.

Found out from his wife, actually, from whom he was neither separated nor in the process of getting divorced as he'd claimed. Dylan's wife, Sherry, had surprised them together, bursting in on them one awful night in Lizzie's apartment, and after that horrid revelation it was of course all over.

Devastated, she'd sworn off him for good. But then Sherry got sick suddenly, and went downhill fast; she'd died soon after he'd left the Boston PD to join the Maine State Police as a homicide cop.

"I don't suppose your little bird got a plate number?"

Now Lizzie was here in Maine, too, lured to the remote, rural northernmost part of the state by vague stories and an anonymously sent snapshot of a blond child who could be her niece, Nicki. Or not. She knew very well that it might not be.

Dylan looked wry. "Oh, yeah. Tag number, sure, he got their Social Security numbers, too," he replied sarcastically.

Outside the front window the brief storm had passed; the northern Maine night turned spangled and sharp-edged. She stared out into it.

"No," Dylan amended more gently when she didn't answer. "No ID, no real proof of anything at all, really. He said it was just that the kid was the same age as I'd told him we're looking for, blond and blue-eyed, and she didn't seem like she belonged with the adults that she was with. Just a feeling he got, he said."

She glanced again at the now-silent scanner, wanting to hear for sure that the fire crews could finally stand down tonight even if by tomorrow all the sleet had evaporated, putting them back in tindery conditions once more.

And she wanted Tara Wylie to be home safe and sound with her mother.

"Where did he see her?" Lizzie asked, meaning Nicki.

If it was Nicki.

"Bangor," Dylan answered. "I've been keeping an eye peeled, I put the word out so the patrol cars and so on know to give me a call if any of 'em notice anything. But with this . . . look, Lizzie, I only told you about it at all 'cause I promised I'd keep you in the loop."

She nodded tiredly, knowing the cold-case drill as well as he did: sifting a lot of chaff in the hope of coming up with even a single grain of anything helpful. It was why she needed Dylan, who had plenty of contacts here in Maine; also, as he'd just proved again, he was the king of schmooze when it came to informants.

Outside, an old pickup truck loaded with firewood trundled past, followed by an even less-reputable-looking clunker whose fenders appeared to be held together by wide strips of silver duct tape, known locally as North Woods chrome.

A wave of discouragement hit her. "Maybe I should go back to Boston."

There, she'd said it. The photograph of Nicki—*if*—had popped up out of nowhere months earlier, mailed to Dylan anonymously, without a return address. Seeing it, she hadn't known at once that in response she would quit the job she had coveted, put her beloved city apartment on the market, upend her whole life. All she'd worked for, all she'd ever wanted . . .

Not until she'd done it. *Blood calls to blood.* But if, as she now feared, the search was hopeless, then it had all been for nothing.

"What, and leave all this behind?" Dylan's gesture took in the whole room, its Sheetrock walls and auto-supply-store shelving as blandly generic as if it had come out of a box marked CONTENTS: ONE CRUMMY OFFICE.

"And what about beautiful downtown Bearkill?" he added with a wave out at the desolate night, the fluorescent overhead lights in the supermarket across the street already snapping off one by one.

It was only 6 P.M. "You'd miss it," he said. "The culture, the exciting nightlife, and what about the glittering social scene?"

Most of the nightlife here consisted of wild animals: deer, moose, even bears. The only sign still lit outside was the one over the door of the corner tavern, Area 51; the glowing panel featured a big-eyed alien hoisting a tilted cocktail glass, its long, slim fingers weirdly articulated and its slit pupils peering expressionlessly.

"Don't make fun," she retorted, her mood changing abruptly at his mocking tone.

Of the town, she meant, or its plus-or-minus eleven hundred citizens; ones she'd sworn to serve and protect when she became Bearkill's first resident liaison officer, charged with outreach activities for the Aroostook County Sheriff's Department. And despite her growing doubts about her decision, for now that oath still held, even if Area 51's idea of a good hors d'oeuvre was a pickled egg.

He eyed her, surprised at her tone. "Don't tell me you're getting hooked on the place? Gone native already?"

"Can it," she snapped back, and was about to say more: that in Boston by this hour she'd be happily tucked into a downtown piano bar, a single-malt whiskey in front of her and a good dinner from some side-street ethnic establishment coming later.

Something spicy from the Szechuan place, she thought, or a plate of piroshki, the rich steamed pastry full of cabbage and egg. Instead, a pedestrian scuttled unexpectedly by outside the office window, glancing briefly in at them before hurrying on.

Pale-skinned and hollow-eyed, the woman wore a puffy winter jacket in shiny black and a red scarf tied under her chin. Black slacks that looked dressier than the jacket-and-babushka combo, heeled leather boots. Like Lizzie's. Or, not *exactly* like.

"Dylan, I have not even a little bit 'gone native,' as you so pleasantly put it." She glanced down at her own sleek Manolos: black, stack-heeled lace-ups she'd paid a small fortune for back in the city.

"Yes, I can see that," Dylan replied admiringly, taking in the rest of her usual work outfit: slim black jeans, a white silk shirt, and a leather belt, brass-buckled.

She ignored his comment, regarding it as merely the standard Dylan Hudson brand of shameless flattery. If you let him, he could oil you up one side and down the other.

Her black leather jacket, tailored to fit her perfectly and as soft as chamois, hung next to Dylan's coat. Pulling it on, she looked around the office a final time.

"Grab that trash bag, will you?" She didn't want the office smelling like a take-out joint when her administrative assistant, Missy Brantwell, opened up in the morning.

He complied obediently, heading out the rear exit with the tied-shut black plastic sack. Now if she could just extricate herself efficiently from the parting dance they'd soon be doing out on the sidewalk—since it seemed that he had no suggestions to make on the missing teenager situation—she'd be home free.

Speaking of which, there was a large black-and-tan hound dog waiting for her there, one who needed food and a good long walk every evening, whatever the weather. And Dylan was not at all a fan of pitch-dark jaunts through half-frozen road slop.

Good, she thought as he came back in without the trash bag, she'd use Rascal as an excuse. But as she opened her mouth to tell him that the rest of her evening would be devoted to dog care, a pickup truck pulled up outside, a shiny red Ram 1500 with a heavy chain winch in the back and a magnetic sign on the door panel:

GREAT NORTH WOODS ANIMAL CARE, TREY WASHBURN, DVM. No cute puppy or kitten illustrations adorned the sign. Trey was not that kind of veterinarian. His specialty was the kind of creature that could kill you by stepping on you: a longhorn steer, for instance, or a six-hundred-pound pig.

Dylan spied the truck. "Well, well, if it isn't our friend Farmer John."

He did not sound friendly at all. But Lizzie hardly noticed, being fully occupied suddenly by the mental equivalent of a punch in the stomach. Now she knew what she'd forgotten.

Dylan eyed her acutely. "You've got a date with him, haven't you?"

"Yes, Dylan. I do. Or I did, anyway." A dinner date, one that had completely slipped her mind.

Jumping down from the cab of his truck, the burly vet came in all smiles. But he stopped short when he saw Dylan.

"Hi." Tall and broad-shouldered, wearing a fleece-lined denim jacket, tan Carhartt overalls, and leather work boots, the big man glanced from Lizzie to Dylan and back.

"Smells good in here." The Thai food. With his thinning blond hair plastered back by the melting sleet and his round, pink face set in a determinedly amiable expression, Lizzie almost couldn't see the hurt in his blue eyes.

Almost. "Trey, I'm so sorry, I just got very involved here earlier, and—"

Yeah, I can see that, his face said. "Hey, no problem. I just stopped by to say that I'm going to be a while anyway. Got some cows at a ranch up the road not doing so well on a diet of trucked-in chow now that their pasture's dried out. So I promised the folks I'd come up after hours and take a look."

If Dylan hadn't been there, Trey would have asked her to ride along, Lizzie knew, and she'd probably have accepted. Now, though, his gaze met hers communicatively: *What the hell are you still doing with this joker, anyway?*

It was a good question, one that she'd also been known to ask herself. And she didn't have a decent answer for either one of them.

"Nice seeing you again," Dylan said stiffly as Trey turned to go.

Damn, she thought again as his sturdy frame bulked in the truck's dashboard glow. But she didn't know what she could have done differently about this and anyway it was too late, she knew, as Trey pulled away with his truck's big tires spewing slush.

Outside, Dylan walked with her to her vehicle, him clomping in his old-fashioned black rubber galoshes while she picked her way cautiously, not wanting to wreck her boots. The night's sleet-washed air tasted good, cleansed for the moment of the stench of burning, not like Boston, where the air was full of exhaust fumes year-round.

"Trey is not," she said firmly, "a farmer."

Dylan shrugged. "Hey, he works with farm animals. Goes home with manure on his boots. No difference."

She beeped open the Blazer's doors, having not yet gotten out of the Boston habit of locking everything she couldn't nail shut. People around here left their cars running, keys hanging in the ignition, even, when they went into the store.

"He's been a good friend. I don't," she added, glancing back at her office once more, "let him bad-mouth you, either."

The office phone's light was still stubbornly not blinking. *Tara Wylie, where the hell are you?* Lizzie wondered. *And why do I have such a bad feeling about you?*

"Sure," Dylan replied skeptically, as down the block a small movement caught Lizzie's eye.

It was the woman who'd passed by her window minutes earlier, ducking fast back into a doorway. And that *was* the same as it had been in Boston: the quick glance, the indecisive lingering.

"You go on," she told Dylan. The topcoat he wore, she was acutely aware, was the same one she used to bury her face in each time they parted.

"Go on, now," she repeated, "somebody wants to talk to me."

Starting back toward her office, she couldn't help feeling a familiar quiver of anticipation. Here in Bearkill she might not see quite the same high level of criminal romping and stomping as she'd been accustomed to back in the city. She might not need her weapon as often up here, either, and even the standard tan deputy sheriff's uniform was mostly optional, much to her relief.

But she was still a cop. "Lizzie," Dylan called after her. "Lookin' good."

"Yeah, sure." She caught her own reflection in the window: short, spiky black hair, smoky eye makeup expertly applied, red lipstick. It was not at all a style that was common around here—switchblade-slim, emphatically female, and with a tight, nervy way of moving that suggested she would deck you, no problem, if you gave her half an excuse.

She carried herself, as she was perfectly well aware, as if begging for a fight. But that suited her, too. *Because let's face it, most of the time, I am.*

Inside, she switched the lights back on, noting that Dylan had left his black-and-white-striped scarf on the coat tree and that there were still no calls, then turned to the visitor who'd followed her silently in.

Late twenties or early thirties, five foot four and a hundred pounds or so, short dark hair, dark eyes, and pale complexion. Both hands were visible, Lizzie noted automatically, even though it was already clear there was nothing threatening about the woman. Her face was a little too thin and her nose too bony, with high, sharp cheekbones and a too-wide mouth. But her plainness was the kind that came almost all the way around to beauty again: simple, serene.

Only right now she looked grim. *Like she's getting ready to face the music. Like she's done something bad.*

Which didn't seem likely, either: that face, those eyes, as if she'd walked through a fiery hell recently and come out still kicking on the other side.

"Have a seat," said Lizzie, pointing to the chair Dylan had used and thinking that despite her bleak expression, this woman hadn't done anything so very terrible, probably.

Still, you never knew.

The phone console on her desk lit up—PEG WYLIE, said the caller ID—just as Dylan came back in, looking for his scarf.

TRANSCRIBED AUDIO OF INTERVIEW W/SUBJECT JANE CRIMMINS, CONDUCTED BY MAINE STATE POLICE DET. DYLAN HUDSON FOR AROOSTOOK COUNTY SHERIFF'S DEP. ELIZABETH SNOW, BEARKILL, MAINE.

CRIMMINS: Wait a minute, you're recording this?
HUDSON: The recording is only so nobody can claim later that either one of us said or did anything we really didn't, okay?

CRIMMINS: Yeah, all right. Can I have my ID back? (pause) Okay. Okay, so I guess I can do this. I mean, I have all the memories so I can ... Enough for all of us, the other ones plus myself.

HUDSON: Other ones? I don't think I—

CRIMMINS: Well, it's, it's like the only way it could be, isn't it? Because *she* thinks it's better to be with *him,* even though I was the one who ...

HUDSON: (pause) Ah, can you be a little clearer on that for me, though? Because this is about Tara Wylie, what we're concerned with here. So I'm not seeing ...

CRIMMINS: I've never told anyone. I'm only staying here now to ... to, ah, tell you about it, because ... (inaudible)

HUDSON: Jane? You all right?

CRIMMINS: (weeping) ... because I'm tired, okay? So tired, and I thought I could just let you take care of it all. Just, I don't know, give up. But it's hard.

HUDSON: Uh-huh. But this was all your idea, though, wasn't it? You came in here to the office on your own to ... (inaudible, continued weeping)

HUDSON: But do you want to take a quick break? Get a coffee, or ...

CRIMMINS: (interrupts) Not because I ... not because I think it'll do any good.

HUDSON: ... or something to eat? Then we could sit down and—

CRIMMINS: (agitated) Because why should anyone listen to me? Why should anyone care what I think about what he did? Oh, no, I'm just the—

HUDSON: Jane? Seriously, you want to take a break now? Put yourself back together a little?

CRIMMINS: (weeping) No. It just gets to me sometimes, that's all. Because I never planned to tell anyone, ever. But now ...

HUDSON: Right. I get that this is difficult for you. But we could be talking about a young girl's life, you know? A missing girl that we need to find, before ...

CRIMMINS: (angrily) Well, isn't that just special. Wow, some re-

ally special little snowflake she must be, huh? The whole
town's out looking for her, I guess.

HUDSON: (pause) Yeah, well, her name's Tara Wylie. She's fourteen, her mom's worried about her. And like I said, we really
appreciate . . .

CRIMMINS: (inaudible)

HUDSON: . . . if you have information. Now, we can do this in
short sessions, we can do it however you like. If you're up for
it now, though, let's try to . . .

CRIMMINS: Sure. Talking about it, making it real, I don't guess
that'll kill me, will it?

HUDSON: Jane? (unidentifiable sound)

HUDSON: (inaudible)

CRIMMINS: (voice rising) Will it? Will it?

TWO

The rural roads around the northern Maine town of Bearkill all looked the same at night, dark narrow blacktop ribbons with no center line or streetlamps. Huge trees crowded up to the edge of the pavement, stiff and silent.

Making her way in the Blazer along the barely familiar route, Lizzie at last found the place where Peg Wylie and her missing daughter, Tara, lived: a factory-built bungalow on a poured-concrete slab sitting on a bulldozed quarter acre way the hell out in the woods. Lizzie had already been there earlier that afternoon, and it looked even more lonely and remote now than it had in the gray winter daylight.

At the end of the long gravel driveway curving between the trees, a DISH TV antenna perched at one end of the bungalow's red-metal peaked roof and a propane tank hunkered under the bathroom window at the other, both illuminated by a pole-mounted yard light that shone bluish white onto the roughly graded bare earth between the driveway and the house.

The yard lamp lit up the graveled dooryard. A snow shovel propped hopefully against the lamp pole was beginning to rust. Lizzie's boots crunched on the gravel as her shadow lengthened alongside her, then fractured on the pressure-treated porch steps.

"Peg?" The porch light came on, the door opened, and the missing girl's mother appeared, looking haggard.

"Thanks for coming," Peg said, leading Lizzie in. "Coffee? Or a beer?"

In the kitchen, a small TV with the sound muted flickered from atop the refrigerator. At the center of a round wooden table with two wooden chairs pulled up to it, a gray cat with a notch out of its ear sat on a sheet of newspaper, washing its face.

"No, thanks." The missing teen's mother was a chunky woman in her early thirties, wearing jeans and a turquoise Bearkill High sweatshirt. Her short bleached-yellow hair was still damp from a recent shower, and her face was taut with worry.

"What's going on?" Lizzie asked, looking around. A heavy canvas jacket hung by the door, flanked by a yellow nylon vest whose back panel was crossed with Scotchlite tape.

A Pathmaker radio stood in a charging base on the counter by the coffeemaker. Lined up under the coatrack were a pair of steel-toed boots, their cap soles heavily scuffed and the yellow cord laces threaded through their metal-grommeted eyelets frayed from use.

"Nothing," Peg replied dully, though her call twenty minutes ago had sounded frantic.

In a shoe box on the counter in a nest of flannel, a striped kitten slept. Beside the box was a saucer that held an eyedropper and a tin marked MILK REPLACEMENT—FOR VETERINARY USE ONLY.

Two cats, but the house smelled utterly clean and fresh, Lizzie noted. "Nothing new, anyway," Peg amended. "I got scared, was all, just so scared, and I didn't have anyone to—"

She pulled out one of the chairs and sank heavily into it. "I'm sorry, I don't mean to be wasting your time."

Then don't be, Lizzie thought. If she'd known this was only a social-support visit, she wouldn't have left Dylan Hudson alone to deal with the woman who'd showed up unexpectedly in the office.

She'd have handled it herself. *And if you were really so worried, you'd have pushed for that Amber Alert,* she thought at the woman slumped defeatedly at the kitchen table.

Instead Peg had balked at the measure. It was as if she didn't want any official publicity about Tara being missing, but why would that be?

It didn't add up. Yet there was no sense antagonizing the woman. "It's okay," she said. "Show me Tara's room once more, why don't you? Who knows, maybe I missed something."

Not that she really thought so. She'd seen enough missing persons' rooms to know what needed looking at and what didn't; the first time had been enough.

But it had been a pain in the ass to find this place again in the dark. So she might as well make this second trip worthwhile, she thought as Peg led her down a hallway lined with unprimed wallboard, past a bathroom furnished with economy-grade fixtures and unfinished tile.

"You doing this work yourself?" Lizzie asked.

Because it occurred to her suddenly that even way out here in the boondocks, a handyman with the hots for the teenage daughter was a classic perp candidate.

"Some. Tara's been helping with a lot of it, actually, she's good that way. And Pup Williams is working on it when he can, you know him?"

"Yeah." Pup was a Bearkill man, ninety years old and maybe ninety pounds soaking wet, whose high-quality work and low rates for carpentry were famous all over the county.

Pup was harmless, though. And anyway, in the unlikely event of a struggle Tara could've taken him one-handed.

The girl's small bedroom and Peg's even tinier one faced each other at the end of the hall. In both, the floor was unfinished OSB— oriented strand board was the cheaper version of plywood, Lizzie had learned back when Pup fixed a rotten floorboard at her own rented house. The pastel chenille bedside rugs lay directly on the rough surface.

"It's why I got the house so cheap," Peg explained. "The guy who built it thought he could save money by doing the finish work himself." She took a shuddery breath. "But he never got around to it, and now I do what I can, when I can."

In Tara's room, colorful posters and banners camouflaged the wallboard tape. A twin bed with a pink quilted comforter and a basic bedside table occupied one corner. On the plain pine desk, with a cork-covered bulletin board above and behind it, stood a laptop computer, a lamp, and a stack of schoolbooks. There was a white-painted dresser topped by a pink dresser scarf, and a closet with a hollow-core wooden sliding door.

Lizzie sat on the bed, trying again to absorb some sense of the girl. She'd checked under the mattress and in the drawers and closets on her earlier visit, but turned up no clue to the young teen's whereabouts; if Tara had secrets, she kept them well.

On a small wooden easel in the corner stood a sketch pad and a box of colored pencils. Tara had left a drawing of a crow half finished, a few swift, dark lines that suggested a broad wing, a sharp beak, and two bright eyes glinting greedily.

The lines were bold, without any wasted strokes, as if from inside the girl a vibrant talent had already begun emerging. Maybe it would get a chance to flourish further, Lizzie thought.

But maybe it wouldn't. Something about this whole situation just didn't compute. Cutting school, for instance. It was a small thing. But the girl had never done it before and she was, as her records indicated, a good student.

"I checked her Facebook again," said Peg, waving at the laptop. "But the only recent activity I can see is from her own friends, trying to locate her."

"You've asked them in person? And talked to their parents?" Lizzie got up.

Peg nodded discouragedly. "No one's heard from her. So they say, anyway, and they're getting scared, too, so I believe them."

"And you still can't think of anyone who might've wanted to hurt Tara? Or maybe just to worry you to death, by taking her? An ex of yours, maybe? Someone like that?"

Peg shook her head. "Her father is dead. He died when she was not much more than a baby. And there isn't anyone else. I'm not," she added wryly, "in the market for any romance."

Something in the woman's voice made Lizzie turn from the bulletin board with its turquoise-and-gold Bearkill High banner, pair of frilly paper-strip cheerleading pom-poms hung from a push pin, and collection of Justin Bieber fan photographs.

"You're sure? You know for certain her dad is deceased?"

"Sure? Of course I am." Peg crossed her arms over her chest a little defensively. "He's dead and I'm glad about it, if you want to know the truth."

That's what I want, all right. So why, suddenly, did Lizzie have such a strong feeling that she wasn't getting it?

On the dresser stood a snapshot of Tara's boyfriend, Aaron DeWilde. Heavily tattooed and grinning smugly, the kid had a neck like a tree trunk and the overbuilt physique that came from a diet of supplements and protein shakes, plus a lifting routine that was not part of any standard high school phys-ed curriculum.

"Still gone, too?" Lizzie waved at the photo.

Peg sighed. "Yeah, and his folks're still ragging on me about it. I told them Tara's fourteen, Aaron's eighteen, so who do you think was doing the leading in this little adventure they're on? If," she added uncertainly, "that is what's happening."

"Uh-huh." Lizzie picked up a school photo of Tara: long, dark hair, bright brown eyes, and a pretty smile. The girl looked like a thousand others, her face not yet fully formed and her eyes brimming with the youthful certainty that nothing bad could happen to her. *Oh, kiddo, I hope you're right,* Lizzie thought.

But more and more she just didn't think so. The girl always called, but this time she hadn't. She never skipped school, but this time she had. And when people didn't do what they always had done, Lizzie knew, too often it was because they couldn't.

Back in the kitchen the kitten cried pitifully. Peg mixed some formula from the can with a little water and drew it into the eyedropper, then began feeding the hungry infant.

"Tara's rescue," Peg explained of the kitten lapping eagerly at the dropper. "She found it last week by the side of the road, all alone. Someone dumped the poor thing there, I guess."

"So now it's your job?" Typical teenager, Lizzie thought, she brings a pet home and then lets her mother take care of it.

But Peg only glanced down fondly at the tiny creature. "Oh, I don't

mind. Cute little thing, and Tara . . . well, she's just a kid, you know?"
Her voice broke. "She's just a little kid."

"Yeah. You're right." Lizzie glanced around once more. The place
was not aggressively spotless, but it was clean, well kept, and orderly.
It looked like a place where two ordinary people, a mother and
daughter, lived decently and without incident.

Until now. "So Peg, why'd you really call me out here in the dark
tonight? On the phone you sounded like you were about to lose it
completely," she added, "but now when I get here—"

She stopped, struck by a pang of sympathy. Peg was all alone out
here on the edge of the woods, miles from anyone and worrying herself sick, comforting herself with an orphaned kitten.

Because her own baby was missing.

"You're sure there aren't any of her friends or acquaintances you
want to talk to me about?" Lizzie asked.

"Or even yours?" she added. "Someone you work with, someone
you might not feel quite right about? Because if there is, I can check
people out quietly, you know."

Sometimes it was a boss at work or maybe someone a parent owed
money to, eyeing a young girl in what ended up being way too friendly
a fashion.

"And they wouldn't have to know," Lizzie said. "You realize that,
right? I know how to check them out thoroughly without anyone
knowing about it."

But Peg shook her head firmly. "No. Really, I just . . ."

She paused, chewed her lip. Then: "Honestly, I just panicked.
Thinking about the possibilities . . . you know, if Tara had any idea at
all what kind of torture I go through whenever she does this, I don't
think she would ever . . ."

But in that belief Peg was just wrong, of course. Kids didn't have
mercy. Back in Boston just before Lizzie had departed for Bearkill, for
instance, a thirteen-year-old girl had stage-managed her own kidnapping, emailed a lot of very convincing-looking faked photos of herself
in distress, and nearly made off with a ransom of ten thousand dollars
in cash, all because a coveted pair of Miley Cyrus concert tickets had
not been provided swiftly enough.

But her growing unease over young Tara Wylie's situation, even though she didn't yet know why, said that wasn't the case here.

"Right," she told Peg. "Tara's a good kid, I get that. About her dad, though . . ." She let the sentence trail off suggestively.

"I told you before, he's dead, all right?" Peg retorted. But as she said this her shoulders slumped under the sweatshirt. Then:

"Okay, look, the truth is I don't know who Tara's father was. I was really young, it was just the one night, I never saw him again after that and I never wanted to. But . . . see, that's not what I told Tara."

Which explained the odd vibe earlier when Peg talked about Tara's father, maybe. Or maybe not.

"Okay," said Lizzie, still not quite buying it. The story was possible, of course, maybe even likely. This stuff happened to people all the time, and it was at least an understandable reason for Peg's reluctance to discuss it.

But it felt way too much like a fallback, the kind of tale a nervous perp tried putting over on you when the first big lie didn't cut it. Or maybe, Lizzie thought, she was just too used to life in the big city, where everybody was lying and everyone, it seemed, had something to hide.

"Okay," she repeated, moving toward the door. "Call me again if anything happens, all right? Anything at all, even if you're just scared. Or—" She hesitated, but what the hell. "—if you just need to talk."

Peg declared that she would, a promise Lizzie wasn't sure she believed. But for now she'd done all she could and it was good to get outside. In the graveled dooryard she breathed in the sharp fragrance of the sleet-slaked pines with a sense of relief.

As she climbed into the Blazer the last of the storm clouds parted, exposing the stars and a slice of moon. But as she drove back to Bearkill in the pine-scented darkness, the white crescent overhead seemed to sharpen unpleasantly into a claw, raking her with new doubt.

Lizzie still wasn't sure why she felt that Tara Wylie was in serious trouble. Maybe she was overreacting. But if the big city had taught her anything, it was that a young girl on her own was the potential star of a world-class creepshow.

And in this world there were plenty of creeps.

Mulling this thought, she rolled into town on Main Street, as silent now at seven in the evening as the remote country road she'd just been on. Slowing between the downtown's two-story wood-frame storefront buildings, she glanced automatically side to side at a row of defunct stores, once-prosperous businesses repurposed into bottle-recycling centers, a videogame arcade, and the local food bank.

A dozen blocks later she turned right onto a dead-end street. Her small rented house was a ranch-style structure with a poured-concrete front step, a rusting wrought-iron porch rail, and a picture window looking out on a postage-stamp yard, just like all the others on the block.

After locking the Blazer and setting its alarms she went up the curved stone walk and keyed the front door open twice: once for the doorknob, and again for the dead bolt she'd had installed after moving in.

She'd already pushed the door open and begun stepping inside when the shape hurtled silently from the darkened interior at her. "Hey!" she managed, and then it was on her, pushing her to the floor.

"Dammit!" she yelled, struggling to right herself. But her attacker was too heavy, his tongue slobbering and his hot breath gusting at her, smelling of dog food as he nuzzled her, whimpering in delighted greeting.

"Oh, all right," she gave in finally, because the dog was unstoppable and because she really was glad to see him. "Okay, Rascal," she managed. "Get off me, you big knucklehead."

The dog groaned with happiness, shoving his massive head under her jaw. One of her first acts after arriving in Bearkill had been agreeing to care for the big black-and-tan hound after his owner's death. But, she'd insisted, it was just temporarily.

She was not a dog person. She'd made that very clear. "Okay, Rascal, you can . . . okay, get off now . . . okay!"

At last the enormous canine backed off and sat, looking proud of himself. Urging him out into the yard, she propped the door so he could come in on his own when he was ready; fifteen minutes later they were both back inside, the door double-locked again and the porch light off. She'd walk him after he'd eaten, she decided.

"So," she said, pouring out his ration of kibble as his thick toenails clickety-clicked impatiently around the outdated kitchen. The cream-colored linoleum, decades-old electric stove, and round-shouldered Frigidaire were all from the 1950s. The only modern item was the police scanner on the countertop.

"How was your day?" The dog plunged his long black snout into his dish to snarf up his evening meal, his ear tips brushing the floor on either side as his eyes practically rolled up into his head with pleasure.

Dylan's Thai food was supposed to be her own dinner, but her stomach wasn't convinced; she was pondering the idea of frying an egg when she noticed the blinking light on her landline phone.

Drat. Only a few people had the landline number. As Rascal shifted to his water bowl and began washing down his meal with a sound like a plunger being used to unclog a stubborn drain, she pushed the PLAY button and heard Dylan's voice:

"Hey, I took your unscheduled visitor to the hospital. She's being admitted overnight for a psych evaluation."

She felt her eyebrows go up. The woman had looked nervous, but not unstable.

"Nothing to do there now," Dylan went on. "She's settled for the night, but you might want to go and have a peek at her in the morning."

Then came the kicker: "She seemed to think she might have something useful to say about your missing girl, but she got upset and never did tell me anything," Dylan said.

"And listen, I got a call," he added, his tone changing. "The little kid I mentioned? A patrol officer in Bangor made a traffic stop and found her, I'd let him know that I was interested so he called about it."

Lizzie's heart stopped. *Nicki . . .*

"The report earlier was a false alarm. It turns out the kid really does belong to the folks she's living with after all. Just thought I'd let you know," Dylan finished, and hung up.

So it wasn't her. *Again . . .*

The woman from the office earlier, though; that was curious, that Dylan's interview with her had gone south so fast.

Frowning to herself, Lizzie grabbed a granola bar, took a sizable bite out of it, and stuffed the rest in her jacket pocket for later; it wasn't the fried egg sandwich she'd had her mouth set for, but it would have to do.

Rascal's walk and the TV watching she'd planned for the rest of this evening would have to wait, too—the first *House of Cards* DVD was already in the player—as would a glass of wine.

She yanked her bag off the hook by the door, reset the answering machine, and wrapped Rascal's collar with its new license and rabies tags around his glossy black neck—Trey Washburn had been very helpful, getting the dog's health status up to date. Outside, she locked the front door twice behind her, then rattled the knob to make sure.

And according to Dylan she said something about Tara Wylie, too. So why didn't he try to follow up on that?

Only one way to find out. In the driveway, Rascal leapt up into the Blazer's passenger seat and allowed his doggy seatbelt to be buckled around him, its lamb's-wool padding crossing snugly over his broad chest. Getting him accustomed to the belt had been difficult at first, but seeing him perched there like a missile ready to be launched should she need to brake or swerve suddenly had been more than she could bear.

"Good boy," she said now, and the dog looked over at her as if in agreement; this, she was beginning to realize, was why they were called companion animals.

On the dark rural highway headed toward the county medical center she hit the gas. The Blazer's big V-8 engine responded with a surge of power, tires whining on the damp pavement and the crescent moon strobing whitely from between the trees.

Nothing to do at the hospital tonight, Dylan had said. She toggled the dashboard's cherry beacon on.

Yeah, right.

The sweet smell of wood smoke mingling with the piney perfume of evergreen trees, the rustle of the nighttime breeze, and the crunch of dry brush breaking underfoot all told fourteen-year-old Tara Wylie that she was still somewhere near . . .

Home! The realization forced a frightened sob from her throat just as someone shoved her hard from behind, urging her along.

Stumbling, she put her bound hands in front of her to break her fall, but at the last instant the rope fastened around her chest pulled cruelly tight again, yanking her back upright.

"Walk," a voice whispered.

Tauntingly, her mind ran through all of the many opportunities she'd had not to be in this situation—chances she hadn't recognized or had wasted when they arose:

On Sunday night—could it have been only two days ago? It felt like ages, but it was Tuesday night now, she knew—Aaron had decided on the spur of the moment to visit a pal of his in Bangor.

And that had been her first chance: not going at all. But on that freakishly warm Monday morning in the early dawn, with a big, handsome boyfriend and his motorcycle waiting, who could resist?

Not Tara, certainly, especially since there was no school that day on account of teachers' conferences, and Aaron promised they would be back by nightfall.

Feeling a spirit of adventure thrilling in her, she'd stuffed a sketchbook and some drawing pens—black ones with points as fine and sharp as hypodermic needles—into her backpack and hurried out before her mother was awake. A few breathlessly exciting hours on the motorcycle later, they arrived at Aaron's friend's place, an apartment on Stowe Street up behind the public library.

Which was her second chance to bail out. The neighborhood was sketchy, lots of mailboxes on each unkempt old three-decker house. Heaped trash bags mounded high in the alleys between buildings, and a general air of deliberate meanness and neglect everywhere had given her the creeps right off the bat.

Hanging out drinking on the front porches were tattooed men and women with ropy arms, facial piercings, and unwashed hair. She didn't feel threatened, exactly; the freedom she was enjoying was too sweetly intoxicating for that. But Tara hadn't liked the porch-people's challenging stares at her at all, and once she got inside she'd liked even less the buddy that Aaron had wanted so much to visit.

At first she couldn't even understand why Aaron wanted to. Aaron was a clean freak, and this guy's cramped, messy apartment had smelled like old bacon grease and dirty socks. Worse, when the friend got a look at Tara his eyes, puffy and sly, had lit up in a way that made her wish she'd waited out on the sidewalk with her sketchbook.

Only needing the bathroom very badly had made her stay. When she came back out, still cringing from the eye-watering filth of the place, *Resident Evil* was already blaring out of the guy's game console, with Aaron and his pal slouched together in front of it unblinkingly thumbing their game controllers.

Sighing, she'd gone looking for something to drink. Which was how, in the grimy disaster of a kitchen, she'd found a syringe lying there on the littered counter with the needle still attached to it. Next to it lay the cotton ball with a dot of dark-red blood staining it.

And even she knew what that meant. She'd been to the anti-drug lectures at school, seen the scary photographs. *Heroin* . . .

She'd felt her shoulders slump dejectedly; so that was why Aaron had wanted to come. He'd always said weed and beer were okay but that sticking things in your veins was for losers.

But people said a lot of things, didn't they? Things that when push came to shove, they really didn't mean. And although she liked Aaron a lot, it didn't even cross Tara's mind to stay and put up with this kind of stupidity.

She wasn't even mad at him, somewhat to her surprise. Just disappointed and suddenly very eager to get home to her own room, to her undone homework and her cheerleading practice tomorrow, and to the new kitten that her mother was having to feed because Tara wasn't doing it, she'd realized with a pang of guilt.

So she'd shouldered her backpack, and when she peeked back into the living room to say she was leaving, neither of the guys had even looked up.

Outside, the unfriendly loiterers watched expressionlessly as she went down the front steps and started off down the street. Feeling their eyes on her back like the laser guns of the aliens in the video-game, she walked faster, feeling her mood improving steadily the farther away she got from them.

Feeling fine, actually. *The hell with them,* she thought as she put her face up into the sunshine. It was a long walk across Bangor to the river, but the unnaturally warm weather made an afternoon in January feel almost like spring.

Once she crossed over the Union Street Bridge she started hitchhiking to Bearkill, walking backward with a smile on her face and her thumb sticking out.

Which was where her next mistake started.

The first two rides Tara accepted were all right: a nice lady in a Kia going to visit her sister in Eddington, then three young guys in a Subaru. The guys were all clean-cut, funny, and nonthreatening, clearly feeling that she was way too young for them and much more interested in one another's jokes and stories than in her.

But they were going only as far as Woodland. So by midafternoon with the sun already low in the sky she was out there hitching again, squinting hopefully into the glare as car after car zoomed by, not stopping. Nervously, she hoped she wouldn't have to walk too far in the dark.

And then the hippies came along. That's what Tara's mother always called people like them, anyway, the men long-haired and the women in flowered granny dresses and leather sandals. Some had come as teenagers to build rugged homesteads, part of a back-to-the-land movement in the 1980s; others were newer transplants. But they all liked handmade stuff, organic food they grew themselves, and marijuana—at least according to Tara's mother.

These hippies drove a little old Volvo sedan that smelled dankly of patchouli oil. Climbing into the backseat, Tara felt comforted by the bearded man's twinkling eyes and cheerful smile. The red-haired woman riding beside him wore a faded T-shirt and tattered overalls brightly embroidered with astrological signs.

They were heading up north, they said, but they needed to stop at their own place first. Did she want to hang out there for a little while, then get a ride all the way to Houlton?

Tara definitely did. It was already getting late, and she had to be in school tomorrow; she'd never meant for her adventure with Aaron to last more than a day.

So she agreed, and minutes later they were bumping down a long driveway through a stand of birch trees whose trunks gleamed whitely in the setting sun. They stopped before a dome-shaped house made of salvaged wood and mismatched windows, festooned with tinkling wind chimes and small, bright flags fluttering on twine.

Half a dozen dogs ran out barking as they got out of the car. Perched everywhere, on the deck that surrounded the house and on junk cars scattered about the yard, cats of every color and size watched, squinty-eyed, as they made their way inside.

The woman, whose name was Iris, had skin so pale you could almost see through it. In the kitchen, which had a wood-burning cookstove and a hand pump but no faucet and smelled of vegetables decomposing in the compost bucket, she handed Tara a steaming mug.

"Thank you," Tara managed, suddenly shy, and the woman beamed at her, waving her into the living room and to a huge, soft chair covered in tie-dyed cotton. Settling into the chair with her tea, she noticed other people: A tall, skinny man sat cross-legged out on the deck, wearing a long caftan and sandals. A woman and a little girl worked at a loom on another part of the deck, and in a chair-swing hanging from a nearby tree a young boy lounged with a baby asleep on his chest.

This was a commune, Tara realized, feeling excited to witness such an exotic phenomenon. She'd been aware that some people got together this way, sharing everything and living in peace and harmony. But she had never seen it, and being here made her life seem bigger, suddenly—more colorful and adult.

She sipped the bitter tea proudly, glad these odd people had decided to allow her into their world. Strange music came from speakers perched on the rough wooden bookshelves, which were full of books she had heard of but never seen: *Our Bodies, Ourselves, Moosewood Cookbook, The Joy of Sex.* The music was droning, atonal, with weird drum thumping and string plucking; gazing about in wonder, Tara supposed that you had to get used to it before you could like it.

She decided to try. Then a woman in a flowing, geometric-print tunic came in, carrying a tray with a pottery bowl of soup, a large piece of black bread, thickly buttered, and a spoon.

"Welcome," the woman said gently, offering Tara the tray.

The soup smelled delicious, and Tara was ravenous. Thanking the woman, she ate every bit of the soup—the broth and vegetables and the tasty bits of green stuff floating in it—and sopped up the last of it with the thick dark bread, which she also devoured.

When she finished and set the tray aside, it was nearly dark out. The man on the deck was gone, as was the boy from the swing. Faint whiffs of marijuana drifted from somewhere.

Then the red-haired woman returned. "I'm sorry, it's taking us a little longer than we thought but we'll just be another half hour or so. Is that all right?"

Tara thought apologizing to a hitchhiker for a delay was not the way things usually worked. But she was content to stay for a while longer, especially if a ride all the way home was at the end of the wait.

Settling back in the big, soft chair that smelled of some kind of herbal infusion, letting the weird, droning music wash over her while the sounds of the communal residents preparing a meal clattered pleasantly from the kitchen, she let one of the cats hop into her lap and curl up there, purring loudly.

Soon she'd be seeing her own little rescued kitten. Poor little Phoenix. She hoped her mother wasn't too mad about having to take care of him while she was gone.

Then she thought of calling home. She always did call when she took off like this. Her cell phone was in her bag, which she'd tucked in beside her in the chair. But if she used it now, she'd have to explain where she was and how she got there, and it would spoil the pleasant atmosphere she was enjoying.

Better to explain once she got home, she decided, which would be in only a few hours anyway.

Thinking this, Tara felt her eyelids drooping. She'd been up very early getting ready to go with Aaron, and riding on the back of a motorcycle was exhausting. Not to mention all the walking afterward. So with the evening shadows deepening to night, she'd let her eyes drift shut.

And when she opened them again it was morning.

THREE

"Over there," said Emily Ektari. Dressed in a scrub suit, white sneakers, and a white lab jacket, the dark-haired young ER physician pointed to a curtained cubicle in the Aroostook County Medical Center ER's small but spotless patient-care area.

The rest of the cubicles, each with its sheeted gurney, shiny metal IV pole, and wall-mounted cardiac monitor, were at the moment unoccupied. In its silence and serene orderliness, the unit was a far cry from the controlled bedlam of a Boston emergency room, Lizzie thought.

"Quiet," she remarked into the fluorescent-lit calm.

Emily looked up from the nursing desk where she was studying a Spanish-language text. "What, you were looking for the Tuesday Night Knife and Gun Club?"

She was repaying a portion of her school loans by working in underserved areas like northern Maine. But her last post had been in Chicago and her next, she'd just learned, would be in the desert Southwest, where a large immigrant population also had few health-care options; thus the Spanish textbook.

"I doubt she'll wake up anytime soon," Emily added as Lizzie turned toward the occupied cubicle. "I think maybe she was on some kind of stimulant. The tox screen I sent off to the lab will tell for sure. But for whatever reason, she was so agitated that I had to sedate her."

Lizzie grimaced, disappointed. No wonder Dylan hadn't gotten anything useful out of the woman. "Did she give you any idea what upset her?"

If she wasn't just reacting to whatever crap she swallowed, Lizzie thought.

Emily shook her head. "Dylan said she'd been trying to tell him something when she just all of a sudden got hysterical. That's all I know. I couldn't get much out of her, myself."

The EKG monitors linked to the bedside units displayed five unlit screens and a bright-emerald one with a jagged up-and-down glowing line marching across it. CRIMMINS, read the inked strip of adhesive tape stuck to the lit screen's console.

Lizzie blinked at the name, recognizing it. *Oh, come on,* she thought. *Could it be . . . because if it is her, then I'll be damned.*

"And he said the more he tried to coax it out of her," Emily went on, "the more she lost her shit."

The curtains around the patient were partly closed. Inside them on the sheeted gurney, a dark-haired woman lay with a white woven hospital blanket pulled over her shoulders, her chest rising and falling with the slow regularity of sleep.

"She wouldn't even let me touch her, other than drawing blood for a tox screen and so on, and starting an IV so I could get some fluids into her. She was pretty dehydrated."

The cardiac line went on moving evenly across the bedside monitor. "You really think she was disturbed enough to—"

"To keep here?" Emily nodded. "Oh, absolutely. She's classic for a moderate amphetamine overdose, actually, and she had herself all wound up. The shot of Valium I finally gave her took care of that, though."

Emily checked the patient's IV, then made a brief note on the clipboard at the foot of the gurney. "I wasn't sure at first that it would and it was more than I thought she'd need, but it took hold in the end. Good old Vitamin V. She'll probably sleep until morning."

Lizzie eyed the figure again. *Crimmins . . .* The name rang a bell, all right; an alarm bell.

"Is her first name Jane, by any chance?"

Emily glanced back, surprised. The printing on the clipboard was too small for Lizzie to have read it from a distance. "How'd you know that?"

"Just a lucky guess." Her unease over the missing Tara Wylie suddenly increased. "Name's familiar from a case that I'd been watching when I was back in Boston."

The heart rate on the monitor increased slightly. "Meanwhile I've got a teenage girl missing," she began, meaning to ask Emily to keep an eye out.

But before she could go on, the heart rate on Jane Crimmins's monitor shot up, the high beep-beeping shrill in the ER's silence and the jagged radium-green line on the monitor's screen zigzagging wildly.

Huh, Lizzie thought. "Tara Wylie," she said experimentally. The monitor's activity revved once more, this time shooting high enough to briefly trigger a jangling alarm.

Emily scowled at the monitor. "Weird. Guess she's not quite as asleep as I thought."

She turned to Lizzie. "Tell you what, though, when she wakes up for real I'll let her know that you were here. If she wants to talk to you, I'll call you, stat."

An upped heart rate could've meant that the woman on the hospital gurney knew something about Tara Wylie's disappearance. But it also could have represented a bad dream or a painful gas bubble, Lizzie supposed.

"All right," she conceded reluctantly. "Or even if she doesn't want to talk, call me anyway. Maybe I can persuade her."

"Dylan gets better looking every time I see him," Emily remarked suddenly as they walked back to the nursing station. Lizzie felt her own heart rate rev up.

"You're *sure* you wouldn't care if I were to start going out with him?" Emily went on.

They'd had this discussion before. *Yes,* thought Lizzie. *I do care, very much.* But:

"No," she said. "Seriously, Em, you want to go out with him, it's fine with me. Be my guest."

But Emily must have seen something in her face. "It was much busier in here a little earlier," she remarked, tactfully changing the subject.

Now Lizzie noticed the large wheeled trash bins awaiting emptying. Stuffed full of paper gowns, latex gloves pulled inside out, emptied plastic IV bags, and other medical-equipment disposables including plenty of stained gauze, the bins testified to some fairly wild ER activity not long ago.

"A compound fracture, couple of soft-tissue injuries, some acute dehydrations, and a third-degree burn," confirmed the ER doc, "from the fire over at Hoverly."

Two miles north of Bearkill, Hoverly was a tiny settlement of wood-frame houses, postcard-pretty antique barns, and the neat-as-a-pin workshops of custom furniture manufacturers interspersed with small dairy farms and vegetable gardens. Inhabited by members of a small, strictly old-fashioned religious group, the town mostly took care of its own needs.

But when several big brush fires had broken out there earlier in the day, horse-drawn wagons and hand-pumped water hadn't been enough; from her office, Lizzie had heard sirens and dispatches on the scanner, and later seen the ambulances speeding out.

"It's bad news out there," said Emily now. "The way things are going in general around here, it's only a matter of time before someone gets really badly injured, or even killed."

She sat behind the desk. "The weather, the forest fires . . . I mean, this is my second winter up here and after the last one I never thought I'd be wishing for snow again."

Lizzie hadn't been here the previous winter, but she'd heard the tales: four feet of snow, blizzards well into April, and cold so fierce that even the old-timers around Bearkill were in awe.

And now this: summer in winter. "It's strange, all right," she agreed. "Like things are going haywire, weather-wise."

Back in Boston it wasn't so obvious; in the city, you heard about global warming and somehow you thought it was only a bad deal for polar bears. You didn't think so much about the fact that what happened to the bears could also happen to you.

Until it started to. Lizzie's turn to change the subject: "So listen, Emily. After you got here, how long did it take you to get acclimated? I mean, to feel at home even a little bit?"

The young MD was from Baltimore, originally; not Boston, but still plenty urban. And she'd worked in other big-city hospitals.

"You mean like I'm not living on the far side of the moon?" Emily pulled a wry face. "I'll let you know if and when. No music clubs, no public transportation. I swear right now I'd kill for a pizza with meatballs that hadn't been poured onto it from a ten-pound bag of frozen ones."

Her expression turned sympathetic. "Why, you having a bumpy ride?"

Lizzie sighed. "To put it mildly." Her own chronic yen was for oysters, washed down with a craft beer from one of the many new artisan breweries flourishing in the Boston metro area. And that wasn't all she missed:

Lights and people, car horns and sirens, exhaust fumes and food smells and dust from the construction sites . . .

"Mostly I'm just treating it like a question on a cop exam," she said. "Like, 'You're working a new case with a newly assigned partner in an unfamiliar and potentially hostile environment, how do you proceed?'"

Emily laughed. "Right, if the partner is an alien from some other planet and the atmosphere is methane. You know why Bearkill would be a good place to be at the end of the world?"

As she spoke, a red light over the automatic doors to the unit began blinking urgently.

"Because you won't even hear about it until a good ten years after it happens," Emily answered herself as the doors swung open to admit a gurney with four nurses pushing it.

Time to go, Lizzie realized. "Listen, Emily, if she wakes up, no matter how late it is . . ."

"You bet," Emily replied, hurrying toward the gurney. "I'll call you if anything interesting happens." But the young doctor's attention was already on her new patient, whose face was covered with a clear plastic oxygen mask and whose chest was even now being exposed for an EKG reading.

Twenty minutes later, Lizzie was back on her own front step with the long-postponed glass of wine finally in her hand, waiting for Rascal to finish mooching around among the shadows on the lawn. The moon had set, darkening the night to soft black velvet, and the only sound was an owl in a tree nearby, hoo-ing softly as if confiding a secret.

"Come on, buddy," she urged, and the massive dog appeared at once from the gloom. She'd tried walking him, but the usually calm canine had startled at every faint sound and tugged persistently at the leash, turning back toward home.

So she'd given in. Maybe he was picking up on the anxiety she felt over Tara Wylie, or more likely the smell of smoke, still drifting faintly from the Hoverly fires earlier, had spooked him.

Whatever you say, boss, he seemed to reply now as he followed her inside. There, once the porch light was out and she'd gone around checking windows and doors as was her nightly habit, she debated a refill on her drink and decided against.

There was, after all, no sense in getting morose, even if she was all alone in a tiny house in the middle of nowhere. Back in the city on a weeknight she'd probably be home by this hour, too, but the windows of her spacious condo overlooking the river there had been a glittering display of moving headlights, brightly lit buildings, and spangled bridges arcing across the sky.

Here the kitchen window was pitch black.

She rinsed her glass and set it in the sink, aware of Rascal's slow, even breathing and glad for his presence as he settled in his dog bed to sleep. On the wall, the black cat-shaped clock that had been here when she moved in ticked through the moments mercilessly, its ceramic tail switching stiffly, wide eyes jerking back and forth.

Too dark, too quiet, she decided. *I should at least put on some music.* She moved toward the radio, which at this late hour on a Tuesday night would be playing cool jazz from a French station in Montreal.

But then she stopped short as the questions that were really bugging her came clear suddenly:

Why the hell is Jane Crimmins, the mysterious caretaker of one of the victims in New England's most notorious recent kidnapping case, asleep in a hospital in Bearkill, Maine? Why did she want to talk to me?

And why'd her heart rate jump when I mentioned Tara Wylie?

Her cell phone trilled, startling her. "Snow here," she snapped into it.

"I'll be at your office in town in five minutes," blurted Tara's mother, Peg Wylie, shakily. "I'm on my way in now, I'm—"

"Peg? What happened? Have you had some kind of news? Or . . . did Tara come home?"

"Just be there," Peg Wylie half sobbed into the phone, then hung up, leaving Lizzie to wonder if maybe she should've had that second drink, after all.

Peg sure sounded like she'd had a few. That, in fact, might be all that this visit was about, Lizzie thought irritably as she headed out into the night and climbed into the Blazer again.

But a few minutes later when Peg's decrepit little Honda sedan roared up to the curb in front of Lizzie's office and the driver tumbled out, it was easy to see that the problem was more than a few too many Budweisers.

At the door Lizzie put a steadying hand on Peg's trembling shoulder, clad in a high school athletic jacket.

Tara's jacket. The girl had been—*still is,* Lizzie corrected herself—a cheerleader. Peg thrust a clenched fist with something in it at Lizzie.

"Take it. Take it, I can't even—"

"Okay, Peg, calm down now." Lizzie led her inside. "Talk to me. What's happened?"

Only a few hours ago, Peg Wylie had worn the anxious but resigned look of a woman whose last nerve was worn to a bleeding nub, but who still believed her missing daughter was probably alive and well.

She did not look that way now. "Please," Peg said, weeping. "I really thought she was okay, but . . ."

Lizzie took Peg's hand, peeled the clenched fingers gently open, and plucked a cell phone from it.

"I tried calling her back but it wouldn't even ring, there's something wrong, *please . . .* "

"Okay. This is your phone, right?" Lizzie asked. Peg nodded numbly as Lizzie turned the phone so the text message displayed on the small screen was visible.

"Okay," she murmured again. But it wasn't. It wasn't okay at all.

The time-and-date stamp on the cell phone's text message read TUESDAY, 9:24 P.M., just half an hour ago. Below that, the message itself consisted of two words, all caps, no punctuation. Centered on the black screen the white letters stood out stark as a scream:

HELP ME

*W*e *didn't want to wake you,* the note lying in Tara's lap had said, in the dome house of the hippies way out in the woods where she'd fallen asleep.

Outside, bright daylight meant it was at least midmorning on Tuesday. She'd jumped up and looked around dazedly, but no one was there, not even the cat. The music had stopped and the dome house, so busy and friendly the night before, shimmered with silence. Panic rushed through her as she realized what had happened. Then she saw the kitchen clock and realized it was nearly noon, even later than she'd feared.

Stay as long as you like, the note said. Which meant they'd gone without her. She'd already missed half a day of school, and she hadn't called home. Fumbling in her bag, she'd found her phone, but no bars showed in the display screen. There were dead areas for cell reception in Maine, and this must be one of them.

She'd hurried through the kitchen, where the sink was piled with dishes. By daylight the dome house's interior looked shabby and careless, the chair coverings threadbare and the floor, made of rough, unvarnished planks, unswept. She'd stopped to fill the animals' water bowls from the hand pump on her way out.

The outhouse was disgusting. She'd crouched quickly among the trees, then jogged down the long dirt driveway to the road. How could they just leave her like that, without a word?

But when a car finally pulled over and picked her up, she'd decided not to worry about it; she would explain when she got home, she'd told herself, which she would very soon because the car was full of more college boys. They were going to help fight the wildfires in Aroostook County, they said.

Tara had thought they looked too soft for it, in their early twenties but already with pouches of fat beneath their chins and the poochy beginnings of beer guts. Of course she hadn't said so, though; they were just boys, after all, goofy and clueless as if fighting wildfires was some kind of an adventure.

And they'd taken her right to Bearkill, or almost. But that's when her next mistake had happened, a big one, and very fast.

So fast, she'd never even had time to scream. *One half mile,* she thought bitterly now, reliving her errors and mocking herself for them as she trudged on through the smoke-reeking night. *They offered to take me all the way but like an idiot I said no.*

Her mother always said if you do something, own it. Don't try to hide it or weasel out of the responsibility later. But she'd also said don't hitchhike. Said it like she meant it, with a look in her eye that had told Tara it truly wasn't negotiable.

So she'd chickened out. She didn't want her mother to know that she'd been hitchhiking, so she told the boys she'd walk the rest of the way home, even though winter's early nightfall had already arrived.

And it hadn't been bad at first; nice night, and her own driveway wasn't far off. But then the van came up fast from behind her, its headlights casting her wavering shadow onto the blacktop ahead.

She'd never seen the driver, hadn't bothered to look around until the van slowed, alerting her too late. Practically in the same instant a pair of rough hands had grabbed her, slapping tape onto her mouth and heaving her into the van's cargo area.

She'd never had time to scream, and the van had taken off fast, lurching forward abruptly while she was still scrabbling for an inside door handle. But there wasn't one, and that's when she had realized: She might not know who'd grabbed her, but she knew what this was, all right.

She ought to; she'd been warned often enough. She'd been kidnapped by a maniac, a rapist or worse. That's what her mother always said would happen if she hitchhiked, and now it had.

The van sped down the road while she screamed as loud as she could through the tape, hammering with her fists on the heavy metal grating between the passenger and cargo areas. Dark cloth draped over the grate kept the driver hidden, but whoever it was could hear her.

She'd made sure of that, even after the van jolted off the paved road, the lurch throwing her to the metal floor. Kicking, pounding, howling through the sodden tape over her mouth . . .

But then through her fright she'd recalled her cell phone and found it in her bag, which her attacker hadn't noticed. She'd kept it turned off to save battery but now, fumbling the phone out with shaking hands, she managed to poke the gadget's tiny, glowing keys.

Her fingers trembled, clumsy and numb feeling. Twice, she accidentally turned the thing back off and had to restart it. But she would get out of this, dammit, she *would*, so she kept at it.

Remembering what her mother always said about sticking up for herself—*You can't be a doormat unless you lie down, Tara*—she held back her sobs long enough to type her mom's number and a message—HELP ME.

There. Gasping with fright, she'd just pressed the SEND button when the van lurched to a halt, slamming her to the floor and knocking the phone from her hands.

The side door slid open. She wanted to start bawling, but she didn't. Instead she grabbed the phone up, stuffing it hastily into her pant pocket. She scrambled to her feet and charged the door opening, ducking and aiming her head at her attacker's midsection.

Because this is it, this is my last chance—

"Oof." The surprised grunt of pain she heard on impact was as satisfying as any stunt in her cheerleading workout. Swerving, she ducked again, rolling to one side and onto her feet on the rough ground, filled with the sharp exhilaration of sudden freedom.

Run, a small, clear voice in her head advised her coldly. But the voice cut off abruptly when an unseen fist slammed the side of her head and she went down hard, stunned silent.

A harsh, unidentifiable whisper came from above her. It was the same voice as before. "Do nothing, say nothing." Helplessly she obeyed, waiting for what would come next.

Please, I'm only fourteen . . . "Look at me and I'll kill you."

Hands hauled her up, shoved her forward. She fell again to the dry, stony earth in the darkness, then struggled up once more. She stood there terrified, dizzy and tottering, until a hard kick sent her sprawling for a third time.

"Had enough? Or do I have to hurt you some more?"

A hand thrust down at her, gripping a shovel. "Take this." Shakily, she obeyed, still flat on her stomach.

"Get up. Put both your hands on the shovel. Don't be stupid and try anything with it."

She hauled herself up by leaning on the tool. It was the only way she could do it. Then she cautiously lifted the thing, ready to fall onto it again if her legs gave out.

They didn't. "Good. Now . . ."

There was joy in the voice, and that scared her the most. *You just wait, though,* she thought. *Wait until I get my breath back.*

Because even though she was still very scared, she was mad now, too. Who the hell did this person think he was, anyway? And now she had this shovel in her hands, a heavy one, its blade sharp and made to cut swiftly through the earth.

Or through other things. "Start digging," the voice ordered, so she did.

Still thinking, though. Thinking hard about the shovel and about the things—*packed earth, dense roots, other things*—that it might cut through. Thinking . . .

Just you wait.

———

Once I saw Cam on TV being led out of the house in New Haven, it all came back to me: The dance at the park. The man grabbing us.

And what happened next. I don't know how long it was after I'd drunk the drugged juice that I woke up in the van's rear cargo area. By then I was hurt and naked, with the greasy taste of the fried chicken he'd been eating smeared on my mouth.

Cam wasn't there. The van had stopped. I didn't know where we were or how long I'd been unconscious, only that it was still dark out.

The side panel slid open. He leaned in and shoved a bunch of cloth at me. It was a dress, a sort of smocklike thing.

"Put it on." He made a hurry-up gesture with his hands.

I didn't want to, but I didn't want him looking at me naked, either. He had my own clothes in his hands, so I did what he said. Then I sat down again as my legs gave way. Through the open side panel I could see that we were on a quiet street in a part of the city where I'd never been, with cracked sidewalks and shot-out streetlights and chain-link fences staggering drunkenly around the tiny, trash-littered front yards.

"Get out," he ordered, but I was too frightened to move. Finally, with a curse he yanked me roughly through the van's side opening, urging me toward a shabby wood-frame house with a sagging front porch and stacked concrete blocks where the front steps used to be.

I began whimpering. I knew that it wouldn't do any good but I couldn't help it. "Quiet," he said, muscling me along.

I should have screamed anyway and taken my chances. But I was so scared; it was as if my whole body were made of pure fright, vibrating with terror. Plus I was hurting all over and still in shock from what he'd done to me, and dopey from the spiked juice.

Using a key from a ring on his belt, he unlocked the front gate on the chain-link fence, forcing me through it and up to the house, which was also locked. I kept thinking that someone in one of the neighboring houses would see us and do something. Yell at him to stop or ask me if I was okay or call the police.

But nobody saw us, or if they did they've never admitted it. When he shoved me through the door I tried a final time to rebel, planting my feet and opening my mouth at last to shout something, make someone hear me.

But nothing would come out except a tiny squeak that made him laugh, like my pain and terror were amusing to him, as if they were what he wanted. He placed his hand on the flat of my back to shove me in, but at his touch my body leapt cringingly forward on its own, nearly falling over the awful threshold.

Then, with the cold, hopeless awareness of a drowning person going down for the last time, I was just where he wanted me to be: inside, where no one could see or hear me.

The door swung shut. He kept one hand tight around my wrist while he relocked it from the inside, using another key from the ring he still held. The keys jingled softly as he prodded me along a hallway smelling of rancid grease, down a flight of unpainted steps, and into what looked at first like an ordinary basement.

A washer and dryer, old tires, and a rumbling furnace were down there. A pool table stood under a dangling lightbulb, a bookcase against one wall was crammed with old magazines, and a heavy orange canvas jacket plus a dusty yellow hard hat and what looked like several small scuba tanks cluttered the rest of the space.

Except for that stuff—old fire department gear, it looked like—it was the kind of cellar anybody might have. But when I saw it, with that weak yellow lightbulb dangling above it, it hit me all at once that I was never going to see anything else again. Not my home or my parents or anybody else I knew.

Not ever. Only him with his small gleaming eyes the color of dark water and his lips slick with grease. The scarred, lumpy knuckles of his fingers were grimy, as if he worked on cars for a living, maybe.

Then I saw the cages. There were two of them over in the far corner of the basement, built up with heavy wood framing against the cinder-block walls. He opened the chain-link cage door of one of them, put his hand on my back again, and shoved me inside.

"Shh," my captor said once he'd slammed the door and locked it. I nearly started screaming again then, but he stopped me by putting a greasy finger to his lips.

"You make a sound, honey, I'll come back here and slit your throat. I mean it. I have done it before," he added chillingly.

As he turned away, chuckling to himself, I felt the contents of my stomach roll over: the dinner I'd had at home, the half of a beer at the park, and the spiked juice he'd made me drink, all of it threatening to come up in a convulsive heave.

And then it did. Panic clutched me; I thought when I was done he'd be standing over me with his knife out. But he wasn't. Instead he was focused on someone else, and God help me but I was grateful for it.

One side of the cell I was in was made of wooden slats as a sort of divider. From beyond them I heard him fumbling with another lock. The lock's hasp clicked open; a girl began crying.

Cam, I thought at first. But it wasn't her; I knew her voice and it wasn't. Next came the sounds of a scuffle in there, a dull smack like a mallet hitting a piece of meat.

"Please," someone whispered.

Twice. She whispered it twice. Then something heavy hit the slats I'd pressed my ear against, startling me backward, and she didn't say it anymore.

The enclosure's door scraped shut and a lock rattled angrily, its hasp snapping shut again with another small click. Feet went up the stairs, one pair unsteady, the other a heavy clomp, and the light went out.

Despair seized me, a feeling like drowning while swirling down a drain faster and faster as the door at the top of the stairs slammed, and then there was silence. I waited in terror for him to come back, but he didn't.

"Hello?" The voice came from the other cubicle. "You okay?"

Peering through a crack between the slats, I saw a primitive room of about ten by ten feet, illuminated only by a small nightlight hanging from an extension cord. Two girls were in there, a dark-haired one and one with that very fine corn-silk hair that was almost white.

The blond girl looked like a long-term disaster victim, big-eyed, skinny, and pale. In there with the two of them were heaps of old, frayed blankets that might've been beds, and a makeshift clothesline with a few stained, shabby items drying on it. There was a small TV and a hotplate, and in a corner stood an old-fashioned sink—the deep, square kind, with a shower hose shoved onto a faucet.

Under the sink stood a bucket; the toilet, I guessed, which accounted for the stink. Biting my lip to keep from howling, I let myself realize at last that the dark-haired girl in the room was Cam.

Sprawled across the blanket-heap bed she lay naked and motionless, one bare arm flung out as if reaching for something.

I couldn't see her chest moving, and that's when I understood she wasn't alive anymore. He must've brought her in here first, while I was still unconscious.

"Is she . . . ?" *Dead*, I wanted to say, but I couldn't make the word come out of my mouth. I felt nothing, like I was frozen inside, but at the same time I knew feeling nothing was a blessing that wouldn't last.

The girl with the white-blond hair nodded, whispering, "I think so. I think she was already gone when he brought her down here, but I'm afraid to find out for sure."

She gulped nervously, glancing toward the stairs as if she thought he might be listening. "It wouldn't be the first time."

"He's brought dead girls down here before?" Now at last I felt a cold, black wave wash over me at the horror of it. That this nightmare was real and I was in it.

And Cam. The blond girl nodded again with quick, tiny bobs of her head, her lips pressed tightly together. She looked toward the stairs again, then went on.

"He . . . he stashes them here sometimes. Then he takes them away after a while, I don't know where."

Cam still wasn't moving. Of course she wasn't; he'd hit her so hard, and the labored breaths I'd heard her taking in the back of the van had sounded as if any one of them might be her last. He'd dragged her in here and thrown her down like trash that he meant to dispose of later.

He would take her back out again and bury her, or dump her by the road somewhere. In a ditch, probably, like my mother always said. Which meant things weren't looking so good for me, either, I realized with another rush of fright.

"Do you have a cell phone?" the blond girl asked.

I shook my head. I didn't own one and neither had Cam; back then generally kids didn't, or at least not so much as now. And anyway, calling for help was the last thing I wanted; even as injured and frightened as I was, I already knew I had to escape without anyone finding out that I'd been here.

Even though Cam was dead. *Cam* . . . my wild, funny cousin, always laughing, brave, and full of mischief . . . *dead*. I couldn't believe it. Still, I was already sure it was true, and there was nothing I could do about it. *Gone.* The word rang in my head like the solemn tolling of the bell at St. Anselm's whenever there was a funeral.

Gone forever . . . But if she were here, Cam would tell me to get a grip, not to be such a baby. She'd say I should look out for myself, wouldn't she?

Of course she would. Even with her body lying motionless only a few feet from me, I could practically hear her. If I meant to obey her, though, I would have to hurry. Because any minute now I was sure that the guy from the van would be back.

And what he would do then I didn't want to imagine. Squinting in the dim glow from the nightlight in the adjoining cell where Cam's body lay, I peered desperately around the cellar, hoping for some tool that I could manage to reach: a crowbar or screwdriver, maybe, the kind of thing that might be lying around down here, and that I could use to get out.

Finally I spied the gleam of metal on the floor. It was a key ring, I realized. *His* key ring. Or was it a trap? Had he dropped it, or had he put it there on purpose to catch me reaching for it? I had no choice but to find out. Behind me, the girl with the blond hair wept softly. Stretched out on my stomach, I slid my hand under the chain link, trying not to hear the sounds from upstairs.

Awful sounds; from what he was doing to the girl he'd dragged out of here, I guessed, and would do to me if I didn't *hurry* . . .

At last my fingers closed on the keys. Somehow in his rush to get upstairs with his prisoner he must have dropped them. Lucky for me, I thought, but now the sharp end of a wire from the bottom of the chain-link enclosure jabbed my arm cruelly, blood running hotly from the gash.

The pain made my teeth clench and my stomach knot up, but I dragged my hand back in anyway. With the keys at last in my grasp, a torn-up arm was the least of my worries.

"Oh," whispered the blond girl, glimpsing what I was doing. "Be careful, if he catches you he'll—"

I pulled the keys the rest of the way under the chain link. They were on a metal ring with a spring-loaded clip; he'd taken them off his belt to let us into the house, I remembered, and used one down here to open my cage before shoving me in.

And then to drag the other girl out. "Hurry," said the blond girl in the next cubicle while the sounds from above, unimaginable to me just hours earlier, went on and on.

"Please," said the blond girl. "You have to help us. We've been here so long."

He'd thrown my clothes into the cubicle with me; shuddering at the thought of his hands on them, I yanked them on anyway, as fast as I could. He was busy now but he would return, and when he did my time would be up.

Hurry. Steadying the heavy padlock as best I could through the chain link, I shoved my hand through a gap in the wire mesh and twisted my hand around to try the first key, jittering it into the lock. But it wouldn't turn, or the next one, either. Or the next. Finally, on the fourth try—

The fourth key turned grudgingly. The lock's hasp snapped open and so did the door, grating against the floor.

"Please," begged the girl in the next cubicle as, weeping silently, I scrambled across the cellar and up the rough wooden stairs. "Please don't leave me here."

But I didn't dare go back to help the blond girl get out, so sure was I that in the very next instant he would appear, see what I'd done, and charge down the stairs just as I was creeping up them.

Only he never did, and when I tried turning the doorknob at the top of the stairs I found it unlocked.

He was in a hurry, said a voice in my head. *Sure of himself and careless with the keys this once ... but he won't be careless next time.*

He'll never make that mistake again. So this was my only chance. Renewed fright hit me as I pushed the door open, peeking around it. The sounds from up here had stopped. I tiptoed into the hall. In the darkness, a loose strip of wallpaper brushed my face and I stifled a shriek.

"At least tell someone," begged the voice from below. "Tell someone we're here."

Ignoring her, I hurried on. No one was in the rank-smelling kitchen, flyspecked and with piled-high dishes teetering in the sink; no one in the den, dark and musty, full of discarded fast-food containers littered around the TV.

Finally came the sprint to the front door, now padlocked on the inside. I thrust another key in—by some miracle it was the right one—yanked the door open, and hurled myself out of the house. In my frightened rush I nearly tumbled down the concrete-block front steps.

At the gate between the trash-littered front yard and the street there was yet another lock; while I was fumbling with it a roar of outrage came from inside. Flinging the gate wide, I ran sobbing down the uneven sidewalk, glancing back just in time to see him charge out onto the porch with his fists clenched and his piggy little eyes glaring around furiously.

But by now it was very late. There weren't many streetlights in the neighborhood, a down-on-its-luck part of New Haven where public amenities, if they existed at all, were poorly maintained. So he didn't see me.

And that was the last time I looked back. All I could think of was getting away—that I was out and free and he couldn't touch me anymore. Even Cam's poor motionless body meant nothing to me compared with my escape. And as for the other girl, by then I wasn't sure if she was real, or just another part of the awful nightmare I'd been in.

All I knew was that I had to run, to get away and not look back. After I'd done that for as long as I could I began to walk, aching and bleeding, still woozy and terrified that at any minute he might appear in his van from behind me, then grab me and bundle me in.

But he never did. Minutes later on the overpass high above the interstate ramp leading into the city I leaned far out over the guardrails. I thought briefly about jumping, but I didn't. Instead I reared back and threw that filthy key ring of his just as far and hard as I could.

FOUR

By seven o'clock on the Wednesday morning after Tara Wylie's desperate text message showed up on her mother's cell phone, the temperature was sixty-two degrees and the only sign that there had been any sleet at all in northern Maine was the mist steaming in gray billows off the blacktop as Lizzie drove out of Bearkill.

"Amber Alert's up." Beside her in the Blazer's passenger seat, Aroostook County sheriff Cody Chevrier tipped his close-clipped silvery head as he listened attentively.

"TV and radio stations've all got press releases, they'll be on the noon news. A flyer with her picture on it is on its way to every cop car in Maine, truck stops got them, hospitals, homeless shelters, and the agencies've all got a heads-up," she recited.

Quickly she summarized the other events of last night: the appearance in her office of Jane Crimmins, Lizzie's hospital visit later after Crimmins's breakdown, and the time with Peg Wylie.

"That cell phone location's being worked on, but no luck so far. Can't say I expect any, either," she finished. Tracking a cell phone wasn't the piece of cake the TV crime shows made it out to be.

"Sounds like you got it all covered," Chevrier said. "That name, though, Crimmins. Why's it sound so familiar to me?"

At his question, her already-solid respect for the rural sheriff went up yet another notch. The kidnapping of three young women followed by their imprisonment in a New Haven basement hadn't been a local crime, and the name Crimmins didn't belong to any of the victims.

In fact, as far as Lizzie was aware it had been mentioned only once, in a human-interest feature that had appeared in New Haven's alt-weekly newspaper, the *Advocate*. Yet Chevrier was somehow aware of it.

"Yeah," he added, snapping his fingers, "now I remember. She had some link to one of the kidnapping victims in the Henry Gemerle mess, right." Surprising Lizzie further, Chevrier went on. "That's it, she was a sort of caretaker afterward for one of the rescued women."

"That's right." On either side of the road, the dry soil was pockmarked by vanished ice pellets. She put the window down; the air smelled like spring, even if a false one.

"Case in New Haven," Chevrier continued, "whole thing started six months ago? Or that's when it came to light," he amended.

"That's when they found the girls," she confirmed. "There was an arraignment pretty quick after that. Then nothing more until a couple of weeks ago, when they started showing the hearings on TV."

She slowed for the GRAMMY'S RESTAURANT sign, then pulled into a parking lot full of pickup trucks and heavy equipment for cutting firebreaks.

Chevrier shrugged. "Hey, I stay on top of all the crime stories I can. You'd be surprised how many fugitives think Maine's a good place to vanish."

He glanced around the diner's parking lot, full of familiar vehicles. "Like nobody here's gonna notice some strange guy the minute he hits town," he added sarcastically.

They parked between a forest service water tanker and an old Ford Fairlane whose rear windows were plastic sheets duct-taped to the outsides of the frames. Into the fuel filler hole, which was missing both its cover flap and filler cap in blatant defiance of DMV regulations, a red grease-rag had been stuffed.

She switched off the Blazer's ignition. "Anyway, like you said, the guy's named Gemerle." It was pronounced *JEM-er-lee*. "The monster of Michener Street, the media called him."

"So what's Crimmins doing here?" Chevrier asked as they crossed the parking lot.

The Fairlane was illegal in too many ways to count, not the least of them being an outdated inspection sticker. But it belonged to a local firefighting volunteer so they let it alone; no doubt Chevrier would have a quiet word with the owner later.

The night before, she'd calmed Peg Wylie as well as she could and then spent the rest of the hours until morning on her to-do list—the flyers, the Amber Alert and agency notifications—and on refreshing her memories of the New Haven atrocity.

There was plenty on the Internet about it, including the *New Haven Advocate* piece revealing that the victim Jane Crimmins had been caring for was a young woman by the name of Cam Petry.

"I'll find out more when she wakes up from the sedation she got," said Lizzie, wondering where Cam Petry was right now.

Homemade posters for church suppers, raffles, and items for sale—snow tires, woodstoves, a shotgun—filled the bulletin board in the diner's covered entryway. Also on display was the freshly posted MISSING flyer for Tara Wylie, crisper and more readable than the ones her mother had made, including a head shot from Tara's yearbook and another of her grinning triumphantly atop a human pyramid of Bearkill High School cheerleaders.

"We're way behind the eight-ball on her now," Lizzie said unhappily, waving at the flyer. Too much time had passed while Peg dithered, trying to pretend that Tara had gone AWOL on her own.

And why was that? Lizzie wondered again as she followed Chevrier into the diner. At the gingham-covered tables and in the booths, fire crews in green forest service uniforms were fueling up for yet another day of clearing and trenching.

They crossed to a booth upholstered in blue leatherette and slid in opposite each other. "Anyway, about Tara's phone. I called the MDEA," she said. The Maine Drug Enforcement Agency had better electronics expertise than anyone else in the state, which they were using nowadays to hunt down more of those meth labs, mostly. "But they've come up empty, too. The phone's not active now. It could've been on just long enough for one call and then turned off again, which makes it a tiny needle in a large electronic haystack."

Or whoever had Tara—if someone did—might have caught her using the phone and done something to it, an idea Lizzie preferred not to dwell on as they gave their breakfast orders.

"Anyway, the Gemerle thing. It was a multiple kidnapping, guy held three girls captive for fifteen years. Kind of like that Cleveland case earlier? Only the Cleveland perp hung himself in jail."

"Yeah. Ask me, that guy got off easy."

Their coffee arrived. "But the New Haven situation, what's the recent action on that?"

"Well, first the court ordered a psych workup."

"'Cause *batshit crazy* isn't a legal term that you can just slap on a guy," said Chevrier, rolling his eyes long-sufferingly.

"Correct," she agreed. "And neither is *low-life scumbag,* if you're on the prosecution's side. So all that took quite a while, because of course both sides had to have their own psychiatrists. But he got judged unfit to stand trial just the other day.

"So he went back to the forensic hospital in Connecticut. He's still there and that's where he'll stay for the foreseeable future," she said.

Hot plates of food came and Chevrier dug into his bacon and eggs. Taking a piece of bacon off his plate, she crunched into it. Then:

"Listen, has Peg Wylie got any good connections around here? I mean is she related to anyone important, or friends with anyone who's got any local influence, anything like that?"

Because connections helped get publicity and when you were looking for someone, every bit of public awareness helped.

Chevrier shook his head. "Peg's a single mom, she moved here a little over three years ago and bought that house out there on the Hardscrabble Road. She wanted a better environment for Tara to grow up in, she said. She's got no important pals that I know of. Lots of friends in the fire department, though."

Lizzie tipped her head questioningly. "She tried joining up, but she couldn't pass the physical," he explained. "Next thing you know, she's on the stair machine at the firehouse every day."

"And she made it through the next try?" Lizzie asked, but Chevrier shook his head.

"Nope. Or the one after that, either. But on the fourth try she racked up the best scores anyone around here ever has. You want somebody to run up five flights wearin' an air pack, drag out some overweight jerk who fell asleep drunk while he was holdin' a lit cigarette, she's your man. Woman. Whatever.

"But remind me about the Crimmins woman again," he said. "How she got involved with . . ."

"Right. The Gemerle thing. After their rescue from Henry Gemerle's basement this past summer, two of the victims reunited with their families. But the third one—"

He nodded sharply. "That's it. I remember now. It was kind of a feel-good story? Some good-Samaritan-type woman took the third one in, and that was—"

"Yup," Lizzie confirmed. "That was her. Jane Crimmins took in Henry Gemerle's third victim, Cam Petry. Who was her cousin, so I suppose that's why she did it. And now she's here, where another girl's gone missing."

"Huh. Well, ain't that a kick in the head. Hudson's got good notes, he documented what happened with her last night? 'Cause we don't need her going around saying that it was his fault the interview went south."

"Yeah, he recorded it. Missy's already typed up a transcript, but there wasn't much of anything in it. Nothing that looks bad for Dylan, anyway. I'm just hoping my choice last night hasn't shut Jane's mouth for the foreseeable future."

Chevrier frowned. "So you think you should've stayed with her instead of letting Hudson take the interview."

"Maybe. It was an option." Or maybe the real reason she'd proceeded the way she had was in the hope of keeping Dylan in town a little longer. But saying that to Chevrier wouldn't accomplish anything useful, so she didn't.

Driving back to Bearkill they passed small houses on rough bulldozed lots, their neatly stacked woodpiles nearly untouched. So far, this winter had called more for fans than furnaces.

At Lizzie's office, Chevrier got out. "So you've looked into Gemerle, right? Current whereabouts and so on?"

"Yeah, he's still safely in the psych unit." It had been a pleasant surprise about the job here in Bearkill that her mind and her new boss's worked so similarly.

"Although it turns out they actually did have an escape the other night, and that guy's still in the wind," she added.

It had given her pause until the supervisor at the forensic hospital had explained. "Different guy, though. Not Gemerle."

Chevrier's white Blazer, the twin of her own vehicle except for the sheriff's insignia on his door, sat in the Food King's lot across the street. But instead of crossing to it he stood watching a stray shopping cart roll slowly across the blacktop.

"Okay," he said finally. Then, turning to her: "I don't want you to make a big deal of this, what I'm about to tell you."

"Of what?" The big window at the front of her office showed Missy Brantwell's blond head bent over an open file folder.

"Peg Wylie," said Chevrier. "Remember I said she moved here to get Tara into a more wholesome place?"

"Yeah. So?" A sharp whiff of smoke tickled Lizzie's nose; bad news for the forest service.

"So before here, they lived in New Haven."

"Oh. Interesting." By which she meant *Holy shit.*

Chevrier eyed her evenly. "Yeah. Fascinating. So handle that information however you want. Don't go crazy with it, is all."

He started across the street. "And keep me up-to-date, hear? We've got no extra manpower, guys're busy tryin' to keep the whole state from burning down."

The smoke smell was getting stronger. A couple of dark-green vans sped by, each carrying a full crew. A pickup truck followed, tailpipe spewing and its bed loaded with open wooden crates piled high with shovels and pickaxes.

"I don't want to hear anybody from the media sayin' we didn't try hard enough to find that girl," Chevrier added as he reached his own vehicle. "So make sure that you do everything, be sure to keep on documenting everything, and don't forget to cover your ass."

Right, she thought as he drove off. But why did she have the feeling that her ass would end up in a sling anyway, whatever she did?

Inside her office, the scanner was alive with traffic. "Team Four, check in. Guys, gimme a callback here . . ."

On the TV that Missy Brantwell had set up on a file cart, the Bangor station's weather graphic depicted the whole state of Maine shaded in red.

". . . can't stress enough that you don't want to be burning anything outdoors," cautioned the voiceover.

Still no scanner reply. "Team Four," dispatch tried again, "come on now, let's hear from you folks. Gimme a shout right now."

The dispatcher's voice sharpened; the only possible reason a team wouldn't check in was if they couldn't. "Team Four . . ."

On the TV screen another graphic showed how much of the state similar fires had destroyed in 1947, when two hundred thousand acres burned.

The scanner spat static. Then: ". . . Team Four here, sorry about that, we're all good . . ."

Lizzie let out a relieved breath. "Someone's gonna get killed out there," Missy groused at her desk, which was covered with notes and paperwork but still so aggressively well organized that it made Lizzie marvel at her own good luck.

Missy might look fragile, with wide blue eyes and curly blond hair framing an always-amiable expression, but her office-management style was nothing short of military.

"I don't care how much training they get," she said, "none of the Bearkill fire volunteers has ever dealt with anything like this."

She plucked a slip of paper from her desk. "Message for you. From some Connecticut guy, he said it's kind of urgent?"

Her heart sinking with the weight of an unhappy premonition, Lizzie reached for the phone. Moments later she was connected with the Salisbury Forensic Institute's chief security officer.

From whom she learned that there had been a mistake.

FIVE

Aching and bleeding, still so scared out of my mind that I could barely recall who I was—*Jane Crimmins,* I kept reciting to myself idiotically, *my name is Jane Crimmins*—I made my broken way home late that night after my narrow escape.

We lived—my parents, my mom's parents, and I—in an old blue-collar neighborhood of New Haven, street after shabbily-neat tree-lined street full of small brick houses built years earlier for factory workers with lunch pails and union cards, breadwinners supporting whole families on a single paycheck.

Although by the time I lived there, that era was long gone. Under the weakly glowing, infrequent streetlights junk cars stood on blocks, torn blue tarps stretched across roofs, and cast-iron railings bled rust onto cracked-concrete front steps.

As I crept guiltily along the dark, silent street I kept waiting for one of the neighbors to call out to me. Old Mrs. Watterston, maybe, whose swollen legs kept her up most nights. Or Finny Brill, a boy from my class whose bad skin and worse breath made him a pariah around school.

Finny stayed up late, too, watching old horror films whose cheesy plots he would recite the next day, trying to convince everyone that he'd made them up himself. He was a braggart, sure he would one day be a famous film director, and always trying and failing to be in on the doings of the more popular kids.

His bedroom window flickered with blue TV light as I snuck under it, feeling like a criminal. Any instant I expected to hear his voice, full of triumph as he caught me doing something that I shouldn't be; Finny was so pathetic, he actually thought he could make friends that way. As if him spying on you was just the same as you telling him your secrets.

If Finny saw me I was dead. But he didn't, and no one did call out. I slunk up to our house, identical to the rest on the street except for the old Chris-Craft motorboat hulking amid the weeds at the rear of our yard, perched atop a rotting trailer whose long-flat tires were peeling away in thick gray strips. The back door was open; I slipped inside.

The house smelled like cat box and the Hamburger Helper we'd had for dinner. Going upstairs I held my breath, not from the odor but so I wouldn't sob out loud. *Cam . . .* But there was nothing I could do for her, and now I heard her voice again telling me what would happen to me if anyone learned what that man had done to me.

"Examine you," she'd said. *"Instruments."* It was as if she'd been cautioning me about what more could be inflicted on me and how I could avoid it: by keeping my mouth shut. And now that she was dead she was somehow even more of an authority than before, so I decided to stay silent.

In the upstairs hall I heard my parents and grandparents, early-to-bedders all, snoring behind closed doors. Not until I glimpsed myself in the bathroom mirror did the fear I'd been holding back hit me so hard again that it nearly swamped me.

My clothes were bloody and torn, nails broken and filthy, and the palms of my hands were scraped raw from scrabbling away from him. Or trying to; bruised, reddened finger marks around my ankle showed where he'd caught me. But my eyes were the same: wide, dark brown, seemingly as untroubled as before. My mouth, a thin pink line just like always, gave me hope as well.

Because it needed not to have happened, this nightmare more terrifying than any of Finny Brill's productions. It needed to be taken back, rewound like a horror film.

Not for Cam, of course. She was murdered, beyond my help. But for me, it had to be made so it wasn't real, and I had a bad feeling that this time, praying wouldn't do the trick.

Or any time, actually, from now on. Thinking this, I took a hot shower, then filled the bathtub and lay up to my chin in it for a long time, letting the hot water penetrate every sore fold and crevice. My father's Gillette razor blades were in the medicine cabinet, I knew, in a small flat dispenser, and it seemed clear to me that if I thought at all it would have to be about them.

So I didn't. Instead I soaked thoroughly, then soaped and soaped again, scrubbing until my skin pruned and the water began cooling. Shivering with misery I dried with a clean towel; then, in my own bed at last, I was asleep almost at once, falling into it with a final sob as if hurling myself off a cliff into the soft black nothingness.

Cam, I thought as the darkness closed around me. *Gone.* And then, *Her mom's going to be so mad.*

And after that I didn't think at all anymore.

Bearkill, Maine's only bar, Area 51, had a griddle, a deep-fat fryer, and a refrigerator—just enough to meet Maine's rules about food being available where alcohol was served.

Still, the burgers were decent, and to Lizzie's surprise it was already Wednesday noon. "An orderly got him out," she said, repeating what the forensic hospital's security guy had told her. *A mistake.*

After that conversation it had taken a couple of hours to get the word out to state and local cops, get a photograph of Gemerle, and start distributing more flyers. The rest of the morning had been taken up with paperwork.

"From what I can understand, the orderly either threatened or bribed another inmate to impersonate Henry Gemerle for just long enough to fool the rest of the staff," she said now. "Not that it was difficult, I guess. It was after lights-out so the other inmate was just a shape in Gemerle's bed. And after that it took a while for them to realize they should call me."

Trey Washburn's lips pursed thoughtfully. "So they thought the wrong guy was gone. And the orderly would do this why?"

Wearing his usual work uniform of Carhartt overalls, boots, and a denim jacket, the burly veterinarian hunched beside Lizzie at Area 51's long, polished wooden bar.

"You got me," she replied. Why did people do any of the damn fool things they did, after all? Like her forgetting her date with Trey last night, for instance.

Now the smell of the french fryer floated unappetizingly from the bar's tiny kitchen, and she wasn't hungry anyway. But at the moment she felt lucky that Trey was still speaking to her, so she'd let him persuade her in here.

The TV over the bar showed a map of the state thickly dotted with blazing campfire icons.

"Anyone seen him?" Trey bit into his burger.

She shook her head. "Seems the orderly got him dressed up in a staff uniform and slipped him past security. Had an ID badge for him, too, they think. Here's his picture."

She slid the eight-by-ten glossy fresh from her office printer down the bar's polished surface.

"Yeah, I see the problem." Trey pushed the photo back. "Guy's got a normal haircut, regular features. Nothing weird looking."

She nodded grimly, chewing. "Uh-huh. Trouble is he's not just anybody. He's a dangerous predator who's already victimized three women that we know of. And he's got at least one connection who's right here in Bearkill."

There was no concrete reason to think Gemerle was on his way here. But she couldn't ignore the coincidence of Jane Crimmins, a close associate of one of his victims, arriving just as Tara Wylie, also a former New Haven resident, went missing.

"You talked to Peg about this yet?" Trey wanted to know.

The bright-blue eyes that met hers in the mirror behind the bar were smart and kind. She looked away, made shy suddenly by the directness of his gaze; since they'd first met he'd made no secret of how he felt about her.

"No, I haven't seen Peg today," she replied finally. "State cops are with her right now making up for lost time, and after that DHHS wants a crack at her."

The child welfare people always got involved when a kid went missing, which when it was a little one actually made sense. But when the missing kid was fourteen and the original theory was that she left on her boyfriend's motorbike, not so much.

"The boyfriend's still gone, too. Aaron DeWilde," she said.

"What do you make of that?" He'd finished his burger and when she looked down she found that she'd eaten most of hers, too, plus all the fries.

"No idea. I'm going to the hospital when we're done here, to try to find out more." By now Jane Crimmins's psych exam should be complete. "And then I'll head up to Cross Lake where the boyfriend lives, talk to his folks."

She wasn't looking forward to it. "They've been watching a few too many cop shows," she added, having spent time on the phone with them this morning.

Aaron's dad in particular seemed fully convinced that there was an FBI lab somewhere that could take a few unrelated bits of physical evidence, punch a set of data into a computer, and come up with the precise current location of a rural Maine kid.

"Listen," she added, "I'm so sorry about last night. Leaving you in the lurch like that."

"Yeah, well." He brushed pale hair back from his forehead. "Things happen." Then he grinned. "Or they happen when you're sweet on a cop, anyway. Want to try again tonight?"

The bar's TV switched to a live shot of racing flames just as a siren howled outside. Beyond Area 51's front window the haze had thickened noticeably again just since they'd come in here.

"What?" She dragged her mind back from the sudden mental picture of a girl dead in a ditch, surrounded by fire. Then:

"Sorry," she said. "I can't tonight. I need another raincheck. With plenty of rain to go with it, if possible."

Trey was the kind of guy who could spend all day wrestling large farm animals into swallowing medicine and holding still for shots, then go home and do miracles with kitchen implements she had only seen used in fancy restaurants: copper whisking bowls and long-handled sauté skillets.

And on top of that, he understood the unpredictable hours of cop work. His own didn't follow a set-in-stone schedule, either.

"Just until this is over," she added. Trey nodded agreeably. Really, it was too bad that agreeable wasn't all she wanted.

Really too bad. Out on the sidewalk she watched Trey's pickup truck pull away. The wood-frame buildings of downtown cast bluish shadows as the winter sun, already more than halfway through its short winter arc, fell behind the high hills to the west.

In the office Missy Brantwell looked up. "Peg Wylie stopped in with more pictures."

They spread across Lizzie's desk: Tara riding a bike, flying along no-hands with her arms spread wide and her eyes as bright as stars. Carving a pumpkin, up to her elbows in it.

"So d'you think she's okay?" asked Missy.

"I don't know." Lizzie sank into her chair. Once upon a time the only predators you had to worry about were the ones who could physically get to the kids. But with computers, an entirely new category of slimeballs was on the rise.

In Boston a few weeks before Lizzie's last day there, a girl of twelve had been found boarding a flight to Brazil. It turned out that a registered sex offender posing as a sixteen-year-old from Rio de Janeiro had bought her the ticket.

"State cops took Tara's laptop this morning," Missy added. "Maybe they'll still get something off that."

But Lizzie didn't think so. An online predator could have deleted his or her Facebook profile by now. If Tara hadn't already cried wolf a few times, the investigation might've begun in time to catch something like that. But Tara had used up all her get-looked-for-right-away cards by running off twice before.

"Uh-oh," said Missy suddenly. Following her assistant's gaze, Lizzie watched a fragment of flaming ash spiral down outside.

"Get your stuff," Missy snapped. Grabbing her purse, she slammed her desk shut and locked it. Lizzie snatched her own bag, too, and all the Tara photos, plus her personal weapon.

Because the early part of a case always felt like wading through molasses, and if you came upon something as you slogged forward, who knew what it might be? Two firearms—her duty weapon and her personal piece—could end up being laughably too many . . . or not enough.

Outside, Missy locked the door as more ash floated down.

"Jeffrey at daycare?" He was Missy's little boy. Lizzie slid her work gun into her duty belt and snapped the safety strap, put her personal weapon into her bag.

"Yeah. I'm going to the daycare to check on him. Probably this is nothing," Missy said, "but . . ."

But no one else thought so. Up and down the street people were shutting up shop and heading for their cars or standing on the sidewalk, gazing unhappily into the blue sky.

Blue except for the ash falling out of it. Another flaming fragment swirled to the sidewalk; Lizzie scuffed it out with her boot as a sick orange glow flared in the west.

"A ridgeline flamed up. They'll do that," diagnosed Missy. "Sulk and smolder out there in the puckerbrush, and then—"

"There's a plan, though, right? I mean, if a fire does get going here in town?"

Missy grimaced. "An *evacuation* plan, yeah. Anything starts burning here, this whole place is gonna go up like a bonfire," she finished, getting into her car.

As Missy drove off, Lizzie's cell phone trilled. "Hey, it's me, Dylan."

She turned her back on the western horizon, where the sight of a line of evergreen trees behaving like turpentine-soaked torches unnerved her more than she liked admitting, even to herself.

"Where are you?" A helicopter whap-whapped overhead, laden with firefighting chemicals, the heavy beat of its rotors blocking out Dylan's voice for a moment.

". . . Augusta," Dylan replied. "Listen, that Crimmins woman? The one from last night . . . have you seen her yet today? And is she by any chance talking about an escaped inmate? Because I just got a call from . . ."

He named the security guy at the Salisbury Forensic Institute, the one she'd spoken to, also. "You talked to him about a perp named . . . how do you pronounce it, again?"

"Gemerle," she said. "Why, what's—"

A Jeep with a cherry beacon on the dashboard roared by, and then a couple of pickup trucks. A windowed van full of a dozen or so dogs came after that; Lizzie recognized Bearkill's volunteer animal shelter staffer behind the wheel.

"Hey, Dylan, just tell me, okay? I got a few things going on here, and—"

". . . spotted him . . ." His voice came intermittently through the buzz and howl of a bad connection. "Car . . . stolen . . . turnpike."

"What, the Connecticut turnpike?" Another loud sputtering of static made her curse.

But then the phone cleared up suddenly. "No. Lizzie, there was a LoJack in the orderly's car. He hadn't disabled it and once they found out the runner was Gemerle, they got a court order and tracked the vehicle all the way to Maine. Took them a while, but they finally picked it up. They found it abandoned at the rest area in Houlton a little while ago."

Houlton was sixty miles from here. An ambulance screamed by. Behind the big plate-glass front window of her office, the phone console started blinking. "Dylan, I've got to—"

"Wait, you need to hear this. There was a gun safe in the abandoned car. Empty. I think Gemerle's gotten a weapon. And—"

And? she wondered a little wildly as the phone console in the office went on signaling.

She turned her back on it, pressing the cell phone to her ear. A missing girl, a rapidly worsening fire emergency, and an escaped human predator who was probably here in Maine; what more could there be?

But when the punch line finally came, it was a killer:

"—and when the trooper popped the abandoned car's trunk, he found a body inside."

"Where is she?" Cam's mother—my aunt Rose—lived only a few blocks from my house in New Haven.

She grabbed my shoulders and shook me, then flung me back down into my chair. "You tell me where Cam is, you—"

Two days had passed since the terrible events of that night: Cam murdered, me brutally assaulted, and then my escape. I'd kept quiet about it all, each passing hour with no one yelling at me or forcing me into a frightening medical examination confirming me in this decision, and now my mother and I were at Cam's house.

"You'd better tell me where she is, you little . . ." Aunt Rose was scared and being scared made her furious.

Everything did. "I—I don't know where she is." Not technically a lie.

I stared at Aunt Rose, so frightened I could barely form words. But at the same time my mind kept working; so far all I'd had to do was keep my mouth shut, but now might be different.

"Isn't she home yet?" The panic had begun the night before, when after twenty-four hours still no one could find her. It wasn't the first time that Cam had taken off from home, usually after a quarrel with Aunt Rose over some stunt Cam had pulled.

But it was the first time she hadn't come back. Aunt Rose glared darkly at me, her meaty arms folded across her chest.

"No, she's not home, you little liar. You're worse than she is, that fake look on your face. Do you see her here? Do you?"

I don't know why she hated me. Not that I was perfect; there had been minor things. Small fires, a choking incident at school.

Little things like that. Now she loomed over me menacingly, demanding an answer until my mother stopped her.

"Rose. Don't scare her, now, you know how she is."

We were in my aunt's living room surrounded by her treasured collection of hand-painted Hummel figurines, sweet little plump-cheeked ceramic children doing sweet little activities: tootling on musical instruments, having confidential conversations with blue-birds, and so on.

I wanted to grab one of those stupid figurines and hurl it through a window, but instead I sat meekly on the cheap woven throw Aunt Rose had draped over the chair. The living room was spotless; not one bit of dust marred an end table or a coffee table, the air reeked of Pledge and Comet cleanser, and we'd had to take our shoes off before being allowed to walk on the white wall-to-wall carpet, her pride and joy.

You know how she is. I shot a dark look at her but she didn't see it, luckily for me; from now on, I reminded myself, I would have to be more careful.

From now on, a lot of things would be different. "She came to the knitting group," I said. "She wanted me to go with her."

Careful, starting immediately. Someone could have seen us together at the dance.

"Go where?" Aunt Rose demanded. She was a stout, broad-shouldered woman with crimson gin-blossoms on her cheeks. Today she wore a housedress with an apron around her middle, rolled-down stockings, and canvas sneakers with the seams split to ease her bunions.

My mother was small and timid, neatly dressed in slacks and a white blouse and with her hair freshly permed. Seeing them side by side, it was hard to believe they had once looked alike.

"The park," I answered Aunt Rose. "We just wanted to—"

"So you lied?" From the look on my mother's face you'd have thought I'd just told her we'd been working as prostitutes.

She got up, shaking her head. "Oh, Jane. You lied? I'm so disappointed in you."

Wow, big surprise, you're disappointed, I wanted to retort, shocked at all these new, harsh reactions I was having but unable to stop them.

Not even wanting to stop them, and why should I? I wondered suddenly. Nothing I did was ever good enough, nothing ever quite right. I could go to confession every day, every hour, and still some small, insignificant sin would manage to smudge the golden perfection of my immortal soul.

Which all at once I did not believe in, either. One minute I'd had faith and the next, presto, all of it was gone. But at that realization there wasn't the sense of release I'd expected, that I imagined whenever I heard about other people's disbelief. All I felt was sad and ashamed.

So ashamed . . . now that the first numb shock of what he'd done to me had worn off slightly, if I could've managed it I'd have crawled right out of my skin, thrown it away because he'd touched it. Being dead made Cam the lucky one of us, it seemed to me.

Dead meant not having to remember. "I tried stopping her," I offered. "But she was going to go, whether I went along with her or not. So I thought it would be better if the two of us . . ."

I was nervous, and talking too much. Luckily, a knock at the door interrupted me. Moments later Aunt Rose led two men in dark suits into the room. *Now you'll tell,* her malevolent scowl said. After trying all Cam's friends and anyone else she could think of, she'd finally given up and called the police.

Once they'd been introduced, they began to ask me a lot of questions, politely and gently. I gave truthful answers until they started asking about the two of us leaving the dance.

No one had been in the parking lot; no one had seen that part. Or so I hoped. But either way, it was a risk I would have to take. I couldn't give them anything to latch on to, to make them think I might be lying about something or leaving something out.

"We walked home together until we got to Evergreen Street," I said. "Then we split up. I went straight home, came inside, and went to bed. I thought she was going home, too."

I glanced at my mother, who was biting her lips to keep from crying and fingering her rosary anxiously, turning the beads over and over in her small, neatly kept hands. Then I looked at my aunt, whose broad, coarse face was frankly murderous.

"Liar," she muttered. "You're a terrible little—"

"I'm not lying," I cried. "Cam went left, I went right. How was I supposed to know she'd—"

"What, Jane? How were you supposed to know she would what?" one of the detectives asked kindly. Not suspiciously.

Sucker, I thought at him. I'd dangled a shred of bait out in front of him and he'd taken it. "That she wouldn't go home. That she'd go somewhere else," I whispered. "Without me."

Because that had to be my story, didn't it? Whatever they asked about what happened to Cam, I didn't know about it because I hadn't been there.

Aunt Rose made a sound of disgust. "That child," she spat venomously at me, "is a sneak, and she's just lying her face off. And if *you* can't get it out of her, I know how to—"

As she spoke she was taking off the plastic belt that she wore around her ample middle, curling it like a whip. "Rose!" my mother breathed frightenedly.

Together the detectives got to their feet, rising in one smooth, decisive motion to block my aunt's attack. "It's okay, we'll handle this," one of them said.

Aunt Rose stepped back grudgingly, her expression thwarted and her eyes telegraphing that if she had her way, I'd be getting the belt and more. But then a question from one of the detectives changed her tune.

"Where do you think your daughter might've gone? Are there any hangouts that she frequents or people she might want to see, maybe that you don't approve of?"

"My daughter," she snapped nastily in reply, "doesn't go to *hangouts.*" She put an ugly twist on the word. "Or see any people I don't approve of, either."

Even scared as I was, it was hard not to laugh. She was so stupid and I felt, momentarily, so exultant. Because so far, the cops seemed to believe I didn't know anything.

"And if I'd had any idea," she added, "I wouldn't ever have approved of her being out anywhere with this little *freak.*"

By now her whole face was so red, you could hardly see the gin-blossoms.

"Oh, you think you're so smart, don't you?" she went on furiously. "Well, I've got news for you, little miss, I'm not fooled by all your la-di-dah *book reading* and your *piano playing.* It's not even *natural,* the way she is, just *look* at her."

At my modest pedal pushers and gingham blouse. At my lack of makeup. I was, after all, a St. Anselm's girl and I tried hard to fit in.

"It's all *fake*," my aunt Rose spluttered, "she's a . . ."

But at this point my mother had finally heard enough. "Rose. Janie says they split up. That she went one way and Cam went the other. So don't you think that maybe—"

That maybe I was telling the truth, she was about to finish. Which was what it looked to me like the detectives thought, too. My dislikable aunt's seemingly baseless accusations just sealed the deal for me, because they didn't want to believe her.

So that's when I knew I was probably going to get away with it. They thought Cam and I had simply gone to the dance together when we weren't supposed to, which was plenty bad enough, and I'd be punished for it.

But if they'd known what happened afterward . . .

Even then all I really wanted was to tell. What had happened to Cam, that she was dead, and what he'd done to me . . . with the detectives standing right there, stopping the words from erupting out of my mouth was like trying not to vomit.

I silenced myself by recalling what Cam had said: about the questions I'd be asked, the violations I'd be made to endure. I'd had much more time to think about it by then and I'd decided that if anyone tried any of that on me I really would come right out of my skin and run away all bloody and screaming.

Not only that, but if I told, I'd be the raped girl, wouldn't I? There'd be the pointing and whispering at school, comments and stares. Bad enough that I was already so different: shy, bookish, all the things my aunt had implied. But if I told anyone the truth I'd be dirty-different, a filthy joke.

And I wasn't going to be, I just wasn't. After all, Cam was already dead. Nothing could help her, and as for the other girls, I was starting to wonder if maybe the drugs in that juice he had given me to drink had made me imagine them.

Probably I had; I'd been so hurt and scared, so messed up that I'd hallucinated them. And besides, all that couldn't really be true, could it? That there were girls locked up in a cellar?

Surely not. It was like things on TV, either made up or they had nothing to do with me.

Nothing at all. "Can we look at Cam's room?" said one of the detectives to Aunt Rose. They were done with me.

Later when Cam still didn't turn up they talked to me again: Had there been anyone at the park that night? Or on the street going home? Was I sure that we hadn't gone anywhere else at all?

But I just stuck to my story, that beyond our going to the dance nothing had happened.

Not that I knew about, anyway.

SIX

Moments after Dylan's call about the body in the car trunk, the phone rang again. This time it was Peg Wylie, demanding yet another meeting.

By then it was Wednesday afternoon. Barely containing her impatience, Lizzie found the worried mother in the white-painted wooden gazebo outside the Bearkill library.

"What do you want, Peg?" Lizzie stomped up the gazebo steps, the news of Gemerle's likely arrival in Maine fresh in her mind, shortening her temper. "What lies are you going to tell me now?"

"What?" Just out of her interviews with the child welfare people, Peg's eyes were swollen and red-rimmed, her short, bleached hair an unruly mess.

She dragged miserably on a cigarette, a paper cup full of water and soggy butts perched on the gazebo's rail. "They said I was lying, too, the investigators from—"

Oh, boo-hoo, Lizzie thought. "Well, they think everyone is lying to them, Peg. Because you know what? Usually everyone is."

It was all Lizzie could do not to shake the woman until her teeth rattled. "Including you. But if you want your daughter back then you'd better drop the game you've been playing with me."

"I don't understand. I'm not playing any—"

Lizzie grabbed the paper cup and hurled it, the wet tobacco shreds and brown droplets of water flying in a shining arc.

"Cut it out, dammit. It's over, okay? I mean it, I don't want any more crappy stories out of you." She stopped, struggling to control her anger, then tried again.

"Peg. A woman by the name of Jane Crimmins was in my office last night. She's from New Haven. Like you and Tara."

A look of stark fear crossed Peg's face before she could stop it. *Good,* Lizzie thought, *now maybe you'll break down and tell me the truth.*

"She took care of one of Henry Gemerle's victims," Lizzie went on, "after the three women he'd been holding prisoner for fifteen years were finally set free. You know who he is, right?"

Peg's frightened look said she did. "Peg, I think the Crimmins woman might be trying to say something about that, and about Tara, too, maybe. But she's so screwed up, she can't."

It was only a guess. But what else made sense? Jane Crimmins wasn't here by accident. "And," Lizzie added, watching for Peg's reaction, "Henry Gemerle has escaped from a locked hospital ward in Connecticut."

This time there was no hiding Peg's reflexive shudder. She knew the name, all right. But:

"Nothing to do with me," Peg said tightly. "Or Tara, either. What, you think I was somehow involved in a multiple kidnapping? Just because we're from New Haven, that doesn't mean—"

Lizzie flung her hands up in disgust. "Right. It's all a big coincidence. Come on, what're you, stupid? Or maybe you just think I'm—"

Peg pulled another cigarette from her pack and lit it with shaking hands. "Do they know where he is?" she asked, trying to make her voice sound casual.

Lizzie had seen this reaction before, too. People got fixed on the story they were telling even when the truth became obvious.

Especially if the truth was bad. "Gemerle's still on the run but the car he was in was found abandoned just off the highway in Houlton this morning."

With a body in the trunk, she added mentally. But there was no use telling Peg so, especially since the revelation might turn out to be useful later. Dylan said the ID in the body's wallet was that of the forensic hospital orderly, a guy named Finny Brill.

So either Gemerle had somehow forced Brill to get him out of the locked ward and drive him here, or Brill had willingly helped Gemerle for some reason and things had gone wrong.

"You're sure, Peg. You're sure you don't have any connection at all with Henry Gemerle. That's not why you called me a little while ago, to tell me about it?"

Peg shook her head stubbornly. "Never heard of him." She dragged on the smoke. "I just . . . I just wanted to know if there've been any developments. Anyway, Tara left home before he ever—"

It was another familiar reaction, this clinging to hope. "I know that," said Lizzie. "He was locked up when she went missing."

So he couldn't have grabbed Tara; not right away, at least. But what about later?

"There's still too much that points to a connection, though, and you think so, too," she told Peg. "I can tell by the way you reacted when I told you about his escape."

The state cops would have the car on a flatbed by now, taking it to Augusta where their techs would go over it for fingerprints and other evidence. Hair samples, for instance.

And blood. "Now, I can find that connection eventually. Tax records, city directories . . . if there's a link between you and that guy, I'll locate it. But meanwhile, Tara's still out there and so is he."

She let her voice soften. "So Peg, if you know anything at all about any of this, you need to tell me now."

Her phone chirped. She let it go to voicemail. "Because Tara could've left on her own or with Aaron, just like you think."

The phone chirped again. "But maybe then she decided to come home again. Walked away from wherever they'd gone together, maybe because they had a fight. Could she have been hitchhiking?"

Peg's face rang a *suspicions confirmed* bell. "Sure. Tara's very independent, so if she didn't like what was going on she'd have left. And . . . and she's hitchhiked before. I've warned her not to, but—"

The phone rang a third time. "What?" Lizzie snapped into it.

"Hey, Lizzie, it's Emily." The emergency-room doc sounded harassed. "Sorry to have to bug you, but things are getting nuts here. There was an accident out on the Ridge Road and we've got a full house all of a sudden."

From behind her in the ER treatment area came a confusion of sounds: a monitor alarm jangling, someone crying out in pain, and someone else shouting something.

"But I thought I'd better let you know the Crimmins woman is getting itchy," Emily said. "I told her you want to talk with her but she wants to leave, and now I'm all out of reasons to—"

Damn, Lizzie thought. "Okay," she said as Peg finished her cigarette and lit another from the end of the first. From her face it was clear she wasn't stepping off that story of hers, that she knew nothing about Henry Gemerle.

Yeah, sure she didn't. "Tell Jane Crimmins I'll be right over," said Lizzie, then stuck the phone in her jacket pocket and spun away from Peg.

"Three strikes, you're out," she called over her shoulder as she stomped toward the Blazer.

"I mean it, Peg. Next time you call me you'd better be ready with the truth. Because if you're not," Lizzie added, swinging up into the big vehicle, "don't bother me at all."

Headed out of town Lizzie passed a small housing development, clusters of small ranch-style houses built around a newly blacktopped circle drive where people were loading their cars full of pets and kids, their faces grim and puzzled. Nothing like the fires had happened around here in living memory and they were having trouble believing it.

But the smoke was convincing them. Thick billows rolled over the roadway, then cleared as the wind shifted. Gripping the wheel, Lizzie peered into visibility that went from fine to zero in the space of a few moments.

Once she nearly missed a curve, the crunch of gravel under the front tire shocking a surprised curse out of her. Loosening her grasp on the steering wheel slightly, she let the Blazer roll along with the right-side tires in the stones until it stabilized, then popped back up onto the pavement with no harm done.

None so far. A heavy burning smell hung in the air, and a thin, smeary ash fouled the Blazer's windshield after each successive drift of smoke. As she neared the hospital entrance she hit the speed dial on the vehicle's console.

"Peg's dug her heels in," she told Dylan, still at the crime scene in Houlton. "I don't know why she thinks that's better than spilling the whole story, but—"

She swung the Blazer around a slow-moving pickup, its bed packed with garden hoses, buckets, and sprayer handles, all with the Agway labels still on them. To protect houses, she realized; it was heartbreaking, the determination these people were showing.

"I'll have another go at Peg later, or the state cops can try again, maybe." She put a hand up in a wave at the pickup driver in her rear-view and got a solemn dip of his gimme cap's bill in reply.

"Right now," she added into the phone, "I'm headed back to the hospital to see the Crimmins woman, she's getting antsy. But how about your end, anything more on that car or the body yet?"

"Yeah." Dylan sounded disgusted. "Looks like the orderly got a blunt-force head injury. Bashed with the butt of a gun, maybe."

He said something sharply to someone nearby, then came back to the phone. "Gemerle loaded Brill into the trunk as a quick way of getting the body out of sight, seems like. Then he took off."

She pulled over as an ambulance roared up behind her and passed, siren shrieking. "You're sure it's Brill?"

"They're confirming the driver's license ID with fingerprints now," Dylan said. "He had to have them taken to work at the forensic hospital. But Brill's been missing since Gemerle left, and so's the spare orderly outfit his work pals say he kept in his locker, shoes and all."

So their theory about the escape was probably correct. Lizzie pulled up to the hospital, a low, yellow-brick structure with big windows and a wide front terrace furnished with café tables and chairs. Under the portico around the side, EMTs from the ambulance that had passed her moments ago were already bringing their gurney back out the ER's sliding doors, having delivered their patient.

"So what's Gemerle using for transportation now?" she asked. In the city there were plenty of ways to get around, but in Maine public transport was absent except in the largest cities.

All three of them, she thought wryly. "No idea," said Dylan. "I hope we don't find another vehicle with another body in it." He fell silent briefly. Then:

"Hey, though, when we get done d'you want to get dinner? I heard," he added, as if as an afterthought, "from another guy who thinks he's seen Nicki. Over in Skowhegan this time."

The town was south of Bearkill, and way over in the western part of the state. To quell the pulse of fury she felt at his words, she tried recalling exactly where. But she hadn't been in Maine long enough to memorize territory that wasn't her own.

"Really," she said at last. She shut off the Blazer, feeling annoyed and like she was being manipulated, like the mention of Nicki was a lure.

He wouldn't lie to me, one side of her head assured her. *Not about that.*

But then the other side chimed in: *Like he didn't lie about his wife? About them being already separated and in the process of getting a—*

"You know what, that's nice of you, but I think I might just stick around and follow up on the Jane Crimmins angle," she said. "I'm here at the hospital, maybe I'll try hanging around with her, take her out somewhere for supper later or something."

From the corner of her eye she glimpsed Bearkill's only taxi driving up to the ER entrance. The old sedan bore a magnetic sign—RIDE THE BEAR!—on the door. Moments later it headed off again down the long driveway and onto the highway toward town.

"I mean," Lizzie went on, "we don't know yet why she freaked out with you, so I think I ought to see her alone and find out if that makes any difference."

"Oh." Dylan covered his unhappy surprise well. Just not quite well enough. "Okay, then," he said. "Well, I'll be around, though. We can—"

Then she realized: *A taxi.* "Dylan, I've got to go."

She crossed the blacktop at a sprint, ran through the sliding glass doors and across the tiled lobby. Down a corridor past shocked-looking nurses and orderlies, into the waiting area, and through the automatic doors while a clerk scurried after her . . .

"Miss? Miss, I'm sorry, you can't—"

The hell I can't. "Where is she?"

All the cubicles in the emergency area had patients in them, all being treated for injuries that, through the gaps between the curtains as she passed, looked bloody and painful.

But the curtains hanging around the sixth cubicle, where Jane Crimmins had been the night before, were closed completely. Lizzie yanked them open, then stopped short. This cubicle's patient lay still, covered by a white sheet. Completely covered.

"Driver from the accident on Ridge Road," said Emily Ektari, coming up to Lizzie with a stack of charts in her hands. "Big-time blunt-force chest injury. He bled to death."

Someone's going to get killed . . . Emily had predicted it hours earlier, and Missy, too. And they'd been right. "Couldn't you—?"

"What, surgery?" Emily blew an exhausted breath out.

"This is a rural hospital, Lizzie, it's not a major medical center like you're used to. We transfer the complicated ones to a trauma center, and even there, what he had, it's fatal more times than not."

"And Jane Crimmins, how long has she been gone?"

"Couple minutes. I tried to stall her for you, but—"

"Yeah, I know. Thanks anyway."

Back in the Blazer she hit the RADIO button, jammed her foot on the gas, and took off. She crushed the speed limit, racing through smoke-billows and yelling for dispatch to alert all patrol units, ordering them to stop that cab. Then, when she was finished using dispatch for a punching bag, she cursed fluently again at herself.

All of which made her feel pretty silly when, outside her office minutes later, she found Jane Crimmins pacing the sidewalk, waiting for her.

"You got a knife or a gun in there, anything like that?"

Driving with Jane Crimmins beside her in the Blazer, Lizzie waved at the faux-leather satchel on the woman's lap.

Crimmins still didn't look dangerous, with her pale, narrow face and short, dark hair, her fragile-appearing hands so small they were almost childlike. But Lizzie sensed some kind of a weird vibe anyway, a bizarre whiff of something she couldn't identify.

"No," Crimmins replied softly. Even her voice seemed that of a child, breathy and tentative. "No weapons."

They drove past the old potato barn on the outskirts of town; the wholesaler's warehouse was a weathered structure with a high wooden false front and a long front porch where day laborers lined up in potato-digging season, waiting to be hired.

Lizzie couldn't help thinking about how fast that barn would blaze up if a spark ever reached it. Out beyond the edge of town, the widely spaced wooden houses and mobile homes looked the same: empty, vulnerable. Between them lay dry weeds and dusty loam, the fenced farm fields bounded in the distance by forests, thousands of acres of burnable timber just waiting for the touch of a windblown ember.

"You know what I'd like?" Jane asked. "A piece of toast."

Whoa, thought Lizzie. Weapon or not, this was one strange ranger.

Jane gazed out at the fields, alive with dust devils whirling across dry soil. "White bread, butter on it. And a cup of tea."

Lizzie had planned to take Jane Crimmins to Houlton. An interrogation room in the county courthouse might convince the woman that the search for Tara Wylie was serious, and that she should cooperate if she could.

Instead Lizzie pulled a U-turn. "I can arrange that."

Because after all, why not? She'd once driven a gang-murder witness around the towns out past Boston for seven and a half hours—she'd eaten enough fast food that day to put her off it forever—until the witness found the courage to talk.

Meanwhile Jane Crimmins was odd and stubborn, but she hadn't done anything illegal as far as Lizzie could tell, and if someone leaned on her too hard she could shut down and simply refuse to talk to any-one. And that couldn't be allowed to happen, even if chauffeuring her around was already driving Lizzie a little nuts.

Jane spoke again. "He's here, isn't he? Henry Gemerle? He's gotten loose somehow, and he's come—"

"How do you know that?" But Jane didn't reply, biting her lower lip as if she'd already said too much.

Back in town, Jane remained silent as they passed Area 51, the cocktail-holding alien on the bar sign peering through the smoke. A few blocks later, Lizzie turned uphill between the Western Auto store and a daycare center that doubled as a job-training office. On a washboard-rough avenue the Blazer juddered past a mix of bunga-lows and factory-built split-levels with here and there a double-wide mobile home set on a concrete foundation.

Crimmins looked impatient. "Almost there," Lizzie assured her as she slowed for more potholes, then made her final turn. In the rear-view mirror, clouds of light dust billowed.

"Where are we going?" Jane's face creased in a frown. She didn't seem worried about the fire. Lizzie was, but since she hadn't yet got-ten an order to evacuate, she'd be sticking around with or without Jane Crimmins's presence.

So if they ended up having to head for the hills anytime soon, they'd just do it together, Lizzie decided. "My place," she said.

She rolled her shoulders and forced her fingers to relax on the steering wheel. "The bar here in town is loud. And the guys in it can get rowdy or intrusive. You don't need that."

She could just about imagine what Chevrier would say about what she was doing now. This maneuver wasn't in any interrogation man-ual, taking a maybe-not-so-well-balanced interview subject to the of-ficer's home, fixing her a snack . . .

But with a person like Jane Crimmins, the only way to get what you wanted was to go slow, lavish her with time and attention until you got close to the information you sought.

And *then* you pounced. Lizzie turned into her driveway, parked in front of the garage. Inside, Rascal sniffed the stranger while Jane stood in the pine-paneled living room taking in the ugly brown sofa, cheap red curtains, and mass-produced pottery lamps.

Lizzie had chosen none of it; the rental had come furnished. She thought of saying so, then decided screw it.

"Jane? How do you know Gemerle's gotten loose? And why would he come to Bearkill?"

Crimmins's face was pale and drawn in the harsh light coming in through the living-room window. She looked a lot better than she had, though, after a night of sleep and Emily Ektari's care.

"She told me he would," Jane answered at last. "The girl that I was taking care of after they got rescued—"

"The girl from the cellar? Your cousin Cam Petry?"

Water in the microwave, tea bag in the water; Lizzie served the tea. "Is that who you mean? Is it why you came to see me last night, to tell me about it?"

Jane Crimmins looked surprised that Lizzie knew so much. But she recovered quickly. "Sort of. But I only wanted to talk to you. Not a man."

"I see. And what did you want to say to me?"

Silence. Lizzie tried again from another angle. "You do know Henry Gemerle has gotten out, though?"

Jane hesitated. "Yes. I . . . like I said, I thought he would do it sooner or later, and then I overheard it at the hospital today, that he really had."

Which made some sense, actually. The accident on the Ridge Road, cops and ambulance personnel afterward in the ER . . . they'd all have known by then about the abandoned car with the corpse in the trunk, and they'd have talked about it.

Jane could have heard them. Lizzie shifted gears a little. "Well, then, you know why I'm interested. Because now we've got a girl missing here, she's the same age as Gemerle's victims were, and that's why we're so—"

"Excuse me," said Crimmins, taking an orange pharmacy bottle from her bag. "Headache." She popped two small white tablets into her mouth, washing them down with tea.

She tucked the bottle away again before Lizzie could glimpse the label. "Now, what were you asking me?"

Lizzie summoned patience. "I was asking about Henry Gemerle.

Who's killed one person already, we think, and maybe taken a girl, and I think your presence here is probably not a coincidence."

"No, of course not."

Rascal came back into the room and began pacing restlessly.

Yeah, you and me both, thought Lizzie.

"All right, that's it," she said abruptly. "You came to me, you know. I didn't go looking for you. Now I want to know why you did, and I want to know everything that you know about Gemerle's whereabouts and his intentions."

She dug her badge wallet from her bag. "All the details, who else might be involved and the reasons behind it," she added.

She lay the badge open on the coffee table between them. "Or I will take you into custody right now. You'll be charged as an accessory in at least one murder, and if anything happens to that missing girl we're looking for, you'll answer for that, too."

All hollow threats; nothing connected this woman to a crime, and anyway the DA decided who got charged with what, not Lizzie.

But even though Jane Crimmins probably didn't know all that, her weird smile didn't waver.

"Okay," she said. "How about this? I'll tell you what I know if you do the same for me."

She paused judiciously, her cup poised halfway to her lips. "Only not if you arrest me, of course."

Jesus. There was something so *off* about this woman. *Okay. Deep breath. Start over . . .*

"Look, Jane, just talk to me, all right? It'll be easy. I'll ask questions and you answer them."

"Okay," Jane said again, smiling sweetly. "I'm ready."

Probably the smile on the face of a tiger was sweet, too, Lizzie thought. Right up until it wasn't. And then . . . *chomp.*

"Jane, we need to find Gemerle. Do you know where he is now?"

Jane's wide brown eyes gazed innocently at Lizzie. "No, I'm afraid I don't. But you're the police around here, aren't you?"

That smile again. "So I was hoping that maybe you did."

Fifteen years after my cousin and I were kidnapped, I saw Cam on TV being led out of that basement prison and knew what I had to do. With only a few words she could turn me into a monster in the eyes of the world, and she would, too. The Cam I'd known had been fun, but not big on forgiveness.

To put it mildly. And probably she still wasn't. Which meant that if I didn't keep her quiet my life was as good as over.

But the next morning I went to my job at the medical center just as usual; I needed a plan, but to make one I required information, and at the hospital I could learn all I had to know.

So at 7 A.M. I showed my ID at the main security desk and went on through the lobby, past the gift shop with its Mylar balloons and stuffed animals and the cafeteria smelling of coffee, then up six floors in the elevator to a fluorescent-lit office space full of partitioned cubicles, each with a screen and keyboard.

After I'd graduated from high school, I'd gotten a job there by showing off my one real talent, which was typing. Eighty words a minute, no errors. Lucky for me, because my parents had left me the house but there'd been no money to go with it.

My desk by the window had a nameplate on it—JANE CRIMMINS DEPARTMENT SUPERVISOR, it said—but for my work I didn't need a name, just ears and hands. All day long I sat at my desk with my earbuds on and my fingers racing while tumors and hemorrhages, seizures and night sweats bypassed my brain and proceeded instead to my hands, and then on through them to my computer keyboard.

Rumor had it that my job would soon be obsolete on account of voice-recognition software. But for now, the technology wasn't accurate enough. So medical transcriptionists like me still typed surgical reports, pathology results, and other dictated materials that were produced by the hospital's clinical staff.

That included emergency-room intake workups, such as the ones I knew would have been done the night before on the rescued girls. When I reached the office I sorted through the wire basket of new assignments recently sent here by the doctors, coming up with the ones I wanted right away.

After that I sat down at my desk and turned on my machines, put my earbuds in, and began typing, just as on any other normal work-day. Only this time I also began listening instead of merely letting the information flow through me.

That's how I learned all their names, where they were from, and every other possible detail about the girls I'd abandoned down in that cellar: their blood types, injuries and illnesses, nutrition statuses, treatment plans . . . everything.

There was a lot of it, too: from their medical care, but also from the social services department. As the days went by and more dicta-tion came in, I learned that two of the victims would go home to the families they'd run away from before they vanished.

The third one, though . . . Cam had no living family to go to as far as anyone knew, and I could have confirmed that. Aunt Rose had dropped dead suddenly of a stroke in the midst of one of her rages. Cam's father hadn't been heard from in years. So far, in fact, they hadn't even been able to identify her; she'd been uncommunicative, either from a head injury she'd suffered or because she was scared, and I certainly hadn't stepped in to offer them any information.

Still, once she was medically stable she couldn't stay in the hospi-tal forever, so two weeks after her rescue from the monster's cellar I began typing Cam's discharge notes. As a last resort, the hospital so-cial workers had set her up with rental vouchers for a place in a New Haven rooming house called the Davenport.

It was all they could do. Residential placement for healthy adults is extraordinarily difficult; that's why there are so many living on the streets. But the Davenport was not much better than the sidewalk, and on top of that there'd been a mistake.

The last building on Skylar Avenue that had not already been torn down for redevelopment, the Davenport stuck up like a rotten brick tooth from the otherwise-empty block. Worse, when I skipped work to arrive there early on the morning after Cam's first night in the place, I found a bulldozer idling on one side of the ratty old structure and a crane with a wrecking ball dangling from it on the other; by some awful mix-up, the city's demolition plans and my cousin Cam had arrived at nearly the same moment.

Inside, the lobby was a dim, rank-smelling cave with peeling green

paint, dusty furniture, and broken venetian blinds hanging in windows that needed no covering, they were so caked by decades of
grime. Peering around, I found Cam slumped moaning in a chair; no
words, just that sound of misery over and over.

She was not, I had learned, in good emotional shape. Also, the
head injury the monster had inflicted—blunt-force injury to the
skull—carried with it possible long-term effects.

"Cam?" I whispered. I hadn't visited her in the hospital in case the
sight of me might trigger something unpleasant, like recognition and
possibly even speech. Now she looked up, her eyes widening and the
knowledge of who I was clearly present in them.

But she didn't scream or begin immediately to accuse me. I held
my hand out; she took it and got up shakily.

"Don't say anything," I told her. Outside, the wrecking ball was
waiting. "Don't even look at anyone," I said, still holding her hand as
we stepped out into the sunshine. "Come with me."

The workmen had been waiting, wondering what to do. Now I
hustled her away from the building just as the crane's big diesel engine roared. Instants later I winced at the explosive crash of a ton of
steel hitting a ton of bricks. But Cam only smiled, her misery-pinched
face softening.

"Like us," she said as the steel ball hit the building again and the
walls began falling.

"Like us," she repeated, and I didn't know what she meant.

But later I did: bashed, broken, ruined.

Oh, yes. Later, I understood just fine.

"Little jerk," fumed Lizzie a few hours after her interview with Jane
Crimmins.

If you could call it that. For Lizzie it had been more like an experi-
ment to learn how pissed off she could get.

"Turns out she's no help, but boy, was she ever happy about the
attention she was getting while I was taking her seriously."

Sipping her wine, she leaned back into the plush upholstered sofa
in Trey Washburn's living room. To judge by the work he did it should

have been rugged, but instead the room was an understatedly gorgeous, impossibly comfortable haven of dark, highly polished wood, thick jewel-toned rugs, and gleaming brass lamps.

In response to his gentle probing she'd spent the early part of the evening telling him about her troubled family history. It was a rough subject, one she usually shied away from: growing up motherless and with an abusive father, then running away from home with her sister, Cecily, and promising to take care of her. After that she'd lost touch and found out too late that Cecily was dead, her body discovered floating in the bay near the quaint fishing village of Eastport, Maine, and her infant mysteriously missing.

But somehow Trey had made it easy. Maybe it was his quiet interest, not interrupting or commenting until she had finished. Or his sympathy when she expressed her guilt over what had gone down when she wasn't paying attention, too busy with her own life to notice that Cecily's was circling the drain.

Or maybe it was that he was simply a genuinely decent guy. "Thanks for dinner, by the way," she said. "It was nice of you to let me cash that raincheck. And I'm sorry I'm in a mood."

The books on the shelves covering the walls were an eclectic mix of history, veterinary science, and popular fiction, and she happened to know that Trey had read them all. Carrying his glass of the good Cabernet he'd opened to go with the tenderloins he'd grilled, he settled beside her on the sofa.

"No problem. Cooking your dinner, that's what I'm here for. Or one thing I'm here for, anyway," he added mildly, then changed the subject.

"But this woman you went to so much trouble over today, you mean she was no use to you at all?"

He bent to smooth the ears of a liver-and-white spaniel, one of the pair he kept. Trey *liked* being helpful and supportive, she realized; he actually enjoyed being a decent person.

She'd heard of that. "Not unless you think there's a revenge plot going on," she replied. "But for that you'd need at least one of his victims to be planning and carrying it out, wouldn't you?"

She closed her eyes and drank a little more wine, trying to let her frustration with Jane Crimmins evaporate. After all, this wasn't the first time a supposedly crucial interview had turned out to be a bust.

"But three of the women Henry Gemerle grabbed and imprisoned all those years ago are down in New Haven where they belong," she went on, "not up here in Aroostook County conspiring to kill him the way Jane Crimmins claims. I know that because I checked."

Trey's pale eyebrows raised skeptically. "But it's still what she says is happening?"

"Yeah, that's her story, all right. And she's sticking to it no matter what." On the hearth rug before a cozily flickering fire in the fireplace, the other spaniel stretched luxuriously in his sleep.

"Jane says the girl she took care of, Cam Petry, wants to kill Gemerle. But not," Lizzie said, "until after she tortures him for a while, as payback for the horrific abuse he put her and the others through for all those years."

"So it's Cam that Jane wants to get out in front of. That's why she was trying to get Gemerle's location from you, to head Cam off at the pass?"

Lizzie nodded tiredly. "It's what she insists, yes."

"And you know that's not true because . . ."

"Because I called Cam Petry at the number listed for her in New Haven," Lizzie replied, "but she didn't answer. So I tried the hospitals down there—according to Jane, Cam's been in very shaky health—and sure enough, Yale–New Haven has her."

Trey poured more wine as Lizzie continued. "In critical but stable condition, unable to communicate, much less travel, according to the admitting clerk I talked to, who had the records in front of her. And since Cam Petry can't very well be in two places at once—"

She took a breath and said, "She's not here hunting Henry Gemerle or anyone else. So you tell me, why is Jane Crimmins lying about all this?"

Trey listened thoughtfully but without any immediate reply. That was another good thing about him, that when he listened, he wasn't just waiting for his turn to talk.

"Not that in general the whole thing couldn't be the way Jane said," Lizzie added after another sip of her Cabernet. "I mean luring your intended victim out of their comfort zone and then offing them . . . it's classic."

Which was also what Jane claimed, that somehow Cam Petry had facilitated the forensic hospital escape, then persuaded Gemerle to come here.

"But as it stands now her story's just not credible. Also, Jane really could have heard all about Gemerle being here while she was in the ER this morning, where the paramedics were probably gossiping about it."

She put her glass down. "She could be on a fishing expedition to find out what the cops already know. Or—"

Another thought hit her suddenly. "Or this is all just a clever smoke screen. What if she does already know his location? And she wants to be sure we don't, so we don't swoop down on him while she's—"

"Doing something to him, herself," Trey finished astutely. "Maybe to get back at him for what he did to this Cam person that she took care of?"

He drank the rest of his own wine. "So she tries to find out whatever she can from you, by floating a bogus story past you."

She nodded, tight-lipped. "That's possible, too. All of which is why I'm back to square one, again, because as soon as she found out that we *don't* know where he is she clammed up again. Got all dithery and indefinite, then complained of a headache."

Trey nodded sympathetically. The dinner, the fireplace, his solid presence . . . relaxed on the soft couch, Lizzie felt she could have stayed forever. But there was still too much to do tonight, she told herself.

"Anyway, thanks for letting me blather on." The clock in the hall struck ten; in the kitchen she sat to pull on her boots.

"So did this Jane Crimmins person say why Bearkill?" Trey wanted to know. "I mean, why Henry Gemerle came here, and what Tara Wylie's supposedly got to do with any of it?"

Lizzie shook her head, yanking on her other boot while the dish-washer across the room hummed pleasantly. "Nope. I asked, but she didn't have any answers to any of that, either."

Pulling on her jacket, she followed Trey out to the enclosed porch that ran along the whole south side of his big, beautifully maintained white-clapboard farmhouse. The porch, a many-windowed refuge of bentwood chairs and wicker plant stands, was cozily lit by wall-mounted hurricane lamps and warmed by a purring propane heater.

"Meanwhile the New Haven cops have been faxing me stuff all afternoon," she said. "So now I'm going home to read all of Henry Gemerle's hearing transcripts and the notes from the investigation in New Haven, and try to come up with something that makes sense." Because the one thing she did know for sure was that Tara was still out there somewhere, missing and almost surely in danger.

"Yeah," said Trey. "Same way in my work. Sometimes the real key to what's wrong is in the history, you know? Not the current com-plaint."

His hands rested briefly on her shoulders as she zipped her jacket. "But isn't the kind of paperwork hunt you're planning sort of . . . cler-ical?" he asked. "For someone with your experience?"

As she turned, he wrapped his arms around her and held her. He smelled like Old Spice, which ordinarily she didn't enjoy.

But when he wore it she did. "You don't know many cops," she said, stepping back from him reluctantly.

The New Haven material she'd requested was nothing compared with some cases she'd had, whose documents filled whole rooms. And the problem with anybody else reading it for you, an assistant or a secretary, was simple:

They didn't know what to look for. Even she didn't until she saw it, sometimes. Even if they did know, they couldn't think about it for you.

"Anyway, I'm just a deputy," she added when she'd explained this, "so officially at least I'm out of the loop on all of it."

Trey followed her to the door, shaking his head in sympathy. "Must be hard having your hands tied like that."

"I'll get over it. Meanwhile I've told all the right people about Jane

Crimmins: my boss, the state cops, and the FBI. And I've got her safely stashed in a motel room for tonight."

The motel was not one of the modern ones near the highway. It was an old relic from the 1950s. Its buildings had been remodeled, an indoor pool installed, and a restaurant added; its hand-painted sign, lit by a string of Christmas bulbs, still read AUTO COURT. But it was more suitable for Lizzie's purposes.

"So with any luck," Lizzie finished tiredly, "tonight will be un-eventful." She looked wistfully back into Trey's large, well-appointed kitchen, gleaming with copper pans and stainless steel.

The fire had backed off again, its whimsical advance-and-retreats driving everyone nuts but so far at least not devouring any houses, people, or livestock. "Anyway, thanks again for dinner."

"My pleasure." He reached out to ruffle her hair, a gesture that if anyone else had tried it they'd have gotten a bite wound for their trouble.

"Stick around longer sometime," Trey said. The moment length-ened. "And listen, I'm sorry about Cecily. That's a tough one, losing a sibling. Still . . ."

It wasn't your fault, he was about to say. But when the moment passed, he hadn't said it, and she liked him for that, too.

Out over the valley the moon hung in a blur of smoke, the hills below black cutouts on the hazy sky. A star peeped through and van-ished.

"I really do have to say good night," she murmured, and moments later in the rearview mirror he was a burly silhouette, waiting until she was safely out of the driveway.

Which is nice, she thought, driving home through the rural dark-ness. *That he cares enough to—*

But the thought got cut off as she neared her own driveway and saw the vehicle parked in it. Lights were on in the house, which they shouldn't have been, and Rascal was out, which he shouldn't have been, either, bounding across the shadowy yard after a glow-in-the-dark Frisbee that someone had just thrown for him.

Slowing, she turned in and saw who it was.

Dylan, of course.

"Hope you don't mind my going in when you weren't here."

And if I did, would it matter? He knew her spare key hung on a nail driven into an old cedar post in the backyard.

"Poor dog was going crazy in there, hearing me," said Dylan, "so I—"

"Don't worry about it." Inside, she hung up her jacket and bag, then went on to the kitchen.

"I see you came prepared." Back in the old days when he let himself in, he brought roses and champagne. Now on the counter she found two liter-sized bottles of Coke and a dozen doughnuts.

Leaving him in the kitchen to wrestle ice cubes out of their trays, she ran a brush through her hair and put on fresh lipstick.

When she got back he'd opened the Coke, filled glasses with ice, and set the doughnuts on a plate.

He'd already spread out his paperwork, too: crime-scene material from the car in the rest area this morning, photographs and DMV printouts and so on. And her own research was there; she'd last seen that material in a jumbled heap on the coffee table in the living room. Organizing all this stuff, he'd knocked hours off her workload and added hours to his own.

"So," he said briskly, "let's review: If Tara left with Aaron DeWilde like we think, that means for at least part of the time she's been gone she was with him. But there's been no sign of him or his bike, no cell phone activity or credit transactions, no ATM activity. And nothing in the hospitals for either one of them."

Of course Dylan would have checked all that. Lizzie nodded, frowning down at a patrol report sheet. "Right. And since they're both gone, you gotta wonder if maybe something happened to both of them. Still, though . . ."

He picked up on her thought. "You're right. Nothing says for sure that's what went down. And I've been wondering too if maybe we should be thinking about something else. What if she was already on her way home when something happened?"

He paused. "And that reminds me, I got news about the cell

phone." But the news wasn't good. "Tower picked it up last night; it was on for about a minute. Local tower. Phone was in Bearkill or right nearby. But since then, nothing at all."

Lizzie sighed heavily. "Yeah, I guess that would've been too easy, huh? Just follow the pings like breadcrumbs, and—"

"Sure. But she was near here. Or the phone was, anyway. So she could've got snatched on her way home. Picked up hitchhiking, or even flat-out abducted."

She nodded slowly. "Okay, let's assume for a minute that's what happened, and it was Gemerle who took her. Why, we don't understand yet. Or how, actually. Like, what vehicle?"

He paged through his notes, looked up. "There was a van stolen in Allagash yesterday. Gray Econoline."

The town was nearby. "Okay, that could be how he's getting around. As for why Bearkill, Jane Crimmins says it's because a woman named Cam Petry lured him here," Lizzie said.

She repeated Jane's story. It sounded just as fantastical as before. "But what if Jane's telling at least part of the truth?" she added. "What if someone really did lure Gemerle here by using Tara Wylie as . . ."

She didn't want to say it. He didn't, either. But it was what they were both thinking, she could see it in Dylan's face:

Bait.

Dark, scared . . . alone. Tara Wylie fought desperately against panic, knowing now how the kitten she'd rescued must've felt when it got dropped off in the darkness by the side of the road.

She'd been here—wherever *here* was—for a long time, all last night and a whole day, too, she thought. *So by now it must be Wednesday night?*

She wasn't sure of that, either. Or of anything, in fact, except that all she wanted was to go home, to feel her kitten's face rubbing against her cheek once more, his purr like an engine of happiness, and his eyes closed in contentment. She wanted to go to cheering practice, do her homework, work on an art project.

She even wanted to watch some boring TV show with her mom in their stupid half-finished living room . . . *Oh, I want to go home.*

Instead she was buried in a box out in a field somewhere, in a hole that was blessedly shallow enough so that some air came in from above, and even a little light for a while, once day came and before it had gotten dark again.

She could have struggled out of her prison easily, in fact, if only she could get the nailed-on wooden slats of the top off. But she couldn't. Flat on her back in a tiny space with not even room enough to turn over, she'd heard through a haze of terror the heavy hammer blows, and had even dimly glimpsed some of the nails coming through, looking as big as railroad spikes.

Whoever had taken her had found her phone, smashed it on a rock, then tossed the pieces into the box and made her lie down in it. After that, the top had been nailed on; finally came the scraping, clattering sound of dirt being shoveled down onto her. Some of it kept sifting through the gaps between the slats, falling grittily into her eyes and mouth until she clamped them tightly shut.

So she couldn't even scream, not unless she wanted to choke. No light, no water, and by now she was very thirsty. *But not as thirsty as I'm going to be.*

Not as scared as I will be soon, either. The words echoed in her head from some hard, truthful place she hadn't even known she possessed.

But now she did. *This. This is how it happens. Buried in a shallow grave.*

Just like her mom had said. *And no one's going to search for me. Not out here in some field, somewhere. Nobody has a clue that I'm even here, so why would they?*

The thought nauseated her with fresh fear. But she couldn't give up yet. If she did, she would die here. Steeling herself, she sucked in a gritty breath. Then fury surged through her. She'd done a foolish thing but she didn't deserve this, she *didn't*.

The anger felt good, like fresh blood pumping through her.

But then another slide of soil poured into her coffin and fright made her chest heave, dragging loose dirt up her nostrils.

Tara felt a shriek building inside her and struggled to keep it back, releasing it at last in a painful sob.

Please, she thought, knowing it wouldn't help. The air in the box was stuffy, smelling of dry earth. This, she thought, is what it must be like when you're in your grave.

But up there in the air and the moonlight, everything that she loved still waited for her, as safe and good as always, and as precious. Putting her hands up, she strained against her prison's lid. But there were too many nails holding it down tight, so it wouldn't budge.

If she kept trying, though . . . Biting her lip with the effort, she shoved upward against the boards and this time was rewarded by the sound of a nail creaking. Encouraged, she pushed again, and one of the boards shifted noticeably.

More dirt slid heavily down onto her face, which should have terrified her again. But somehow it didn't. She was too tired and too overwhelmed to be scared.

And too pissed off, she thought, surprising herself.

Her mom got pissed off when things got very hard. When money was short, or Tara had done or not done something, her mom started screaming about it. Blowing her top, her mom called it.

But then the hard thing got dealt with. The thought sent a strange calm flowing through Tara. It was the feeling she got when she was drawing in her sketchbook or practicing with her cheering squad, both things she hadn't been very good at, either, at first.

She'd tried a hundred times before doing her first cartwheel. She remembered the sharp, sweaty smell of her own body while she sat there in the school gym, blubbering in frustration. And now she was the team's captain, cartwheeling and somersaulting like she'd been born to do it, the phys-ed teacher said.

Oh, yeah? she thought at the stubborn nails holding her in. *You think you can stop me from getting out of here? We'll just see about that,* she thought furiously at them. *We'll just see.*

Then she forced herself to relax, breathing slowly and evenly as she lay there alone in the cramped, stifling darkness.

Resting. Only for a little while, though. Just until she was ready to try again. She let her hands lie at her sides, opening and closing them slowly, preparing herself.

And then she felt it, right there at her fingertips. Sharp, pointy-ended . . . a smile spread on her face as she identified the thing she had found.

It was a large, jagged-edged plastic shard of her broken cell phone.

SEVEN

Fifteen years after I'd left her for dead and eight weeks after I brought her home from the hospital following her stunning rescue, my cousin Cam had her first major seizure.

By then it was late autumn, the streets slick with fallen leaves and the branches black scrawls on the gray sky. Cam and I walked together each day, working on getting her strength back, but that afternoon we had an extra reason to go out: It was the first step in the plan we'd developed for punishing the monster, Henry Gemerle.

"You're sure he'll show up?" Cam asked as we made our way into Yale's campus, past Gothic towers and elaborately scrolled iron gates, among the hurrying students in their bright scarves and jackets.

"He'll be there," I assured Cam.

Finny Brill, I meant, the odd-duck boy from our old neighborhood. He still lived there, caring for his aging mother, and while I was back finishing the process of selling my own parents' house—Cam didn't like the place, and I didn't like her being there, either; it was full of memories, and the less she thought about the old days the better. I'd run into him.

Still odd, still desperate for friends, in his rush to update me on the facts of his lonely life Finny had dropped one fascinating bit of information: These days, he worked as an orderly at the Salisbury Forensic Institute.

"Just until I get my big break, of course," he'd added. He still dreamed of being a filmmaker; I listened politely while he went on at length about his current project.

Around us in front of the house I'd just sold for a tidy sum, young mothers in leggings and long, baggy sweaters jogged along briskly behind three-wheeled baby strollers, while hipster dads in fedoras and horn-rims circled them on vintage bikes. It seemed that after years of slow decay the whole neighborhood had become trendy all of a sudden, and this turned out extremely well for me; the old house had been bought almost the minute I listed it, and for even more money than I'd been asking.

But while I listened to Finny, all I could think of was that Salisbury Forensic was where they had Henry Gemerle locked up until the courts and psychiatrists decided: Would he go to prison or remain in a locked hospital ward for the rest of his life?

And that's how I first got the idea of another fate for him. After all, what I wanted was to hurt him and for Cam not to hurt me. So, I wondered while Finny kept yammering on about that break of his, why not kill two birds with one stone?

"But how do you know?" Cam persisted now. "That this Finny guy will show up like he said he would?"

The way I'd presented it to her was that together, she and I would get revenge on the monster. She was on board with it right away, too—or seemed to be. What I didn't say, of course, was that my having something bad to hold over her head—that she'd helped me torture Henry Gemerle, for instance, at length and eventually to death—would in turn keep her silent about me: that I'd left her with him.

And then there was what I didn't say to myself: that I wanted Cam back. My old, funny Cam that I loved so much, whose world, so much brighter and livelier than my own, she'd let me into; I wanted that world again, and her with it.

I had, after all, no life of my own; Gemerle had taken care of that. Not that I'd ever been much for trusting people or letting them get

near, even before. But now except for work and a few casual acquaintances I was as solitary as a nun in a cloistered convent, only without
even the consolation of religion. He'd killed that, too.

Mostly though, what I didn't want her focusing on was my leaving
her for dead. It was our revenge against him that I needed her to be
thinking about; that, and my part in getting it for us. But before we
could do anything to Henry Gemerle at all, we had to *have* him, and
that was where Finny came in.

"He'll come," I said again. "And when he does, you leave the talking to me." I knew how to persuade poor Finny.

Silently she nodded agreement. Even after all she'd been through
she was still very pretty with her short dark hair, pale skin, and cameo
features. But her big dark eyes, once sparkling with fun, were somber
now with the terrible things they'd seen and the worse ones that
she'd had done to her.

"Leave it to you," she repeated softly. "All right."

She wore the smart red wool coat I'd bought for her, with the
curly lamb collar and black buttons, stylish new leather boots, and a
soft, black cashmere beret; beside her I felt like an ugly stepsister.

But I didn't care. Even though I was still afraid of her, the past few
weeks had been the happiest of my life, first renting her an apartment
in an old but nicely maintained building just off Whitney Avenue,
then moving in there with her. The place had big windows, two bed-
rooms, and a leafy view, and by living there I could take care of her
and at the same time keep an eye on her, I thought; not until much
later did it occur to me to wonder who, exactly, had been keeping an
eye on whom.

But that was later. At the time, we never talked about that night.
She never asked me about it, and I didn't bring it up. For all I knew she
didn't even remember; she'd had that head injury, after all, the result
of the bad beatings he'd given her. Certainly she never asked what it
had been like for me, grieving her loss in silence, enduring my own
guilt and my mother's intense vigilance, even more constant and
overbearing than before Cam's disappearance.

Feeling so sinful and no longer believing in redemption; knowing
(I thought) what had happened and not being able to tell—I wanted

very badly to talk about it now with the only person who could possibly understand. Still, I couldn't take a chance, since if Cam did recall, and if she told anyone what I'd done, every finger in the world would be aimed accusingly at me. My quiet, private life, the tiny safe place I'd carved out for myself, would be over. So most of all I had to keep her silent about it, and that was my real purpose that day as we carried our espressos to a table by the window.

She twisted a sliver of lemon peel between her fingers, the penetrating fragrance floating sharply up from the strong brew. Through the windowpane beside us, the blue light of autumn shone slantwise onto her face.

"Oh, I love this place," she said, and then Finny arrived.

A loose-lipped grin stretched his freckled face when he saw us, his white-lashed eyes crinkling as he brushed back his fiery-red hair with an awkward gesture. In baggy jeans and a frayed sweater with his bony wrists sticking out of the cuffs, he still looked like a middle school kid and was as easy to persuade. Moments after joining us, he had eagerly endorsed my ideas for a documentary film about the notorious Henry Gemerle, the monster of Michener Street, as the press was already calling him.

To be directed by Finny, of course, and full of the cheesy horror elements he'd always loved. Naturally I had no such plan, but he didn't know that, and as enthralled as he was by the idea of finally becoming a real filmmaker he'd have done anything I asked; the whole thing took only a few minutes.

"Wow. Cool," Finny said, jumping up and in his enthusiasm nearly knocking over the table. "I'll get started right away."

Already mentally getting his gear and a shooting script ready, he didn't even seem fazed that when the time came, the first thing he'd need to do was break a violent sociopath out of a mental hospital. All he'd said about it was that he could definitely get Gemerle out of his locked ward and off the grounds of Salisbury Forensic whenever I gave the signal.

It would be easy, he said, as if for an artist like Finny it was just another creative challenge; Cam looked bemused.

"Interesting guy," she remarked when he was gone, her arched eyebrows expressing clearly what we both thought: that Finny Brill was a complete buffoon, but a useful one.

"Yes." I felt my worry dissolve a little. Working with me on this, she'd have little reason to tell stories about me. I'd be too useful to her—she was turning out to be just as vengeful as I remembered—and afterward she'd be as guilty as I was.

And maybe . . . just maybe . . . once it was all over she would love me a little, too. Forgive me, and love me.

But even without that, she'd keep her mouth shut. "How do you feel?" I asked.

At my urging she'd worn lipstick, just the tiniest touch; it looked good on her, and after a rough few weeks I thought that against all the doctors' predictions she might have turned the corner at last. Music came on, Ravel's "Bolero," and the stainless-steel coffee machine behind the counter spewed steam, foaming someone's latte.

A girl laughed, and a horn honked out in the street. With a happy sigh Cam lifted her cup to her lips. Then:

"Cam?" She stared fixedly out through the café's front window but there was nothing there to see, only the constant stream of students and professors hurrying to and from the nearby Yale libraries and dining clubs. The pale stone dormitories with their arched granite entries and leaded-glass windows looked as if they dated from medieval times.

"Cam?" Her eye twitched, and then one whole side of her face cascaded into a series of grimaces, half her mouth snarling at me while the other half was as still as all that old stone outside.

Her arm spasmed violently so the espresso in her cup flew upward, the lemon peel falling into her lap. White foam seeped from between her clenched teeth, and her eyes rolled back.

The barista hurried over. "Everything okay?"

"I . . . I think so," I said. It all went so fast; by now Cam already seemed to be coming around, blinking and trying to get her bearings.

"What happened?" she murmured, glancing guiltily at me as if she had somehow spoiled our outing on purpose.

I mopped at the spilled coffee, feeling the stares of other café patrons while trying to reassure Cam that she was fine, that I was with her and everything was all right.

But of course it wasn't. The damage the monster's beatings had done to her brain, as the doctors had already warned her, was getting worse. There was a blood blister in there, as dangerous as a hidden time bomb.

"I want to go home," she whispered, and once we got there I made her lie down, of course. But she wouldn't let me phone her doctor, and against my better judgment I finally gave in, hoping it would be okay.

Later when she announced that she was taking a shower I had further misgivings, and when I heard the wet thud of her body slamming against the tiled wall I knew I never should have let her go in there alone. And naturally she'd locked the door . . .

"Cam!" I pounded on it while the spasms shook her. All I could think of was that her face might be under the water, that while I stood there helplessly she might be drowning.

Finally I ran for a hammer from our toolbox, the one that we'd laughed over as we stocked it with the kinds of tools we thought two women living on their own should have. With the hammer I bashed on the hollow wooden door until a hole opened in it and I could reach through to the knob inside.

"OhGodohGod," someone kept saying, and as I scrambled across the wet tiled floor toward her I knew it was me.

"Cam." Her eyes were rolled back again so only the whites showed, her whole body jerking like a fish dying on a hook.

I cranked the water off and grabbed a towel, covering up the freckles on her arms and legs. I'd only seen her naked once before, back in Gemerle's basement cell, and I averted my eyes from the sight as much as I could while I hauled her out of the tub, laid her on the tiles with a rolled towel beneath her head, then ran to call for help.

Even as I dialed 911 I knew she'd hate it, my seeing her like that. Cam was always as clean as a cat and as private about herself, too. But she was beautiful, the curve of her hip sloping gracefully to her thigh, her leg smooth as an artist's drawing. Even the midline scar on her belly looked perfect to me.

Afterward, when the ambulance had raced her off to the hospital where she would remain until the surgeons had their way with her, opening up her skull and removing a piece like somebody lopping off the top of a soft-boiled egg, I recalled that scar again. But the long curved line of her body kept superimposing itself on my real-life vision of her, marred only by my memory of a monster who'd seen it all, too, while he'd done whatever he wanted to her.

I despised him for it as sincerely and ferociously as anyone could. But mostly I recalled how lovely she was, even though I couldn't say so while I sat by her hospital bed. I was waiting for her to wake from a complex surgery—clipping the leaky blood vessel, cauterizing the ends, installing a shunt to keep the swelling down, and then repairing her opened skull with a surgical-grade metal alloy patch—that both she and I had feared she wouldn't survive.

Later I might have tried telling her, I suppose. But by that time she wasn't listening. Not to me, not to anyone at all.

No one but him.

"Inmates at the Salisbury Institute aren't supposed to have computer privileges," said Dylan, leaning back in one of the ugly plaid chairs in Lizzie's living room. "So how'd he even know what Tara Wylie looks like?"

By now it was early Thursday morning and they'd been going over the case for hours, the half-empty doughnut box and the remaining bottle of warm Coke shoved aside on the coffee table.

"They're not supposed to have escape privileges, either," she retorted. But somehow Gemerle had managed that, too.

They'd reviewed all the facts: that Tara and Peg Wylie were from New Haven, just like Jane Crimmins, Henry Gemerle, and the hospital orderly, Finny Brill.

What connected them all, though, was still a blank. "They're all linked somehow. We just don't know what the link is yet," she said.

By lamplight the room was almost cozy, she noticed, the dark wood paneling and deep-red draperies giving it a denlike feeling.

"Yeah, you're probably right," said Dylan. "Hey, this is just like the old days, though, isn't it?" He pulled his iPad from his soft leather briefcase, twiddling with the icons on the screen.

Back in the city they'd had brainstorming sessions like this often. "I've missed those times," he said.

She missed them, too, and she especially missed what came after, the night paling to dawn through the windows of her bedroom overlooking the Charles, his arm flung out across the pillow with the day's first gray light brightening behind it.

Remembering, she took a doughnut and bit into it, then had to wash it down with a gulp of lukewarm soda to get it past the lump in her throat. The swirly red script on the Coke bottle's label blurred suddenly through her tears.

She cleared her throat. "What're you doing?"

He shrugged. On his iPad's screen the familiar Facebook page layout had appeared. "Probably nothing. But I dropped in on Aaron DeWilde's folks earlier tonight. Any particular reason no one's been hunting very hard for him?"

Damn, she thought; Peg Wylie's games and then Jane Crimmins's antics yesterday had knocked Lizzie's own planned visit to the DeWildes off her to-do list, and then with the fires going on, too, she'd forgotten about the missing boy's family.

"Well, for one thing, he's got no violent history with Tara or anyone else, nothing to suggest he'd harm her," she replied. "And he's an adult, at least legally. Although the DeWildes have been pestering Peg Wylie," she added, "accusing Tara of leading their innocent little boy astray."

Dylan made a face that echoed her own opinion. First of all, the DeWilde boy's age made a charge of statutory rape possible, a fact his parents didn't seem to have thought of. And anyway, no kid was as blameless as the DeWildes made theirs out to be.

"But they haven't even filed a missing persons report on him yet," she finished.

Which was actually kind of odd, now that she thought about it.

"Why, did they say something that made you think they really don't want cops looking too hard at him?"

"Not in so many words. They're too far into denial for that." Dylan did something on the iPad, cursed, and backtracked. "They just kept saying how the Wylie girl was a bad influence on him, that whatever he might be into—not that he is, but if he were—it's all her fault."

He went on navigating his way around the screen. "Kid's no angel, though, I'll bet, and if he ends up in a jackpot his folks wanted me to know she must have put him there. Okay, here's his Facebook page."

Just as in the photo in Tara's room, in this one Aaron was a big, good-looking kid, but here he held a shotgun. Correctly, too: muzzle up, open action, finger well away from the trigger.

In other words, for a Bearkill kid he looked perfectly normal. But: "Huh. No recent activity."

She scanned the screen. A dozen messages showed, all of the *hey, bro, where r u?* variety. But there were no answers, not for the past two days. "Is part of it set to private?"

Dylan shook his head. "Nope. Looks like everything's here. Kid's got no secrets, supposedly. Or if he has, he's smart enough not to put them online."

He scrolled up and down once more, then closed the Facebook icon and snapped the iPad's cover shut. "His folks both said he's usually on here every few hours or so. But now . . ."

He got his phone out and punched in a call. "Yeah, Bruno, you know the kid we're thinking that the missing Bearkill girl went off with, that Aaron DeWilde?"

Dylan got up, his long stride carrying him to one end of the living room and back. "Right, that's the one. Listen, I know he's already on our interview list but can we maybe—"

Dylan was about to ask his colleague to move the search for the kid nearer to the front burner. But as he listened again Dylan's face changed.

"Really. Yeah. Motorcycle still with him, you say. And money still in his pocket."

These things ruled out robbery. And if you couldn't ask the victim about them, it meant nothing good had happened to him.

Dylan put his phone away. "Patrol cops just now found Aaron DeWilde's body. Mall security phoned it in, it was lying behind a dumpster around the back of the Sears store in Bangor."

He was pulling on his coat. "ID's not a hundred percent yet. They'll want his folks to do a visual identification in Bangor tomorrow, before the body gets sent to Augusta. But it's him, the description fits."

He paused at the door. "Do me a favor and call them, let them know I'm coming? I need to notify them in person."

"Sure." She didn't envy him his errand, telling a teenage boy's parents his body had been found. "Good luck," she added.

He laughed without humor. "Thanks. But I'm pretty sure that train has left the station for tonight."

Or it had for the DeWilde family anyway. She watched from the doorway as Dylan went away down the front walk and his car backed out of the driveway, pulling off down the silent street. Then at a sound from behind her she turned to find Rascal in the act of gobbling a doughnut, the box overturned and his grin white-ringed with powdered sugar.

Not until much later, after she'd called the DeWildes, straightened the living room, showered, and made her way at last to bed, did her eyes snap open suddenly in the darkness.

A soft, faintly musical note had just sounded from somewhere outside the house. Or . . . had it been from inside?

Probably not. Rascal lay sprawled at the foot of her bed, and he always sprang up if she so much as dropped a tissue. So maybe the alarm was from her own raw nerve endings still twitching with the urgency of so many unanswered questions.

But whatever it was, there'd be no more sleep tonight. In the kitchen she snapped on the coffeemaker, let the dog out, then blearily spied her own open laptop's screen saver looping and relooping on the kitchen table.

Then she recalled the soft *ping!* of her email program. The new-mail alert sound was what had yanked her awake.

New info, please call, read the email's header. It was from Peg Wylie; Lizzie grimaced tiredly at it.

Peg had already sent alarm flares up too many times. Besides, letting people think you were at their beck and call day or night was how you got a life with nothing in it but work, a situation she'd known only too well back in Boston.

It was just past 4 A.M. The dog ducked back in through his door. "What d'you say, Rascal? Should I at least get dressed first, and maybe eat some breakfast?"

At the word *eat,* he made a beeline for the kitchen, and by the time she'd fed him and herself and put on clothes and done her hair and her makeup, it was nearly five. She gave herself a last look—black jeans, white silk shirt, leather belt, and boots, a lower-heeled pair this time in deference to the early hour and her uneasy sense of how this day might go. She checked her bag for her badge and duty weapon on her way out.

The sky was still dark, the smoke-tinged air silent and the temperature strangely mild, like spring instead of midwinter. In the Blazer she swiped her phone's screen to the mail function and found Peg's message again just as another came in, this time from an unfamiliar sender. *Call me. Urgent.*

Sure, Lizzie thought tiredly, everyone's messages were always urgent when they wanted something. But then it hit her who EEKTARIMD was: Emily Ektari. And if Emily said it was urgent, then—

Pulling over, Lizzie punched in the number Emily's message supplied. "Hey. You're up early."

Emily laughed without humor. "Yeah. Listen, remember I drew blood on Jane Crimmins yesterday? I got her blood type."

Lizzie hit SPEAKER, then pulled back onto the pavement. "No, I don't think I did know that."

She needed to check on Jane soon, too, she reminded herself, in the motel room. "But how come you drew blood on her at all?"

"Long story," said Emily. "I'd have drawn a tox screen on her anyway, as agitated as she was. Which, by the way, I was right about. She had stimulants on board. Not an overdose per se, but plenty."

"And by stimulants you mean . . ."

"Amphetamines. But you can see positives if the patient's on prescribed Ritalin, the attention deficit disorder drug, too. So take that for what it's worth."

"Got it. And the second part of your story?"

"Okay." Emily took a breath. "The blood-type part. See, I got a guy in my ER once, had a rash. I gave him Benadryl and steroid cream and sent him home."

Lizzie turned onto Main Street. "Sounds reasonable enough to me."

"Textbook," Emily agreed. "But two hours later he's back and now he's vomiting bright-red blood. Large amounts of blood."

Lizzie pulled to the curb. It was way too early for Missy Brantwell to be at work, but that was her yellow Jeep, and behind that was parked Peg Wylie's crummy little Honda sedan.

"Real shocker of a bleed," Emily continued. "The kind nobody ever gets used to, just a remarkable volume of . . ."

"Yeah, okay." Lizzie parked.

"Turned out the rash was part of a weird hemorrhagic syndrome and if I'd just typed his blood the first time around, I might've bought him enough leeway to save his life. As it was . . ."

"Huh." Lizzie got out of the Blazer. "Emily, listen, I don't want to be rude, here, but—"

"Okay." Emily cut to the chase. "So on Jane Crimmins, I got her blood type because I always do, nowadays. And then a little while after you'd left, her old records came in."

"You mean her medical records? But how did you get—"

"The federally funded rural health initiative in northern Maine has us on their network," Emily replied. "Links people's medical records from anywhere in the world. I can get your medical history, any medications you're on, lab results, all right off the computer."

Inside the office, Peg looked ghastly, her blunt-cut blond hair unkempt and her fireplug-shaped body clad in a rumpled shirt and baggy jeans.

". . . so I put her name into the system, along with her Social Security number. Card was right there in her wallet," Emily said.

A new thought struck Lizzie. "Wait a minute. If you can get lab results from the computer, why'd you bother testing her blood? I mean, wouldn't the computer tell you what her blood type is?"

"Aha," said Emily. "That's just my point. You see . . ."

Lizzie, phone in hand, locked up the vehicle, and strode toward her office.

". . . you see," Emily went on, "it turns out that the blood type on the computer and the type that the patient really had . . ."

"Hi," Peg Wylie uttered dully as Lizzie came in.

". . . they didn't match," said Emily.

"What?" Lizzie threw her jacket and bag at the coat tree and nodded to Missy, gesturing for Peg to sit.

"The blood types," Emily said. "The medical records say Jane Crimmins is B-negative. But the blood that I drew here, that got tested right here in our lab, is O-positive."

Missy had made coffee. Lizzie poured a cup gratefully.

"I guess there could be a computer mistake," said Emily, "but it's not likely, and a lab error here is out of the question. We rechecked twice."

Peg's skin looked claylike, her eyes sunken with fatigue. She bit a thumbnail nervously, waiting for Lizzie.

"So you're telling me the woman you saw in the emergency room is not Jane Crimmins."

"That's what it looks like. And before you ask who she really is, I'd love to tell you but the computers aren't that good yet."

The TV in the office was on, and the weather guy was saying something ominous. "Listen, if you find out anything else—"

"You got it," the ER doc agreed, hanging up.

Lizzie turned to Missy Brantwell. The background check she'd asked Missy to do on Jane had come back clean: no wants, warrants, or priors. "Call the motel in Houlton, will you, and get Jane Crimmins on the phone?"

She paused, searching her memory for yet another name that the locals had all probably known since infancy. "What's it called again, not one of those motels right out on the highway but the other one, off on the side road . . ."

She struggled for the name but all she remembered about the place she had chosen for Jane Crimmins was that the hodgepodge of buildings around the big gravel parking lot had sported a fraying banner: EAT SLEEP AND SWIM IN OUR POOL!

"Treetops," Missy pronounced at once, then dialed the phone on her desk and spoke briefly into it. But a moment later she looked up puzzledly.

"Jane Crimmins isn't there. Or at least no one answers in her room."

"What does that mean?" Peg put in nervously, looking from Lizzie to Missy and back again.

"She isn't, huh? Well, isn't that just special." Lizzie frowned down at her two hands and very carefully did not punch or strangle anyone with them.

"You go on outside and wait for me in the Blazer," she told Peg, who looked mutinous. But she went. Peg's email had mentioned *new info*. Lizzie supposed she'd better find out what it was.

Besides, something about Peg just wasn't hitting Lizzie right. A little time alone with her in the Blazer might help uncover the reason for that, too. "You okay?" Lizzie asked Missy when Peg was gone. "Your mom okay, everything all right with the baby?"

"So far." Missy smiled tiredly. "Fires are still far enough from our place so I'm not too worried. Mom's never really asleep these days. People with her condition tend to wander at night, but I had the sitter come out overnight to keep an eye on her."

She sighed resignedly. "Turned out that I couldn't sleep much, either, so finally I figured I'd just come on in here."

With a confused mother and a lovely but demanding toddler son, the office was about the only place Missy could get any rest at all, lately.

Not that she'd be getting much today. "Okay, I'm on my cell. If you need to head home, just go, and call me when you can."

The smoke hadn't gotten any thicker overnight. But all it would take was a stiff breeze to whip things up again. "I'm going to take Peg with me down to the motel. Maybe my little pal Janie, or whoever she is, left something behind."

Like a notarized affidavit saying what the hell she's up to, Lizzie thought. But that was too much to hope for. *If she's left anything in that motel room, I'll bet I'm not going to like it.*

Which for ordinary life was way too pessimistic, of course. But when a murder cop expected the worst, in Lizzie's experience he or she turned out to be correct more times than not.

Like this time, for instance.

When you've worked in a medical center for as long as I'd worked at the one in New Haven, you can do almost anything in it: take showers and change into clean clothes, find food, watch TV, or even sleep overnight in a bed if you're careful and you know how to pick your spot. It's like a small city, containing everything needed for life.

You can learn almost anything about any of the patients in there, too, especially if you're the one creating their medical records, like I was. Place and date of birth, all the vital statistics, next of kin, medical or surgical history, any drugs prescribed now or in the past, allergies and precautions . . . it's all recorded, and not just in their charts.

Because the thing is, when I typed a report I made a hard copy that would be returned to a physician, a social worker, a therapist . . . whoever had sent in the dictated report in the first place. But it wasn't the only place the information went; as I sat at my keyboard and typed in the material, a computer file was also being created.

That computerized file could be retrieved and sent anywhere in the world electronically; for instance if you developed a heart problem or any other illness or condition while you were on vacation, the doctor wherever you were could consult your file via computer. It took a password to do it, of course. You couldn't just waltz in off the street and snoop in there. But the needed credential was gained easily by emailing a request for one to the database administrator.

Or by being me.

I actually was one of the administrators, and I accessed the medical database all the time, to create, update, or correct a medical record. As a result it was simple for me to access the data of anyone who had ever been a patient in the network, to request anything I wanted, and—in a near-instantaneous twinkle of electrons—get it.

Or change it, which I thought might come in handy once Cam and I began working on our plan. That was why, soon after Cam and I had set up the orderly Finny Brill to get Henry Gemerle out of the forensic hospital for us—and while Cam was in the very same medical center where I worked, recovering from her brain surgery—I tried altering a few things in the medical records on my own.

To find out, I mean, whether or not I could get away with it. And when I did, I got more ambitious. For starters, I decided to try ordering a few drugs.

Sitting beside Lizzie in the Blazer that Thursday morning, Peg Wylie said nothing as they drove out of town. Instead she gazed silently at the dried-out winter landscape that was coming to be the new normal around here: cracked mud in place of pasture ponds, dust where there should be snow.

The sky went on brightening, revealing old fence posts now weathered to silvery gray with shreds of rusty barbed wire still clinging to them and nests of bittersweet vine crowning their tops. Then:

"I lied to you," Peg said suddenly.

A hawk soared above, wings outspread, then dove fast, some rabbit or other small, soft mammal in the dry weeds having a bad morning suddenly.

"About Tara's father, I mean," said Peg.

Lizzie wasn't sure if the shriek as they passed was real, or if she'd imagined it. Either way, though: Bye-bye, rabbit.

"I had a boyfriend, and I got pregnant," Peg said. "And then I got married. I was sixteen."

The road south of Bearkill ran along a high, narrow ridge with views east across the St. John River to New Brunswick, Canada, and west to the northern reaches of the Appalachians. At this early hour the mountain peaks were indistinct humps against a dull sky, their eastern slopes covered with now-leafless hardwoods.

Lizzie pulled into a scenic bypass overlooking the river. The land past the trash cans and picnic tables dropped away to a vista of water and small islands far below, stretching to the horizon north and south. Directly to the east, a pale-pink line appeared on the horizon.

"Okay," said Lizzie. "And then what happened?"

Peg lit a cigarette. Her blond hair was bleached, a line of darker roots showing her natural color, which was light brown with a few gray streaks, and her eyes in the growing dawn were blue.

Pale, not-a-cloud-in-the-sky blue. She dragged nervously on the smoke. "And then his unit got called up. Military, he was in the National Guard. They got sent to Iraq."

Lizzie nodded, waiting. The pink line to the east turned pale yellow. A breeze, freakishly warm for this time of year and smelling freshly of the river, sucked the rank cigarette smoke out the passenger-side window.

Peg took another drag, pinched the butt with her thumb and index finger, then tucked it into her cigarette pack—there were no ashtrays in vehicles anymore, and around here lately no one flicked cigarettes out windows, even on gravel parking lots.

But finishing the cigarette seemed to have shut off Peg's speech-switch, too. She fell silent again, her face desolate.

"So?" Lizzie prompted finally, restarting the Blazer as a thin orange disk peeped up from the trees on the far side of the river. Then it jumped up, its light turning the hills to the west to gold while she turned back out onto the highway, once more heading south.

On the outskirts of Houlton they pulled off onto a side road, drove half a mile, and found the wide gravel driveway of Treetops. The colonial-style house, white-clapboarded and with the traditional green shutters at the windows, was the central hub of an elaborate series of more recent additions: a two-story brick unit housing the lobby and combination bar and restaurant—HOT BEEF SUB WITH AU JUICE SAUCE! read the yellowing placard propped in the window—and three one-story windowed spokes radiating outward from the central brick section, each spoke containing a dozen guest rooms.

At the rear, just visible over the guest-room sections, was what Lizzie assumed was the pool building, a blue-domed structure resembling a miniature covered sports arena.

Peg had stayed silent for the last part of the trip but now the sight of the motel seemed to get her going again from where she'd left off.

"Then he came home." She sighed. "Freaked out, hooked through the gills on heroin, and all pissed off at the whole damn world. At me, too. Tara was three months old."

Peg stopped, turning to stare out the window. Lizzie decided to give the woman a minute to collect herself. She hit her phone's auto-dial.

"Missy, do me a favor? Drop the New Haven cops a request for more records. Any priors on Henry Gemerle, and ask them for all of the unsolved stranger-rapes in the area from—" She specified the years she wanted. "Oh, and you know what? Ask them if there's a yard behind the Gemerle house, too, and was it investigated at all."

She listened a moment. "Yeah, investigated as in dug up, or if ca-daver dogs were ever in it. Or," she added, "GPR."

Ground-penetrating radar was a near-prohibitively expensive way to look for evidence. But Yale was in New Haven and probably had an archaeology department, so the cops there might have access to the technology without having to buy the gear.

She turned back to Peg, who'd straightened in her seat looking ready to talk again. "So then what happened?"

Around the back of the motel, four huge metal dumpsters and an industrial-sized propane tank formed an L-shaped service area. She parked next to it and got out, fishing around in her bag for a magnetic-stripped rectangle of plastic.

The employees at Treetops were just as cash-strapped as the minimum-wage workers back in the city had been. Getting the extra key card from the desk clerk last night had cost two folded twenties wrapped in a ten—the same price as Boston.

Lizzie hadn't even been sure at the time why she'd done it.

Force of habit, probably. But now she was glad.

"Then I left," said Peg, as if this must be obvious. "He was just get-ting impossible to live with."

The key card opened the motel's rear outer door. Inside, the hall stank of chlorine from the indoor pool.

"Last time I heard he'd just gotten out of jail again. And I don't want him to find us here. Not ever," Peg went on.

"Right," Lizzie said tiredly, but she didn't believe a word of it. What Peg had just told her might be a decent reason to keep your head down, keep your troubles from going public. A guy with a heroin habit was no one's idea of fun.

But it wasn't enough when your kid was missing. Lizzie punched her phone's REDIAL button. "Yeah, Missy, one more thing. Sorry about this, but call the New Haven cops again?"

She turned to Peg. "What's his name? Your ex, his last—"

Peg looked startled. "Zimmerman, his name is Mitch—"

Lizzie repeated this to Missy. "I'll hang on," she added, then listened while Missy relayed the information from the NHPD: brown/blue, six foot two, 190, muscular build, forearm tattoos.

Right now he was in custody on armed robbery charges, Missy said. So at least Mitch Zimmerman existed. Peg might even have been married to the guy like she said, not that it mattered. She was still lying; for one thing, the story was so harmless that if it were true, she'd have offered it earlier.

The room Lizzie had checked Jane Crimmins—or whoever she really was—into the day before was the last one on the corridor, adjacent to a whirring, clattering compressor of some kind, perhaps connected to the pool.

She slid the key card in and the door swung open; as the standard motel-room interior with its heavy drawn curtains came dimly into view, Peg stopped.

Lizzie did, too, glad suddenly for the chlorine reek. "Stay behind me, don't come in."

"Tara?" Peg's voice rose. "Oh, my God, is that—"

"No." *I hope not, anyway,* Lizzie thought. She flipped on a light switch. The room was a battle scene: chairs overturned, lamps broken, blankets torn off the bed.

The heavy ceramic lid from the toilet tank lay near the far wall. Lizzie crouched next to the bloody heap by the dresser, her heart slamming in her chest. Being a murder cop was like being an ER physician sometimes, she supposed: You could cultivate all the calm exterior manner you wanted.

But as Emily Ektari had said earlier, no one ever got used to the sight of a lot of blood all of a sudden.

A *lot* of blood.

EIGHT

Lizzie looked up at Peg's horrified face. "Take it easy. It's not
Tara, okay? I don't think anyone's here at all."

Lizzie scanned the carpet, looked under the beds, noted the disar-
rayed bedclothes, and checked behind the overturned TV.

Nothing. "Peg, go down to the lobby and ask to use the phone,
okay?" Lizzie scribbled on the desk pad.

"Call this number, a guy named Dylan Hudson should answer.
When he does I want you to tell him that you're with me and that I
need him to come out here."

Peg nodded dumbly but made no move to obey.

"Hey, you okay?" Lizzie peered into Peg's shocked face. "'Cause
this really isn't Tara, you know that now, don't you?"

"Yeah," Peg managed shakily. "Just blood." Her gaze flitted around
the room. No clothes or other personal items were visible, and nothing was on the bathroom counter but unopened soap and the standard tiny bottles of motel toiletries.

"But whose blood?" Peg whispered.

That was the big question, all right. "Just go, Peg. You want to help
Tara, you do what I asked."

Finally Peg obeyed, and once she was gone Lizzie knelt and peered
under both beds again, into the entryway closet, and all around the

bathroom. She checked all the dresser drawers and the bedside table, too: Bible, a sheet of TV instructions, and a menu from the motel's restaurant, nothing else.

In the wastebasket she found the unopened pack of pajamas and the toothbrush that she'd bought for Jane at the dollar store on the way here yesterday. In the desk was nothing but a few sheets of paper with the Treetops logo on them, a silhouette of a fancy cart with two high-stepping black ponies pulling it.

Nothing else; no shred of evidence to say what the pill-popping not-Jane Crimmins had been doing in here, or what had led to this scene of carnage. Then, just as Lizzie dropped to her knees again and spotted something she'd missed, a voice interrupted.

"Can I help you?" In the doorway stood a tall, pear-shaped man with a receding forehead, droopy eyes, and a ratty mustache. He wore baggy tan slacks with sneakers and a plaid collared shirt. The small button pinned to his frayed gray sweater-vest read LIVE LONG AND PROSPER.

He leaned forward, his eyes avid, taking in the scene of past violence like it was vital oxygen. "I'm the manager. What's going on?"

Lizzie stood up. "I'm a cop. This is a crime scene."

Unlike Peg, the motel manager seemed unfazed by the blood. But then who knew what he got used to, working here; all it had taken to give Lizzie a permanent motel-room phobia was a single demonstration of a forensic device that made body-fluid stains glow in the dark.

"I checked a woman in here yesterday," she said. "By the name of Jane Crimmins. Now she's gone, and I find this."

She waved at the mess. "So was there any disturbance? Did anyone complain about noise, a fight, anything like that?"

But probably that loud compressor next door had muffled it, she thought. The manager drew himself up primly.

"Now, Officer, I'm very sure this motel has no responsibility whatsoever for what any of our guests may choose to—"

Lizzie's patience for fools, never well supplied anyway, fizzled out abruptly. "Hey, dickwad, how about you just answer my question and save the legal opinions for later, okay? You had any complaints for anything at all, like maybe a visitor from the Planet Vulcan you haven't felt like mentioning? 'Cause it looks to me like somebody got all of the blood let out of 'em here. You sure you don't know anything about how that happened?"

The plump hands pressed together in a praying gesture. "No! I most certainly don't—"

Peg stepped past the motel manager. She looked as if she had managed to calm herself somehow, and sure enough those were booze fumes on her breath; the bar here opened early, apparently.

"Detective Hudson's coming," she said. "Ten minutes."

Lizzie turned back to the manager, whose ghoulish eagerness had evaporated. "Go on back to the front desk and stay there," she told him.

A flash of rebellion at being told what to do showed in his glance, but he went. "Peg, d'you want to go get the yellow tape from the Blazer?"

Kneeling once more, she peered under the desk chair. Taped under the seat was a large tan manila envelope. Dry-mouthed, she pulled the envelope out, opened the loose flap, and peered inside.

Pill bottles, the small orange plastic pharmacy kind like the one the supposed Jane Crimmins had taken from her purse earlier, filled the envelope. Without touching them she could see that the labels were of two kinds: Some said diazepam, which was the generic name for Valium, and others were for methylphenidate.

Which Lizzie knew was pharmacy-speak for Ritalin, an often-abused stimulant used for attention deficit disorder. Emily had said it could cause false positives on tests for amphetamines.

There were perhaps a dozen small bottles labeled for each drug in the envelope. Uppers and downers, in other words; a mental picture of a woman who was so badly agitated that she couldn't take questioning from Dylan popped into Lizzie's mind.

"What are you doing?" Peg stood in the doorway again, yellow tape roll in hand.

Jane had taken pills from a bottle like one of these back in Lizzie's kitchen, she recalled, saying they were for a headache.

"Just making sure we haven't missed anything." Lizzie caught the tape Peg tossed at her and laid the envelope casually on the dresser.

Maybe Jane had crammed all of her pills into just a few bottles so they'd fit in her purse, then put the emptied bottles in the envelope and hid it; speed freaks were compulsive that way sometimes, Lizzie knew. Jane would have meant to get rid of the bottles more permanently, but whatever went on here had happened before she could.

That was one theory, anyway. "On second thought, let's just let the state cops handle it," Lizzie added, glancing around a final time at the bloody mess. "It's their department."

Outside, she moved the Blazer around to the front parking lot so Dylan would see it when he arrived. Getting out, Peg pulled a cigarette from her purse and managed to light it.

"Did Tara get hurt in there? Do you think—?" She blew out a plume of smoke.

"I don't know." Lizzie punched her phone's buttons again. Time to give her own boss a call, assuming Mister Magoo out there at the front desk hadn't done it already.

But then from the corner of her eye she caught sight of something odd in a car parked by the motel's restaurant. There was someone inside it, small fists hammering at the window of the midsized sedan.

Hurrying toward the car, she shoved her phone back into her bag. "Help!" the child in the vehicle cried as Lizzie assessed the youngster: female, moderate distress, no obvious injuries, maybe ten years old. Her hair, pulled into a ponytail, was light blond.

Nicki's hair was blond, too. And she'd be the same age . . .

"Help, they locked me in here! Let me out, help!"

The little girl wore a white blouse and navy vest, like part of a school uniform. Scanning the child's face, Lizzie looked for the tiny birthmark Nicki had just in front of her right ear.

A fairy's touch, Cecily had called the mark. But through the tinted glass Lizzie couldn't see well enough to tell for sure if it was present on this child.

"Peg, go on inside the restaurant," she said. "See if someone there left a kid out here in the car."

The vehicle's doors were all locked. "Hang on, kiddo," she told the little girl, "I'm a police officer, I'll get you out."

She knew the odds of this being her own long-dead sister's missing child were heavily against. *Still, stranger things have—*

Peg returned shaking her head. "Nobody in the restaurant at all."

Or in the parking lot, either. "Okay, then, go on back to my vehicle. Inside you'll find a windshield hammer under the driver's seat, you know what one looks like?"

Peg nodded briskly and obeyed at once, about-facing yet again back toward the Blazer despite her own ongoing distress. Under other circumstances, Lizzie thought—ones in which Peg was not lying her head off, for instance—the Bearkill woman would make a good team member.

"Help!" the little blond child cried hysterically. "I can't unlock the doors! They left me in here, I've been here for hours and I'm suffocating, help me!"

"Calm down, I'll get you out." The girl wasn't suffocating, clearly. But she seemed thoroughly frightened, and besides, Lizzie wanted—needed—a better look at her.

Peg returned with the hammer. "Okay, now," Lizzie told the child, "you cover your head with your arms and close your eyes."

The car's door locks were electronic. She raised the hammer. "Wait!" A man strode hurriedly out of the restaurant. "Wait, what are you doing, that's my car!"

Sport coat and slacks, white knit polo shirt, wristwatch. Behind the man hurried a woman in a navy pantsuit, wearing a lot of jewelry and a heavily sprayed platinum hairdo.

"Wait, wait, what's going on?" she cried anxiously.

Lizzie lowered the hammer. Inside the car, a fleeting look of thwarted malice crossed the little girl's face and was gone.

The man rushed up, pressing his key fob. The car's window lowered: no birthmark, and the girl's eyes were hazel, not blue.

So: not Nicki. Lizzie quashed disappointment; after all, what had she been expecting?

"What the hell?" the man demanded as the door locks popped. The woman yanked the rear door open and seized the little girl's arm firmly.

"What did you do?" she demanded of the child. "For heaven's sake, I leave you here for five minutes and when I come back—"

Lizzie produced her badge and identified herself while the woman dragged the unwilling child out of the car. When the kid's feet hit the ground she started yelling again; close up, she did not look so angelic.

"Liar! They left me for hours!" She jerked from the woman's grasp. "You hurt me! Help! These aren't my real parents!"

She looked, actually, like a world-class brat. Lizzie turned back to the man, whose flat, sad expression said this wasn't the first such scene he'd endured. "Sir, I'll need to see some—"

"Identification," he finished for her. "Sure." He produced a driver's license, handed it over with an air of resignation. "My daughter," he added quietly, "is disturbed."

Meanwhile the woman spoke evenly but furiously to the child. "We were in the restrooms, for heaven's sake. And I warned you when we got here, if you made a big fuss in the restaurant you'd have to sit out in the car. Didn't I?"

Lizzie handed back the man's license, about to tell him that she hoped he understood but she would have to check further.

Because she was pretty sure she understood the situation now, but that wasn't enough when a kid was involved.

"It's okay. I know them," Peg said quietly. The man looked gratefully at Peg. "He works for the highway department, based out of Houlton, and the little girl goes to a—"

"Walthrop School," the man put in. "It's a residential place for emotionally disturbed girls. In New Hampshire." He glanced over at his wife and their child. "We were bringing her home for a visit."

Then he looked down at his shoes. "I guess maybe that wasn't such a good idea," he added. "I'm very sorry for the trouble."

On the other side of the car, the little girl stamped her feet, then hauled off and took a solid swing at her mother, who sidestepped it expertly. "I hate you!" the girl shrieked.

"Excuse me," the man said, hurrying over. Moments later he had his arms wrapped tightly around the child, restraining her while she kicked and struggled; with his wife's help he at last got the girl back into the car and her seatbelt fastened.

As they drove away, Lizzie watched with a mixture of painful emotions. It hadn't occurred to her to wonder what she would do if she found Nicki and the child had significant problems.

But now it did. "She was hurt in there, wasn't she?" Peg quavered, pulling Lizzie back to the present. "All that blood in the room. It's Tara's, isn't it?"

Lizzie finished leaving a message on Sheriff Cody Chevrier's voice-mail. "We don't know that."

But Peg wasn't having any. "Oh, come on. You think I'm that stupid? Somebody bled to death in there, bled like a—"

Dylan's car pulled in. Lizzie turned to Peg. "Okay, then. You're right. Someone's dead, probably. Or nearly dead. I don't know who or why."

Dylan parked and got out, sliding on his dark glasses as he crossed the parking lot.

"But what I do know is that this whole morning, you've been trying to feed me another load of horsecrap about your daughter."

Caught, said the sudden expression on Peg's face.

"Not only that, but I don't know where *you* were or what *you* were doing when whatever happened in there went down."

Peg looked shocked. Too bad, Lizzie thought. She took a deep breath to calm herself, let it out slowly.

"You know, Peg, everyone working on this case has their own reasons. Things that *they* want, besides finding Tara."

Watching Dylan stride toward her, his black topcoat swinging open over his dark wool suit and his oxblood wing tips glinting in the morning sun, she added: "Maybe it's good for their career, or they just want a perfect case-clearing score, whatever.

"All but me," she went on. "I can't benefit from Tara's case. I'm not even assigned to it."

She plucked the cigarette from Peg's fingers and dragged on it. "I'm just a lowly sheriff's deputy, so all I'm in it for is to try to help."

The smoke was like a kick to the head; another drag and she'd be hooked again. Some primitive self-preserving instinct stopped her from taking it.

"So when you decide to stop lying to me, give me a call. Otherwise—"

Dylan was near enough now so she could smell his cologne, like vermouth with a twist of lime.

"Otherwise," Lizzie finished, dropping the cigarette and crushing it decisively with the toe of her boot—

"Otherwise, go fly a kite."

"What's she doing here?" Dylan asked. Across the parking lot, Peg Wylie hoisted herself up into the Blazer's passenger seat.

"Blowing smoke at me," Lizzie replied. "And not just from her cigarettes, either."

The aftertaste of the drag she'd taken was disgusting. "Don't ask me why, though," she added, "because I still have no idea."

She angled her head at the motel's main entrance. "Meanwhile there's a room with a lot of fresh blood in it in there, a real horror show. Also—"

She told him about the pill bottles. "I'll bet that's why she flaked out on your interview, too."

Gazing past Dylan at the distant hillsides, she wondered yet again how she'd gotten herself stuck in a place where there were more trees than people. On the other hand, at least trees didn't look you in the face and lie.

"Peg's still hiding something," she said. "Like she thinks the truth is even worse than Tara being AWOL, somehow."

Dylan's eyebrows went up. "And you know this because?"

It had hit her while she was looking at the child in the car: the obvious reason why Peg's most recent story was unlikely to be true.

"Okay, so you saw Tara's missing person flyer, right? The description on it?"

He nodded. "Teenager, brown hair, brown eyes . . . so what?"

"So Peg says she's on the run from Tara's dad. But he's got a sheet, and I got his description from the New Haven cops earlier. Hair brown, eyes blue . . ."

"So? What's your point?"

"So Peg's eyes are blue, too," she said, then watched as he got it and shook his head ruefully.

"Oh, man. High school biology, huh? Two blue-eyed parents, a brown-eyed kid, small chance."

He grimaced, thinking about it. "So, what, do you think Tara's not really hers, like maybe she stole the kid or something? Maybe that's why she didn't want any publicity about it?"

"I don't know what to think. But somebody needs to go at her again 'cause so far I'm getting zilch."

She filled Dylan in on Emily Ektari's blood-type mismatch discovery, which meant Jane Crimmins wasn't who she said she was.

"So even though she's got the right ID, she's also lying. And now she's in the wind, on top of it," Lizzie added.

"Great," he said, shaking his head in disgust. "That's just what we need. But listen, there's something else. A fire crew was out in the puckerbrush early this morning getting the jump on some embers."

Finding and dousing any smoldering bits that might blaze up later was a part of the crews' morning routine.

"And they found a freshly dug hole in the ground out there," he said.

"Like, a hole with someone in it? As in buried in it?"

"Yeah. Looks like it. The thing is, whoever was in the hole isn't in it anymore," he said.

"Grave-sized hole, wooden box like a coffin in it," said Dylan. "Wooden top, couple short nails sticking out of it, lying on the ground by the hole."

By now it was nine in the morning, the unseasonably warm sun well up in the winter sky. In the parking lot by the motel, the state's white mobile crime-lab van arrived.

"Fire crew's chief says there's a busted-up cell phone in the hole," Dylan added. "I don't know whose it is, yet, but I'll bet I can guess."

"Yeah," Lizzie agreed. "Tara maybe used it once somehow to send that text message to her mom?"

He nodded. "Yup. That's my thought, too. And then it got noticed, and broken. Although it could still be that someone else sent the text," he added.

"To what, torment Peg? Yeah, I guess that's a possibility." Either way, Lizzie refused to let herself imagine being buried in a box in an active fire zone. *Vehicles, voices . . .*

But no one to hear you scream. *No rescue.* "And you found out about the cell phone and the rest of it how, exactly?"

Dylan watched the crime-scene tech climb out of the van and start across the parking lot toward them. "Fire crew's team leader called Cody Chevrier. Cody must've figured this'd end up being mine, so he called me."

And that in a nutshell was Aroostook County sheriff Cody Chevrier, who felt no need to visit a crime scene just for ego-boosting purposes, or God forbid to create a photo op. *Your job, you do it,* was his motto, though if you needed any backup he was there in a heartbeat.

"Cody got me up to speed on what the fire guys found and I was on my way up to that scene when you called," Dylan said. "The county's so strapped for personnel right now with the fires going on, he doesn't have anyone else to send."

Which was why there weren't volunteers out searching for Tara Wylie. The battle against the brush fires was a holding action and every available man or woman who wasn't tied down somewhere else was busy battling to keep it that way.

The crime-lab technician strode toward them. She was in her late twenties, Lizzie estimated, tanned and athletic looking with bright, smart eyes and wavy auburn hair tied up in a scarf.

"Hi," said Lizzie, not sticking out a hand because the tech was already all gloved up. Besides, she didn't feel like it.

"Hi," said the tech with the barest glance at Lizzie. "See you inside," she told Dylan with a brilliantly white smile.

Lizzie watched the technician return to the motel. "Isn't it amazing what diet and exercise can do for a person?"

"Yeah," said Dylan, still watching, too. She was about to ask if he wanted a can of Alpo to go with his houndlike tendencies, but Peg interrupted.

"What's going on?" she demanded, squinting suspiciously from Lizzie to Dylan and back again.

"I'll tell you later," said Lizzie, and Dylan shot her a look of gratitude, having no wish to explain to Peg now about the hole in the ground where a broken cell phone had been located.

"You've got this other thing?" Lizzie added to him, meaning the bloody motel room.

"Yeah." His grim nod confirmed her own earlier assessment that this was his case. There'd been too much blood in that room to believe otherwise, and she could see from his face that he was already making his mental to-do list.

Then he caught her expression. "Something wrong?"

The crime-scene tech had already entered the motel but her image felt burnt on Lizzie's retinas; that and the way Dylan had watched the young woman's lithe figure as she'd departed.

Lizzie shook her head irritably. "I gave the motel manager more grief than he deserved in there, that's all."

Dylan's eyebrows raised. "You could apologize."

She turned. "I don't feel that bad about it," she said, and stalked away from him.

But by the time she reached the Blazer with Peg Wylie already in the passenger seat, she'd cooled off enough to think straight again. Today wasn't about Dylan, or about Nicki, either.

It was about Peg's missing daughter, Tara, and Peg was still lying about something. Which was why, on Lizzie's own to-do list, changing that fact had just become job one.

On a cold December morning in New Haven two weeks after her brain surgery, I brought a still-recuperating Cam home from the hospital. The cab let us out in front of our building. I'd bought a car by then, a nearly new Lexus, with some of the money I'd gotten from selling my parents' house. But I didn't want to watch out for traffic or pay attention to street signs that day; I wanted to focus on her.

Gripping my arm, she made her halting way up the front walk; inside, she stood gazing around as if to make sure she was really there at last. She went into the kitchen where everything gleamed, to the living and dining rooms bright with fresh flowers in readiness for her, and at last to her own room with its familiar braided rag rug, low wooden bed, and white chenille spread.

I'd thought about new curtains but when I saw her I was glad I'd kept the old lace tie-backs, merely washing and ironing them to pristine whiteness. Only when she was satisfied that everything was as she'd left it did she let me take her coat and carefully lift her soft knitted cap from her head.

The staples from surgery had been removed and prickles of new hair had begun sprouting on her bluish-white scalp. She would need help with bathing, I'd been told, and there was a whole long list of other things she wasn't yet allowed to do alone, too.

"This is an elaborate care plan," the nurse had said, "which must be followed strictly. Are you certain you can handle it?"

But in fact the only hard part was hiding my happiness. It would be like when Cam first got freed, I thought. When she could barely do anything on her own and had turned to me for everything.

And it was that way, too, for a month while I nursed and cosseted her. Dainty sandwiches, nourishing broths . . . nothing was too good for her. Even the plan to punish Henry Gemerle was put on hold, waiting for her recovery. But then:

"Oh, my *God*!" In the kitchen I was making a mushroom stew with cream and shallots; dropping the spoon, I rushed in to find her already halfway out of her chair, her lap robe fallen to the floor.

"What is it, what's wrong?" I put my arm around her to guide her down again. She was not supposed to get up unaided without her walker, which I'd left out in the hall because it took up so much room in the apartment.

And besides, she had me. She gestured at the TV. "He . . ."

I followed her anguished gaze to the screen, where a courtroom news story was being reported. Then I saw the prisoner in his bright-orange jumpsuit being led in between two bailiffs.

It was Gemerle. Cam turned accusingly. "You didn't tell me."

I hadn't prepared her for this new torture, that he might suddenly appear right there in our own living room.

"I didn't know," I whispered, and truly I hadn't. For weeks all I'd thought of was Cam's surgery and her recovery . . . it was as if nothing else in the world existed.

For me, nothing else had. True, there had been calls on the answering machine from the district attorney's office, asking if Cam would testify; at the very hearing, I realized, that we were watching on TV right now.

But she couldn't, of course, and not only because she was so ill. After all, who knew what a clever attorney might manage to coax or trick her into saying?

Fortunately, her surgery had given me a perfect excuse to tell them that she wasn't able to talk on the phone, that she was much too ill to appear in court, and that she would be that way for the foreseeable future.

And her doctors had backed me up on this. Still, to make absolutely sure she'd keep silent when I wasn't around, I'd been sedating her with Valium tablets when I went to work. Orders for prescriptions, I'd found, could be put into the medical database like anything else, then filled at the hospital pharmacy.

But now Cam was wide awake, staring at the TV as Henry Gemerle shuffled to the defendant's table, his wrists manacled and his ankles in chains. Seeing him I turned, expecting to find her hatred of him mirroring my own. Instead, though, her face was full of sorrow and yearning. After a moment of utter confusion I believed I knew why.

It had been in the news that there'd been infant things in that cellar—tiny clothes and other items moldering in a storage cabinet. But no infant anywhere.

"Cam," I said gently, sitting beside her. "Where is . . . ?"

That old midline abdominal scar I'd seen explained her look of sorrow now, I thought.

. . . *your baby?* I was about to finish. But before I could do so, Cam shook her head impatiently to silence me.

"There they are," she whispered as the camera panned over the courtroom spectators, and then I saw them, two young women in the front row. They were flanked on either side by a pair of guardlike older ladies in dark business suits, the kind of outfits that frilly blouses are meant to soften but don't.

"Victim advocates," Cam said contemptuously of the women. She'd never spoken to another social worker after the Davenport fiasco. The crawl at the bottom of the TV screen read, EXPERTS SAY ACCUSED UNFIT, JUDGE TO RULE ON ABILITY TO ASSIST DEFENSE.

"The girls look all right," I said. Cam shrugged, waiting only for the moment when the camera found Gemerle again, his lips curved in a smirk I recalled too well. No shame troubled his face, only a kind of puzzled curiosity, as if he didn't understand what everybody was so upset about. Those deep-blue eyes of his glinted with the same cruel glee I'd witnessed at his house that night.

Seeing him, I knew suddenly that the experts were wrong; Henry Gemerle was no more unfit to stand trial than I was. At the thought that he might fool them an awful drowning feeling went through me, like I was falling down a dark well.

Still gazing at the TV, Cam reached over and put her hand on mine. She'd never done such a thing before.

"He looks just the same," she said, not removing her hand.

"Yes," I replied faintly, still fearing that before we could team up to punish him she would tell, that with a word she would ruin my life. Seeing him would remind her, I thought, of what had happened to her.

And why. That it was my fault. "Yes," I repeated, dry-mouthed with fear suddenly. "Older. But the same."

The yellow hair, thick swatches of blond eyebrows, and once-slim build now gone a little to flab since he'd been imprisoned were all the same as I recalled.

"Cam, is the baby still alive?"

She looked startled. I was, too; I hadn't known I would say it. But she nodded in the affirmative. "Oh, yes."

"Do you . . . do you know where?" But to this she gave only a small, negative shake of her shaved head.

A smell came from the kitchen, of frying potatoes needing to be turned. I got up, letting Cam's hand fall. The TV crawl read, JUDGE OKAYS CAMERAS IN HEARINGS RE ACCUSED'S TRIAL COMPETENCY.

So we would see him again. I hurried back to finish cooking our dinner, my heart thumping wildly at the memories that his face had brought on; for Cam, too, I supposed.

But seeing him had brought on another feeling, also. Stirring the soup, I imagined future evenings when Cam and I would sit together watching the court proceedings on TV, sharing memories that only we two could possibly understand.

Let the other girls be there in person, I thought, in front of the greedy cameras where merely by tuning in, the whole world could gawk at them. We had each other, Cam and I, and despite my fear that she might still turn on me, for now that was enough.

Or it was until I realized the enormity of what she'd told me. That with it I had the means, finally, to cement her loyalty to me permanently. The thought came suddenly as I laid the soupspoons on the dining-room table, lining them up carefully atop the linen napkins and then filling the wineglasses.

Because the two of us punishing the monster together was one thing. But bringing Cam's lost child back to her would be another, wouldn't it?

After all, for creating the ties that bind there is nothing like flesh and blood.

"You know what I think?"

Lizzie gripped the Blazer's steering wheel as the vehicle bounced along; not many roads led out to the brushland where the gravelike hole had been found, and of those none was paved all the way to the end.

Peg listened stonily as Lizzie went on: "I think *you* think Tara will be in worse trouble somehow if you tell the truth than if you don't."

No answer from Peg. On either side of the washboard-gravel road, teams of men and women dug firebreaks, swinging at them with pickaxes and shoveling dirt onto hot spots. The air smelled like ashes mixed with exhaust from the constantly howling chain saws, as workers cut brush and whippy saplings and hauled them away before the fires could use them for fuel.

Chevrier had said he'd let the workers up here know to expect her. Now a guy in a yellow vest spotted her and waved her forward.

"Up there?" She stuck her head out the window.

"Yeah! Quarter mile or so!" The guy wore bulky ear protection and an air pack strapped to his back. "Over on the right you'll see a red bandanna tied to a sapling? Turn in there!"

She buzzed the window back up and switched on the Blazer's air-conditioning to clear the smoke from the cab; not cigarettes, this time, but the real deal.

"I've brought you here to show you something," she told Peg.

The missing teen's mother spoke resentfully. "You've got the wrong idea. I'm telling the truth, I don't see why you think—"

"Hold on." Lizzie hit the brakes as a girl in an orange slicker stepped onto the dirt road, hands up in a *halt* gesture.

Flames lapped at the road. They'd already eaten right up to the gravel edges, leaving black ash. Two guys beat monotonously at the flickering remnants that kept springing up again.

Peg scowled as the girl in the vest waved them by. "Why are we even out here?" she began again.

Lizzie pulled onto the blackened grass. The red rag fluttered from the trunk of a small tree. "Just get out."

She led Peg across soft, powdery soil, its burnt structure falling away beneath a solid-looking surface.

Finally she stopped, putting a hand out, and then Peg saw it, too. A hole gaped in the baked earth, and beside it sat a wooden box about six feet long and half as wide.

It looked like a coffin except for the slats that lay around near it. From the nail holes in them, it was pretty clear they'd been nailed crosswise onto the box.

Peg dropped to her knees. "Oh, God . . ."

From around them rose yells from the fire volunteers trying desperately to keep one another in view in the smoky conditions, or at least within shouting range. A pickup truck moved slowly on the dirt road, barely visible through the haze, the support teams perched in the vehicle's bed handing out water and fresh bandannas to the ground crews.

"Oh," Peg said helplessly again. The hole was only a few inches deeper than the box itself.

So you put the box in the hole, then the person into the box. Threatening them with a weapon, maybe, to make them get in, Lizzie thought. Then you put the separate boards of the lid on, fastening them with what looked like . . . yeah, those were roofing nails.

Whoever had been in this box had been let out again, though. She knew from the two sets of human footprints in the ashy soil of what had been pasture, leading away on a trail deeply trodden into the soil by—Lizzie supposed—animals.

Sheep, maybe. Or cows. "Jesus," Peg whispered faintly. "She was in there? You think Tara was—"

The feds working the kidnapping would arrive soon. Chevrier had already put them in the picture, which was fine with Lizzie. Not having to do crime-scene chores meant she could use the time instead to try again at getting something useful out of Peg.

The truth, for instance. "You're still lying to me, Peg. You know it and I know it. Two blue-eyed parents are very unlikely to have had—"

"Don't lecture me, all right?" Peg retorted. "It was all I could think of on short notice."

She fumbled in her shirt pocket for a smoke and cursed when she was out, then rummaged angrily until she located a loose cigarette in the bottom of her purse. "Tara still thinks she's my ex's kid, I don't want her to—"

"But what's so bad about that? I've heard worse, and at her age probably Tara has, too."

Peg only shook her head stubbornly, blowing out smoke. "I don't care, I just don't want her to know."

Lizzie scanned the makeshift grave impatiently. What Peg was saying didn't make sense. For one thing, sooner or later the girl would figure it out. "That hers?"

It was a cell phone, badly smashed, one large daggerlike shard the only recognizable piece. It had been left here because it was evidence for the crime-scene team to process.

"Yeah," said Peg shakily. "It used to be mine but she really wanted one, and—"

"Okay." Lizzie counted to ten, controlling her temper.

Turning, she herded Peg along. The smoke was eye-wateringly thick. "While we drive back to town, I want you to think hard about where Tara might be right now."

Peg nodded mutely. Lizzie could see that the sight of the hole and the broken phone had shocked the woman, knocked all the magical thinking or whatever it was right out of her head.

But it hadn't yet persuaded her to tell the truth. "And who she might be with," Lizzie added cruelly.

Her boots raised small clouds of parched dust. "Because I don't know yet how he found her here, but I'm pretty sure Tara's the reason why Henry Gemerle came to Bearkill."

Hopping into the driver's seat, she slammed the heavy door. The vehicle felt soundproofed suddenly, the whole outside world held off by a couple of tons of steel and glass.

Too bad the feeling couldn't last, she thought as she turned the Blazer around on the gravel, aiming back downhill through the smoke. Not until they bumped back onto the paved road once more did she speak.

"Look, Peg. I told you this once, but I need to be sure you understand that I'm not on Tara's case, officially. It's the state cops and the FBI who—"

"I'm not telling them anything," Peg cut in flatly.

Lizzie counted to ten. "Peg. You called me, remember?"

On the highway they passed a farmyard where a dozen brown cows walked up a ramp into an enclosed trailer. The drought meant local feed production was way down, and if they couldn't buy feed for the animals the farmers had to sell them.

"You wanted my help," Lizzie went on, "but I guess now you've decided that confiding in me will only hurt Tara somehow."

In the farmyard, two small children watched the herd being loaded, waving farewell as the trailer's doors swung shut.

"Still," Lizzie went on carefully, "I get the feeling you're leaving the door open a crack."

Silence from Peg. But a *listening* silence. Lizzie took a deep breath. "So here's the deal. If you tell me the truth about what's going on I . . . I'll keep it to myself."

It was maybe the worst idea she'd ever had, and for sure it was illegal. But Tara Wylie was still out there somewhere and in danger, if she was even alive.

So never mind the rules, Lizzie thought, or the job. What mattered was the oath she had taken: *to serve and protect.*

Nothing else was working for her in Bearkill; not finding Nicki or settling things with Dylan, not even playing straight with Trey, one of the most decent guys she'd ever met. He deserved better from her; everyone did.

"I don't get it," Peg said.

"Yeah, I don't, either." Because what she'd decided was wrong and yet at the moment, it felt like the only possible thing. So she would hear whatever Peg said, act on it as best she could, and figure out on her own when or whether to confide in anyone else.

So maybe I'll tell. And maybe, she thought, feeling suddenly much better about everything—

Maybe I won't.

NINE

Patient confidentiality doesn't only mean not talking about what you know. It also means not trying to find out things that are none of your business.

That's why what I did next was against the rules: I had no job-related reason for retrieving the records of cesarean births that occurred in New Haven hospitals during the relevant years. But I did it anyway, since for the sort of plan I was devising now I couldn't rely just on Cam's word.

Once I'd gotten the birth records I wanted, I narrowed my search to brown-eyed mothers like Cam. I could also have sorted them by zip code, ethnicity, or a dozen or more other delimiters used mostly by public health researchers. But all I really wanted was my cousin Cam's medical history, and finding that, too, was surprisingly easy.

I simply searched for it, and the information came scrolling up on the computer screen in front of me. From it I learned the child's birth year, a scant nine months after we'd both been abducted, and that when she went into labor he'd brought her to the ER, signing his own name as the supposed husband of the patient and father of the child. He must have threatened her to keep her silent, I guessed, and afterward he took her and the new baby back to the Michener Street address, in a run-down part of town I'd studiously avoided all that time.

She never kept any follow-up appointments, and I could find no vaccination records for the infant. Fifteen years later at my desk in the medical records office, I gazed out the high window overlooking New Haven. From it I could see all the way across the Yale campus and in the other direction across Long Island Sound.

Out there, somewhere . . . The baby was a healthy girl: She'd gone home with Cam and the monster, but she hadn't been there—she'd have been fourteen by then—when Cam and the other women were rescued.

So what had happened? Cam didn't seem to know—pressing her for theories had resulted only in stubborn silence, at any rate—but there were two other women who might. That was why, on the Monday morning after I learned that Cam's baby had definitely been born, I took a bus downtown to the courthouse.

Gemerle's competency proceedings were about to begin their second day of hearings, and his other two victims would be there; I'd seen them on TV, sitting with the victim advocates.

Of course I was terrified to approach them. All I wanted, as I stepped off the bus in front of the courthouse building, was to jump right back on it again and go home, to be there with Cam.

But the girls might know something about Cam's lost child, so I didn't.

"He's my cousin," Peg whispered to Lizzie. "Henry Gemerle's mother and mine were sisters."

By now it was late morning. Smoke drifted lazily from the fire zone they'd just been in, hazing the blue sky over where they sat parked outside Lizzie's office.

"That's good, that's a good start," Lizzie said. "Now, do you want my help with any of this? Because that's what I'm offering to you here. All you need to do is take it."

Sniffling, Peg yanked a wad of tissues from her purse. "I swear when I get that kid back I will never let her out of my sight again."

Lizzie ignored this. "So the cousin thing, though. You want to expand a little on that?"

Peg nodded brokenly. "Like I said, our mothers were sisters. Both dead now. We lived only a few blocks from each other in East Haven."

"I see." *Take it slow,* Lizzie reminded herself. *Circle around a little.* "So did Tara ever meet any of your family members?"

Peg laughed bitterly. "No, none of them. And she won't if I have anything to do with it."

She turned to face Lizzie. "They all thought Henry was a good guy because he was working steady. I'm the only one who thought he was weird. He gave me the creeps. I kept away as much as I could."

"Uh-huh. The rest of the family still saw him, though? At his place, or yours?"

But Peg wasn't listening. "I mean of the whole bunch, there's not a one who wasn't short a few marbles, if you know what I mean. To them, Henry was just fine. But then . . ."

Missy came to the office window and spotted Lizzie, nodding as if the sight of her was expected. Which reminded Lizzie: She'd promised to be here by noon to cover the phones for an hour.

". . . then I started hearing about this baby Henry had somehow gotten hold of," Peg said.

Lizzie waved at Missy to say she'd be coming in shortly, as they'd agreed.

". . . said it was his girlfriend's baby," Peg went on, "even though nobody could remember Henry ever having a girlfriend."

Missy turned away from the window and went back to her desk. "Peg? Let's go inside, okay?" Lizzie interrupted reluctantly.

Once a subject started talking, you didn't stop them if you could help it. But as it turned out Lizzie might as well have tried damming Niagara Falls.

"He really wanted to get rid of it," Peg continued as they went in. "The baby, I mean. A baby girl. And I wanted one. My mom came home talking about it and I said I'd take it. And I did."

"Really." Inside, Lizzie sat at her own desk with Peg in the chair across from her. "Nobody thought that was unusual at all? No one from any health department or anything?"

Peg made a face. "Please. The last thing we wanted was to get family services involved, nosy social workers or whatever."

She dug in her purse for a cigarette, found none. "We knew girls who'd had their kids taken away by the welfare people. So, no. No social workers, anyone like that."

It still sounded odd, though. "What about your mother, didn't she have something to say about it?" Because if Peg was thirty or so now—younger than Lizzie had first thought, just aged by worry—that would've made her, what, fifteen?

"Yeah, well," Peg replied with a shrug. "My mom didn't have too much input into my decisions. She had a big pill habit to take care of."

"Sorry. That must've been rough. But . . . come on, Peg, even you didn't think it was strange? A weird cousin with a girlfriend no one ever saw, and then a baby?"

Peg sighed. "Maybe if I'd thought about it I would've. But I was just a kid myself. I had this fantasy of being some kind of a storybook heroine, saving a baby from the kind of life I had."

She shook her head ruefully. "I had no idea how hard it would be. Or that . . ."

Her voice dropped to a whisper. "Or that he'd come back."

Now they were getting to it. "But you were afraid he would?"

Peg nodded, her eyes downcast. "A few months later I saw him downtown. He looked . . . I don't know. Wrong, somehow. Like he was plotting something. He didn't see me or Tara, though, and I was glad. He scared me."

She looked up. "That's when I decided that I didn't want him around her ever again."

She broke off suddenly, her desolate gaze looking past Lizzie out into the winter day. "I should be out with the fire crews, you know. I'm a volunteer myself, I should be there with my crew."

Lizzie recalled the boots and hard hat in Peg's kitchen, the radio on the counter. "I think under the circumstances they'd cut you some slack."

She leaned back in her chair, trying to make sense of what Peg had said. The likeliest explanation for what they'd found on the ridge was that Gemerle had moved Tara. Maybe he'd worried that her cries for help might be heard by the fire volunteers.

Which if it was true meant at least that she was alive, or had been when he did it. But why he was keeping her that way—why he was doing any of this at all—Lizzie still had no idea.

Turning, she was about to say so, to offer at least as much reassurance as she could. Instead, a stray gleam of sunlight from the office's big front window hit Peg's eyes at an angle, revealing the faint line of something curved on the left one, a pale iridescent blue against the white part of Peg's eye, just the narrowest edge. But it was enough, and from it suddenly Lizzie knew two things:

Just as she'd thought, Peg Wylie had indeed been lying about everything, all along.

And she was lying now.

It had been dark in that cellar of his, and it was years ago. So going into the courtroom that day, I felt sure that neither of the girls I'd left down there would recognize me.

The metal detector and security screening held no terrors for me, either. The guards in their navy-blue uniforms seemed to sense this, already looking past me as I approached. Once cleared to go in, I moved along with dozens of others down the linoleum-tiled corridor to the door where a clerk was handing out paper tickets with numbers on them.

The hall was jam-packed; it seemed half the world wanted an in-person look at the awful criminal they'd seen on TV, and I had a moment of panic when I thought I might not get admitted. But in the end I was issued one of the last passes being given out that morning, and with it I made my way into the rear of the chamber.

The room was warm, smelling of dusty radiators, damp coats, and the pungent hair pomade of one of the courtroom clerks. As the judge entered we all stood, then sat and waited some more while up front the attorneys put their heads together and argued over some procedural business.

At last all the rustling and murmuring went silent. In the upstairs gallery the news cameras stood like three-legged aliens, each aimed at the bench where the judge glanced once more at the bailiff, then looked out over the spectators.

His gaze lingered a moment on me, I don't know why, and the sudden notice, so much the opposite of what I'd been expecting, brought my heart up into my throat. And then, before I'd even had a chance to recover, *he* came in.

Henry Gemerle, the monster of Michener Street . . . At the sight of him my whole body went rigid with fright, my gut rolling over as if getting ready to turn itself inside out. Then I caught sight of the girls. They sat nearer the rear of the courtroom today and the cameras were all aimed at Gemerle, so I felt safe.

Getting up, I moved toward the girls. Neither of them looked anything like I remembered from the brief glimpse I'd had of them, which renewed my confidence that they wouldn't know me, either. Reaching the bench where they sat—the victim advocates weren't present today—I slid in beside them and whispered:

"Hello. You don't know me, but I'm taking care of Cam."

Slowly the young woman nearest me turned her head.

"Cam Petry?" I said. "You remember her, don't you? And I want to ask you about—"

She just stared. It was Nancy Shields; I'd learned her name back when they were all first let out of the cellar.

"—about Cam's baby," I said. But then before I could go on I felt Henry Gemerle's eyes on me, his lip curled in obvious fury at the sight of the one who got away.

Me. Hastily I turned away from Nancy Shields and scrambled backward.

But it was already too late. Gemerle's clear interest in me and my frightened reaction made people wonder about me. Many of the observers in the courtroom turned curiously, a low murmur spreading around me. Even the judge glanced up, and everyone stared: the lawyers and court employees, onlookers on benches, and psychiatrists in suits, all slicked up and ready to give their expert testimony about Henry Gemerle.

No, I thought desperately, *this isn't what I wanted.*

Gazing around wildly I searched for a rescuer, someone to save me. But there was no one, only a chunky blond woman wearing a blue sweatshirt staring down at me from the gallery, looking as if she might have wanted to help. But she couldn't.

So I did the only thing I could do. I ran.

By the time I got home that Monday noon, Cam was throwing things into a duffel bag any which way.

Luckily only Gemerle had recognized me; I'd given only a single interview right after Cam and I moved in together.

A feel-good human-interest story, the pesky writer from New Haven's alt weekly newspaper the *Advocate* had said it would be, a heart-warmer about cousins reuniting after a tragedy. I'd been reluctant; the flurry of interest surrounding the girls hadn't yet died down, and the last thing I wanted was any publicity.

But if we were boring enough—I refused photos, and didn't let the reporter come to our apartment—the rest might leave us alone, I'd figured, and in fact that was what happened. I'd played dumb and Cam had been legitimately stupefied, both from shock at her experiences and from the pills I'd already begun feeding her.

But what had happened in the courtroom was still bad enough. Cam had despised the idea of my talking to the alt-weekly reporter. Being stared at and questioned was torture for her, even in the hospital when it was only for her benefit. Now I'd risked drawing attention to her again.

Or at least I thought that was the reason for her anger. "Cam," I begged once I got into the apartment. "Please listen."

But she didn't look at me, just kept throwing things into her bag.

"Cam, I never meant to—"

She whirled on me. " 'I never meant to,' " she mimicked cruelly. "I didn't know, oh, I'm so innocent, please feel sorry for me."

She threw the duffel into the hall. "Funny thing about you. You never mean any harm, but somehow you always do it anyway."

She'd swept her dresser top clean of her hairbrush, a tray of pill bottles, and an envelope containing her medical history.

But she'd left a picture frame with a snapshot of the two of us.

"I just wanted . . ." I began. The snapshot was like a window into a happy world; here in this one, Cam's energy frightened me.

"Right, *you* just wanted," she snapped back at me. "Can I ask you something, though?"

She turned to face me. "Have you ever thought for a minute about what *I* might want? I mean, how exactly did you think this thing you did today was going to turn out?"

I took a deep breath. "I was just trying to help."

She smiled nastily. "Yeah, right." Brushing past me to the hall, she went on waspishly.

"You're a fool, Jane. You think that being dull and stupid hides your bad side, but you're wrong. It just makes you even less attractive, if that's possible."

Behind her the neat, spare room with its white curtains and narrow bed looked suddenly as if no one had ever slept in it. She pulled on her coat; I stopped myself from helping her with it.

"Cam, please. You can't just leave me like this. After all I've done . . ."

My voice trailed off; I could see her thinking of something else she wanted to say and deciding not to.

"Look," she began finally. "Maybe you really didn't mean any harm."

The words burst out of me. "When have I meant you harm? I've done everything and never wanted anything in return because I—"

But then I stopped. She was looking at me with an odd expression. Or . . . not *at* me. *Past* me, at her bedside table where dozens of Valium tablets were piled in a little heap.

I used to crush them but after a while I'd stopped bothering; she'd always swallowed what I gave her without question. But now I saw that she must've hidden them, then spit them out.

That she'd been doing it all along. "I went to the court hearing because I thought," I said through the sudden tightness in my throat, "that I could find out about your baby."

She stared incredulously. "Where it was sent to," I went on, "and who has it. Her, I mean," I added desperately.

Cam was eyeing me as if I were some strange zoo animal. "And if we found her, then we could bring her home," I rushed on. "We could be a . . ."

"A family," she finished for me, and it was her tone that did me in, finally: incredulous, like everything I'd said just made it all worse.

"You left me with him. Left me for dead," Cam said icily. "You were so fucking scared somebody would find out what happened to you, you forgot about what was happening to me."

"Cam . . ."

"Or no. You didn't forget. You didn't care. I should have been the one who had a life, you know, I'd have known what to do with it. Not sitting all alone in a dinky house, dumb job, no friends, not even a man to keep you company . . . you didn't even need Henry Gemerle to make you a prisoner," she ranted viciously. "You did it to yourself!"

"Cam," I tried again hopelessly, and then I saw my laptop sitting open in the living room with an email on the screen. To Finny Brill; a *sent* email.

Horror pierced me. "Cam, what've you done?" I rushed to the device, but of course there was no way to take it back.

Since the delays surrounding Cam's surgery, Finny had been getting increasingly impatient to move forward with what he called "our creative project." Now . . .

Finny, the email read. *It's time. Tell him Cam is coming to be with him the way we planned. Ask him where he wants to go and let me know ASAP. Then—do it.*

Below that was Finny's near-instantaneous reply: *Bearkill, Maine.*

Finny had said he could get Gemerle out of the forensic hospital practically as soon as they sent him back there from the courtroom, and we'd had no time to—

"Cam, we're not prepared," I protested. She must have sent the message as soon as she saw me on TV. "Why would you get this all started now when we're not—"

But then I understood. She was ready; I didn't need to be. Our plan had been to punish Gemerle, but she was doing something else. Then I understood, as the import of her email finally struck me. It wasn't a punishment she had planned at all.

Not for him, anyway.

"I have to go now," she said flatly.

I swallowed a painful sob. "I was never going along, was I?"

She shook her head at me almost kindly. "No. You weren't."

Now I got it: that she'd been using me, playing the helpless invalid to keep me devotedly caring for her, all the while getting stronger and more determined to leave me.

And now she was strong enough. I'd forced her hand, but she'd been meaning to do this anyway.

"But he hurt you." I pointed to where the purplish marks of surgical staples still showed through her short fluff of returning hair; her eyes darkened defensively.

"He didn't mean it. He never did. He just lost his temper, he was always sorry for it later. And he only took the baby so she could have a better life."

Remembering, she looked away from me. "The other girls were glad he liked me the best. It meant he paid less attention to them. Then when the police came and arrested him, I promised I'd get him out, that we'd be together again. But I didn't know how."

She turned to me again. "And then you came along. Like," she added, and her sarcasm nearly killed me, "an answered prayer."

A sound outside sent her rushing to the living-room window, which looked out over the sidewalk. "What were you *thinking*?" she spat furiously at me again as she peeked between the drapes.

I looked, too. There was a man down there, and after a moment I recognized him. It was the reporter I'd given the interview to when Cam first got released from the hospital, the guy from the independent newspaper. He must have recognized me at the courthouse. Now he was pressing the bell, wanting to be buzzed in.

"He'll go away," I said helplessly; her answering glance was scathing. She snapped the curtains shut.

"I'm sorry," I said miserably again. Then: "But how will you get anywhere?" I'd never even seen her call a cab.

"I bought a car. What, you thought you were the only one who could do it?"

I must've stared. She had money; I'd never made her pay for anything, and a victims' fund sent her a check each month. But—

"And I got a driver's license," she added matter-of-factly. "What did you think, that I just sat around doing nothing while you were at work all day?"

Actually, it's what I had thought. I'd dosed her well enough every morning to keep her muddled and unambitious for hours.

Or so I'd believed. Her bag stood by the door. By now it was afternoon, the winter sun already beginning to fall toward the horizon. In a few hours it would be dark. Eager to go, she peeked out the window again and sighed in annoyance.

"This is ridiculous. He won't give up, why should he? And it's your fault. I don't care how sick I was, I should've known better than to get involved with a fool like you."

Her words felt like punches I couldn't fight back against, her gaze like an ice pick stabbing me. But even then I wanted to help her somehow.

I could have told her how to get out of the building unseen. From the basement there was a service exit to an alley behind the buildings, over to the next street.

But she never gave me the chance. "But what am I afraid of, anyway? He can't hurt me. I can just walk right out past him," she said angrily, and turned sharply away from me.

Fool, fool, I heard my own voice howling at me in my head. With the doomlike thudding of my heart pounding in my ears, I followed her down the hall.

Halfway to the apartment door we'd set up a telephone table with a landline phone dating from the 1960s, with a pink plastic receiver on a metal base encased in matching pink plastic.

A princess phone, it was called, and as she stomped past it she ripped the cord out and smashed the base against the wall so hard that broken parts flew everywhere.

That's when I knew how furious she must have been with me all along—how vengeful and full of hate. She'd loved that phone. Crouching, I picked what was left of the heavy base off the floor as she spun and faced me.

"You just couldn't stand it, could you?" she accused. "You wanted some of that oh-so-special victim-sympathy that the other girls had. So you toddled on down to the courtroom to get some."

Her lips twisted. "It wasn't enough to be Saint Jane. *Oh, I take care of her every need, I'm so goody-GOOD!*" she mocked.

"Cam, it wasn't like that. I only wanted what was—"

"Never mind." She picked up her duffel bag. "I'm going to join Henry. Our daughter is already there, it's why he picked the place. That's where he must have sent her, don't you see?"

Her eyes glowed with the certainty of delusion. "He loves me. I was special to him. So now we'll be a family, the three of us."

The three of us . . . her, Gemerle, and the baby, who by now would be a young teenager. "Cam, how can you believe that?"

But of course she could. In a part of my heart, in fact, I understood her behavior completely: She'd started out young and feisty, convinced she'd get out of there.

Convinced, probably, that I'd send help. Only I hadn't, and over the years she'd been so broken and stripped of all hope that she'd believe anything just to avoid another session of his abuse.

She'd even come to believe he loved her. Which I understood, too, I supposed; there's only so much fear a person can live with. She'd eased hers in the only way she could.

Now, though, when I'd done so much for her and we'd made *plans* . . . She spoke harshly again. "It wouldn't have worked anyway, you know. That dumb scheme of yours."

She made an ugly face. *"Oh, I'm going to get revenge,"* she mocked. "Sure, only not after your stupid stunt today. He saw you in the courtroom, you know. And he recognized you, I could tell.

"And he won't trust you. Not that you'll really try, you're such a coward. And even if you do, you'll never get near him. I'll make *sure* you don't."

Now I was the angry one. After all I'd done for her, that she should *spit* on me this way . . . as the immensity of her betrayal struck me and she reached for the door to go, I rose up behind her as smoothly and silently as I'd ever done anything.

Then I hit her very hard on the back of her shaved head with the heavy base of the broken princess phone.

"Unh," she said as the weight of the thing struck something solid; bone, I supposed. Then her knees buckled and I caught her under her shoulders and lowered her the rest of the way down.

Blood spread across the hardwood. She was still breathing, but no one bled that much and lived, I was certain.

Which meant it was only a matter of time until I went to prison. Meanwhile Gemerle was free now, and he was the cause of all this, not me.

It just wasn't fair. But if no one ever found out what I'd done, then maybe things still could be put right.

I dragged Cam back into her room and laid her on her bed. I put a thick mat of towels under her head to absorb the bleeding, and spread plastic trash bags to keep it from soaking the mattress. Then I cleaned the rest up as best I could, which was not very well; the blood had splashed everywhere.

Until finally it was nearly midnight.

From the bedroom, Cam took another loud, hitching breath, her death seeming to take forever. That was his fault, too, I thought resentfully. And what else might he do now that he was loose?

To Cam's teenage daughter, for instance, whose whereabouts I now believed I knew. Probably he'd want the girl with him as a way of controlling Cam, I thought; by threatening the girl, he could make the mother do anything. Though Cam had already proved her willingness to do anything for Gemerle.

The more I thought about it, in fact, the more sure I became. Why else would he make such a remote place—Bearkill, Maine, had a current population of only eleven hundred according to its Wikipedia entry—the meeting spot?

I slapped the laptop shut. That's why he'd picked Bearkill, of course: because of the girl.

Which meant that to trap him, all I had to do was get to her first.

"Contact lenses?" Dylan looked incredulous. "Come on, Lizzie, you mean you can really do that? Change your eye color well enough so that no one will realize it, just by . . ."

"Yup." Area 51's Thursday-afternoon interior was empty except for the two of them, the bartender sitting at a table in the back doing a crossword puzzle.

"Buy 'em online, get any kind you want," she said. "Cat's eyes, reptile eyes, black, red, yellow . . ."

Peg's were a shade called Blondie Blue.

"Especially if you don't need any vision correction," Lizzie added.

She finished her Coke and slid off the barstool; when she'd found him here Dylan had been about to order lunch, but the way she felt right now, any minute she'd be drinking her own.

"Hey, don't feel too bad," Dylan said. "I've looked right at her, too, you know, and I didn't tumble to it, either."

"I guess," Lizzie replied. She glanced at the bottles lined up behind the bar, reminded herself just how lousy a daytime drink would make her feel, and headed for the door.

Outside, the air smelled like burning weeds. "Meanwhile I get that she's lying," Dylan went on as he followed her out. "I'm just not sure the reason is to hide that Tara is Gemerle's kid."

In the Blazer he turned earnestly to Lizzie. "Who cares who her father is? I mean, if all we're trying to do is get her back?"

But to that Lizzie had no answer. They drove across town in silence, and when they got out to her house the air smelled like soapy bleach from all the chemicals the firefighters were dropping from helicopters, half a mile away.

So far, though, no mandatory evacuations had been ordered, and until they were, Lizzie didn't intend to join the people who were leaving ahead of any official announcement. Chevrier would tell her when it was time, she figured.

Inside, she got out the eggs, bread, and butter. "So did you talk to the DeWildes last night?"

Rascal had burst through the opened front door to gallop around the yard a few times; now he returned, pleased and panting.

"Yeah," said Dylan, smoothing the dog's ears. "They're . . ."

He spread his hands helplessly to indicate how destroyed the bereaved parents were. "They're in Bangor now, identifying him."

"Poor people." She dropped bread into the toaster. "Anybody had any more sightings on Gemerle or Jane Crimmins?"

Or whoever she was. Dylan shrugged. "They're still working the motel room. No results back from any blood evidence yet. And some of my guys went to the burial site in the fire zone, to start processing that. But no, no sightings."

He put coffee on. "As for the DeWilde kid, Bangor's got its own homicide cops. Them and Portland, the state stays out unless they want help, and then it's my problem."

She sank into a chair. "You know, though, I'm still the one who knows all the ins and outs of all the different relationships."

The toast popped up. "Yeah. And it would make sense to have you coordinating all these investigations. But since when did this job ever make sense?" he said. Then: "Not to change the subject. I haven't had the chance to mention this before now, but I figure you should know. I'm seeing someone."

"Good for you. That's . . . good," she finished idiotically. She fought to produce a smile. "So who? Somebody on the job?"

"A woman from my apartment building. No cop connections."

"Oh." Their eyes met across the table. She wondered what he saw in hers and got up hastily so he wouldn't see too much.

"Sorry to spring it on you," he said. "I just didn't want you to find out some other way, is all."

"That's okay," she managed lightly, pouring more coffee. "I guess I just thought it would be Emily Ektari if it was anyone."

His look turned speculative. "You think she might—"

At which a laugh burst out of her; good old Dylan, he was a handsome dog and a charming one, too.

But a dog nonetheless. "Don't you ever quit sniffing around at every woman you see? Really, Dylan, you're . . ."

Before she could finish, though, his cell phone chirped and then his face changed in a way she recognized.

"Right, I know where. Be there shortly," he said.

"*We'll* be there," she corrected, pausing only to put the food away where Rascal couldn't get at it before following Dylan out.

TEN

"Come on, Lizzie, this isn't fair. Don't freeze me out," Dylan added as he muscled the Crown Vic up the same bumpy gravel road that Lizzie and Peg had traveled earlier.

Lizzie sighed. Behind them dust billowed in grayish clouds; ahead in the blasted landscape heaps of blackened sticks smoked sullenly where groves of saplings had been just hours earlier.

He'd made no promises; not lately. Still, it was sinking in now: He was seeing someone else.

"Dammit," he said, trying again, "you know it's not that I don't love you. I do. But if it's never gonna happen for us, then . . ."

Which infuriated her all over again, because if he hadn't lied to her back when they really were together, she wouldn't be so hesitant to trust him again now, would she?

He swung onto a patch of miraculously unburnt grass, then forward onto blackened earth when a volunteer firefighter in a yellow vest waved urgently at him.

"Hot muffler'll torch that grass up," the kid explained as they got out. "Over here," he added, leading them from the road.

A dozen yards distant the soil was still loamy, the fire of hours earlier hopscotching whimsically to scorch some areas and leave others untouched—so far. They were nearly to the site where the hole with the box sitting next to it had been when the kid stopped.

"Okay, so I have not touched him, and I haven't told anyone else about him, either," he said. The kid looked a little shaky but he was trying to be manful about the sight of the body.

Lizzie crouched. In jeans and a gray sweatshirt, the deceased was a middle-aged white male with light hair and freckled skin now bluish in death.

"Not what we were expecting. Or rather, who." Lips pursed, Dylan stared down at the body as if it might tell him who had done this to it.

"So," she asked, "this junior firefighter here, he knew to call you because . . . ?"

Dylan kept staring. "Told 'em all earlier, a call to me gets 'em fifty bucks if it pans out. Think it's Gemerle?"

"Description's right," she allowed. "Think he's been here all along?" She scanned the parched soil around the body.

"Hard to say. Maybe. In the smoke and so on, he could've been missed until now."

She prodded at the victim's neck, found the likely cause of death buried in the cool flesh:

"Huh. Length of wire." Straightening, she tipped the head sideways with the toe of her boot and spied the two cutoff wooden mophandle sections tied to the wire, one at each end.

"A homemade garrote," she said, unwillingly impressed. "That takes strength. Or some excellent motivation," she added.

Dylan frowned down at something dark peeping from between the body's clenched teeth. Producing a latex glove from his coat he pulled it on, then touched a finger to the victim's lower lip.

The thing in the victim's mouth slid out on a gush of dark blood; Lizzie repressed a shudder. It was the victim's tongue; in his agonized struggle he'd apparently bitten it off.

"Mm-hmm," Dylan said clinically. Only if you knew him well would you detect the jagged edge of something else in his voice: sorrow, maybe. Or pity.

"Yes sir," he went on, "this guy is the best argument for not escaping from your friendly neighborhood forensic institution that I personally have ever seen *in* my *life*."

He thought for a moment. "But what I still want to know is, why help him escape? And after that, why kill him?"

But before she could voice the answer that had already begun percolating in her head, Dylan turned toward a dust cloud boiling up near the main road. Soon Cody Chevrier's white Blazer appeared through drifting smoke, light bars flashing.

"You thinking what I'm thinking?" she said as the vehicle sped uphill toward them.

Dylan nodded. "Gemerle had a pretty cushy situation where he was. Locked in, but Salisbury Forensic is a medical facility, not a prison-type environment."

If Gemerle got caught after an escape attempt, he'd get sent to a worse place, in other words.

"So maybe somebody made it worth the risk? Maybe like we said last night, lured him out. And made sure there was something in it for the orderly, too," Lizzie theorized.

Chevrier got out of his vehicle, approached Dylan, and stuck his hand out; they'd worked together before. Then, taking in the scene expertly, he turned to Lizzie.

"So what's the deal here?"

She didn't hesitate. "That's Henry Gemerle."

She could feel Dylan's eyes on her; they hadn't made a for-certain ID yet. But:

"Guy did a runner from the Salisbury Forensic Institute. Seems he had a helper. We think Gemerle killed the helper, stuck the body in the trunk. They found the vehicle in Houlton."

Chevrier listened skeptically, glanced at the body again. "And you've identified him how?"

"Fits the description, for one thing. Also if you lift him a little, you might find a plastic ID bracelet from the hospital," said Lizzie.

Crouching, Dylan raised the body enough to expose the plastic strip still wrapped around the dead wrist.

"We think Tara Wylie might be his daughter," she added. "Why he took her, we don't know yet. Or even if he did, for sure."

Chevrier nodded. "Yeah, well, I might have an idea about it. This came in to your office. Missy wanted me to give it to you. I guess you asked the New Haven cops for more Gemerle stuff?"

She peered at the sheet of names and addresses Chevrier gave her. The final name on it was familiar: Peg Wylie. "Jesus."

She passed the list to Dylan. There were about a dozen names on it. Some addresses had been crossed out and replaced with new ones, a few of them several times.

And some were crossed out altogether. "Gemerle wrote this?" Dylan asked.

Chevrier nodded as Lizzie went on scrutinizing the fax sheet. "He didn't have to find Peg," she said. "He's been keeping tabs on her all along, right up until he got arrested. And on these other women, too."

She turned to Chevrier again. "But why would this give you an idea of why he might've taken Tara?"

"It doesn't, by itself. But your pals in New Haven also sent along some court documents, including this roster of witnesses who testi-fied in his competency hearing last week, some privately and others in open court."

He handed it over; she scanned it quickly. Peg Wylie was on this sheet, as well. "Oh, man. Now I get it. She must have pissed him off by testifying. So he was punishing her."

Lizzie pulled her phone out. "Missy, did New Haven send you any-thing about Gemerle's old place being dug up yet? The yard?"

But they hadn't. She stuck her phone away again. "Gemerle's got no priors. But that doesn't mean he wasn't active. I'm guessing these women on his list are ones who never reported what he did to them, because he threatened them. Peg, too, probably."

Dylan's eyes narrowed. "And maybe some of them are crossed off because they aren't alive anymore?"

"Right. I want to know what's in that backyard of his. If it's not already dug up then it needs to be."

Chevrier eyed the corpse again. "So if you think he moved her, where do you think Tara Wylie is now?"

"Who knows? And he can't tell us. Damn." She turned away in frustration. It was just midafternoon but already the low sun was sinking toward the mountaintops to the west.

"Meanwhile there's a woman in the area using the name of one of his victims' close associates, Jane Crimmins," she said. "We know it's not her, we've got lab evidence saying so. But again, we don't know why."

Chevrier drew an Altoids tin from his shirt pocket and popped one into his mouth. "Sounds like a mess. Hudson, you got all this okay?"

Dylan caught the sheriff's drift on the first bounce.

"I could sure use Deputy Snow's help," he answered smoothly. "She's got homicide experience and we've worked together before."

He glanced at Lizzie. "Also, she's up-to-date on all aspects of this case. The local aspects, especially."

Chevrier popped another mint and chewed it vigorously.

"Okay, then," he said. "Snow, you can work with all of 'em as needed, right? Feds, state guys . . ."

"Yeah, boss." She shot a look of gratitude at Dylan.

Not that this all couldn't still turn into a huge pain in the butt. As if to emphasize the fact, Chevrier aimed a warning look at her as he strode back to his vehicle:

Don't screw this up.

t was almost midnight, and there'd been no sounds for a while from Cam. But I felt frozen until the door buzzer made me jump.

"Miss Crimmins, do you remember me?"

It was the reporter from the alt-weekly who'd been downstairs earlier.

"Go away," I shouted.

A business card slipped under the door. "Okay, I understand you might want to think about talking to me. But I want your story and you know from before you can trust me. I'll write it all just like you say."

I said nothing but in the bedroom Cam chose that moment to make a loud gurgling sound.

"Miss Crimmins, are you all right?"

"Go away or I'll never talk to you!" I told him. This late at night one of the other tenants would get fed up with this guy in the hall and then *they'd* call the police. "I'll talk to you tomorrow!"

When I peeked out a little later I half expected to see him down on the sidewalk, but he wasn't there so when I'd finished packing a bag, my laptop, and a big manila envelope full of Cam's pills, I hurried out of there. I paused only to take two of Cam's stimulant pills and grab a barbecue skewer from the kitchen drawer.

Cam was still breathing, but shallowly and not often; I thought she didn't have much longer to live. They'd know that she'd been murdered, surely.

But no one would know where I was. They could pound on the door tomorrow, I thought as I rushed down the stairs and out the service door to the alley. They could pound all they wanted but no one would answer. Eventually they'd get in, and Cam would be here, of course; cold, silent.

But I'd be long gone.

It was late Thursday afternoon when Dylan summoned the crime-scene techs from the motel where they'd been finishing up and spent a few minutes with them. The pretty one wasn't among them, Lizzie noticed, annoyed with herself for caring. Then he and Lizzie went back down the gravel road in the Crown Vic.

"So," he said as they bumped onto the paved highway, "you think Peg might finally come clean now?" He turned toward town, leaving the ashy zone of fire devastation behind.

"Beats me," Lizzie said. "Now that Gemerle's dead he can't hurt her—or Tara, either—but . . ."

But there was more to it than that, she was sure of it. And the girl was still missing. A dagger of renewed anxiety for Tara Wylie pierced Lizzie as Dylan aimed the big sedan toward Bearkill and hit the gas.

"If Tara was coming home just around the time Gemerle got to Bearkill, the timing's right," he mused. "But how'd he find her?"

Lizzie turned from the depressingly dry rural landscape going by. "Easy. He cruised her neighborhood. If she was headed home by then, which based on her past behavior we think she probably was, he'd have come across her sooner or later."

Back in the city among so many people the idea would've been far-fetched, but not here. "Probably he even knew what she looked like, since he was apparently keeping tabs on her mother for all those years," Lizzie said.

Surveillance from a distance was easy. Even the pictures on Tara Wylie's official MISSING posters had been downloaded from the Internet. Identifying her would've been a snap.

When they drove back into Bearkill the downtown streets were nearly empty, people either staying close to home or leaving town altogether on account of the fires. Dylan pulled to the curb.

"So does your new girlfriend know the kind of hours you work?" Lizzie asked suddenly. "And what you're doing while you work them?"

He glanced at her. "Why, you think she needs warning?"

But then his face went rueful. "I don't know. Maybe she does. Just . . . but look, probably we shouldn't talk about it."

"Yeah. Probably we shouldn't." It was none of her business.

"Anyway, I've got to go," she said. "I sent down a separate request to the New Haven PD earlier, asked them to get in touch with the real Jane Crimmins. And with the other girl, the Gemerle victim that Jane Crimmins took in. She's in the hospital."

"So we'll see what they have to say. They're working on tracking down the stolen van, too. As far as whatever vehicle Gemerle was using, there's plenty of them in the fire zone. Volunteers' cars, work-crew trucks, people bringing food and water . . ."

One more wouldn't be noticed. She got out, bent to the open car window. "Listen, you might as well know something now. When this is over I'm out of here. I'm going back to Boston. I'll tell Chevrier once things settle down."

He stared for a moment. Then: "But what about Nicki?"

She forced herself to answer calmly. "Dylan, I can't search the state of Maine inch by inch. I need some kind of a lead, and there aren't any. Like it or not, she's a cold case."

When he didn't reply, she went on. "And there's nothing else for me here. If something substantial about Nicki needs looking into, you can call me about it."

A muscle jumped tautly in his jaw. "Didn't take you long to give up."

She couldn't believe it. She kept her voice even. "Oh, that's what you think I'm doing? Really?"

Luckily just then Missy Brantwell came outside and spotted Dylan's car. "Sorry to interrupt," she said, hurrying over. "The NHPD sergeant called you again," she told Lizzie. "About someone you wanted checked. Jane Crimmins? He said no one was home at her place but the uniforms got the super to open it."

Missy took a deep breath. "And it looks like somebody got killed in there, he said."

Outside our building in New Haven I called the reporter who'd showed up earlier, reading the number off the card he'd slipped under the apartment door. It was past midnight and he sounded half asleep, but he perked up when I told him I would talk with him after all.

Only it had to be now, I said. I'd meet him in East Rock Park; if he brought anyone else, though, it would be all off, and Cam was refusing to talk to him at all.

He could get the whole story, every lurid detail, I told him: Cam's victimization at the hands of Henry Gemerle, her rescue, and our lives together afterward.

But he'd have to get it from me. The reporter agreed, the same terrier tenacity I'd heard in his voice earlier drawing him now, and ten minutes later I was waiting by the playground where the swings and jungle gym stood half lit by a single streetlamp.

He showed up on foot and came over to my car, a skinny young guy in a tan knitted hat and black hoodie over a T-shirt, a wispy reddish beard and thick horn-rims completing his hipster look.

I gestured for him to get in, and he did. "Hey," he said, taking the horn-rims off to wipe them.

"Hey, yourself." I felt bad about it, but he'd heard Cam's labored breathing and he seemed smart. He might get to thinking about it, later; he might even call the police.

He could do it soon, and I needed a head start. And I'd come this far, hadn't I? Isolating Cam, lying to her and drugging her—or trying— then attacking her and leaving her to die . . . it wasn't as if I didn't know what I'd already done, and what I'd become.

What, like it or not, I was. So I turned quickly while the reporter was still busy polishing his glasses, and gripping the metal shaft of the barbecue skewer I'd taken from the apartment, I drove the tip of it into his left ear canal as hard as I could.

He stiffened, his arms jerking up and his clenched fists slamming his chest. He'd already begun convulsing as I grabbed his phone out of his pocket, leaned across him to yank the door handle, and pushed him out. When I pulled out of the park his body was visible in the rearview mirror, still moving.

So that was done, his foolishness ended for good. But I still couldn't leave town; not yet. Instead I drove to the medical center, walked through the dim, silent parking garage to the hospital's main entrance, and crossed the echoingly empty lobby.

There was no one at the security desk. The cafeteria was closed, and in the gift shop the Mylar balloons floated eerily, pressing shiny faces against the windows as if trying to escape.

I took the elevator upstairs, entered my office, and logged onto the medical database system as ADMINISTRATOR. Locating Cam's file, I changed her status from DISCHARGED to ADMITTED and listed her condition as CRITICAL.

That way if anyone went looking for Cam, they'd have an explanation for why no one answered our apartment door. If they looked hard for her, of course, it would be a different story. But this would slow them down. Exiting the database, I left the office and the hospital building as unnoticed as I had arrived.

The drive through the silent city felt surreal, as if the dreams of the sleeping people all around me were in my own head.

At the service area in Branford I saw only the slack-faced servers at the food counters, moving like zombies to the beat of piped-in music under the fluorescent lights. I bought doughnuts and sandwiches, washing another of the Ritalin pills down with a swallow of Big Gulp soda; minutes later the car was gassed up, the tires checked and reservoirs filled, so there was little chance of my becoming disabled by the side of the road.

On the turnpike once more, I glanced a final time in the rearview mirror at the city's late-night glow, sodium yellow on the charcoal sky. After that I drove north, not stopping until I entered the state of Maine.

By Thursday evening, a few hours after Henry Gemerle's body turned up in the fire zone, a high-pressure system that had been stalled north of Montreal got a reluctant move on, sliding east. Behind it a line of thunderstorms promised relief for parched, fire-plagued Aroostook County.

But ahead of the storms came lightning, long wriggling lines of blue-white light crackling hotly through the night sky around Bearkill. Next came bright, yellow-white flares shooting up from the tinder-dry evergreens on the ridges around town, their pitchy sap so flammable that it might as well have been gasoline.

"It's happening." Trey Washburn blew an unhappy breath out. The burly veterinarian stood with Lizzie on the sidewalk in front of her office. From there the sky's orange glow made it clear that in a supreme case of irony, the weather they'd all been hoping for had touched off the major blaze they'd been fearing.

"Looks like I'm going to have a long night," Trey continued. Not everyone in the area had moved their livestock yet, and plenty of animals still needed coaxing into trailers.

"Me, too." Another bright flare sprang up on the horizon as here in town more cars and pickup trucks zipped by, heading for the volunteer fire crews' staging area.

"You okay?" Missy called, driving up in her yellow Jeep.

In the backseat, Rascal drooled happily, his hound-dog head hanging out the open car window; of course Missy had thought of going over to Lizzie's for the dog.

"Heading to my gran's," she called. Trey's big red pickup truck had already departed. "Unless you need me?"

"Nope. You go, I'll hang out here," Lizzie replied. "Stay safe with your family."

A whiff of burning creosote stung her nose as Cody Chevrier pulled over, his face grim. "Everything under control?"

She stepped up to his vehicle. "So far. I'll keep the office open as long as I can. Unless there's something else you need?"

Chevrier shook his close-clipped, silvery head. "You're doing it. Give yourself time to get out ahead of any flames, you hear?"

The fire was visible between the rooftops, moving inexorably closer. Chevrier eyed the blaze uneasily while from his dashboard a stream of urgent dispatch transmissions crackled.

"Things get dicey, you hit the road," he said. "This here's for an experienced crew, Lizzie."

On his radio the dispatcher's tone changed suddenly. "Fire One, choppers report you have flame approaching your position on your west, over."

Fire One was the on-air name for the all-volunteer Bearkill Fire & Rescue. "Fire One, do you copy?"

Still nothing. "Answer back, Fire One." Chevrier pulled away abruptly, the Blazer's cherry beacon swirling.

Experienced, she thought, watching him go. Which she wasn't, and it made her feel even more out of her element here than usual.

But as she turned back to her office she spotted Peg Wylie leaving Area 51, under the glowing sign of the big-eyed alien with the tilted cocktail glass.

Peg looked as if she'd been tilting a few cocktails herself, wobbling unsteadily toward her old Honda. So instead of going in, Lizzie fired up the Blazer and drove alongside Peg.

"Hop in," she called, and Peg obeyed; booze fumes filled the passenger compartment.

"Take me out there," the inebriated woman demanded thickly.

"You lied." Aiming the Blazer out of town, Lizzie gripped the wheel so hard her fingers ached.

"I was about to commit a crime for you, you know that?" she went on as she swerved hard onto the old Station Road just past the Bearkill town limits sign, bumping on the broken pavement.

"Tara's not the result of any one-night stand. She's not your ex-husband's kid, either. And Gemerle didn't give her to you.

"She's yours and Gemerle's, isn't she? You didn't want an Amber Alert because you were afraid that the Gemerle connection might surface."

Peg rubbed her eyes with balled fists; she could do that now because the contact lenses weren't in. When she gazed imploringly at Lizzie, it was with eyes that were a deep, rich brown.

"What I still don't understand," Lizzie finished, "is why."

In the past couple of hours Peg had cried too much, and drunk too much, to keep the lenses in. She'd taken them out in Area 51's tiny restroom, Lizzie guessed, because they hurt and because she'd figured no one would see her anymore tonight.

But about that, as about so many things recently, Peg Wylie had been wrong. Another pang of anxiety for Tara stabbed Lizzie.

"No," Peg protested again. "It was only that Tara's run away before. And she's always come home, so I just didn't think—"

Lizzie shook her head exasperatedly. "Yeah, right. Stick with that stupid story, Peg. Because, you know, it's worked so well for you, so far."

Ahead in the murk the skeleton of an old gas station hulked by the crumbling roadside, saplings thrusting up through what had been the service area. A maple tree grew in the mechanic's bay and the antique gas pumps were all shotgunned to scrap.

Lizzie pulled onto the disintegrating tarmac. The gnawing urgency she felt, that Tara was still out there and in danger—*but alive, she could still be alive*—kept ratcheting upward.

But the mother of the year here, just went on lying about it. Lizzie turned in the driver's seat.

"Give me a break, Peg, okay? She's your child and his. And you wanted to make sure no one would suspect that."

She forced down a surge of fury. "Because he threatened you, and Tara, too, and you're still scared of him. But now what you feared is happening, because you gave a statement about him in New Haven."

Peg shook her head in silence as Lizzie went on: "But what I don't get is, why would you do that?"

More silence from Peg. "He's dead, you know. Gemerle is. We found his body up in the fire zone. We think he was killed last night. From the condition of his body we think it was almost certainly his blood in the motel room, not Tara's. We'll know for sure when lab results come back."

At the news Peg looked up wonderingly in relief, but not for long. "Then where is she?"

She was sobering up fast. "Why hasn't she come home yet if he hasn't . . . if he hasn't hurt her?"

"I don't know. But I think maybe he had her and now that he's dead he can't say where he put her." Cruel, but Peg's dawning look of simple fright in response gave Lizzie a way in at last.

"So you've got to tell me the whole thing, Peg. All of it, or we'll have no chance of finding her.

"Everything you remember or that you even suspect," she went on. "Then maybe we can still get Tara out of this."

Peg finally spoke:

"No. She's dead, isn't she." A flat, despairing statement, not a question. "He killed her, hid her body."

"We don't know that. Look, why are you fighting me on this? Just tell me—"

"And you won't tell anyone else? Before, you promised that you wouldn't tell—"

Lizzie shook her head. She'd had a chance to think some more about the deal she'd offered. "No. I should never have said that."

Peg slumped in defeat.

"What difference does it make?" She seemed to be asking it of herself. "Without Tara, I don't care about anything, anyway."

She straightened, steeling herself. "Okay. Like I said, we were cousins, Henry and me. And he drugged me. He put something in a wine cooler, and then . . ."

A terrible little laugh escaped her. "And then he raped me." She forced the word out.

"And you got pregnant."

Peg nodded. "Yes. But I was too afraid to tell anyone how I got that way. He told me if I ever said what happened . . ."

She turned miserably. "See, he'd give us money. Our family, we were penniless. I can't even express it, how poor. But Henry had dropped out of school and he was working steady. He even had his own place, a foreclosed house he'd bought near his mom's."

Peg sucked in a shaky breath. "He said if I told anyone, he wouldn't help us out anymore."

Lizzie watched a raccoon waddle into the gas station ruins. "Did you know about the girls? In his cellar, did you know about them?"

Peg shook her head emphatically. "No! Of course not, I . . . he was always after me. Then all of a sudden he quit bothering me. I didn't care why, I was just glad. I didn't know it was because he had someone else to torture. I only found out about all that stuff when everyone else did, last summer when he got caught."

Lizzie thought about this. Something was still not quite right about it, but what? "Okay. And you didn't want Tara to know who her dad was. That's why you changed your eye color, right?"

Peg looked taken aback. "What? Oh, no, it wasn't like that at all, it didn't have anything to do with that. It was about me."

Her face grew thoughtful. "I'm not even sure how to say this. But see, even after I got away from him, every time I looked in the mirror I saw the girl he'd made a victim out of."

She shook her head again, remembering. "I changed my hair, cut it, colored it, dressed different ways, wore makeup or not. But still there she was every time in the mirror, his . . . *thing*. His filthy toy. Only then one day I tried on the blue contact lenses."

"But why didn't you tell me about them?"

Peg blew a breath out. "I don't know. I guess I just didn't believe it mattered. Or I didn't want to believe it."

Lizzie started the Blazer again and put it in gear. "So there was never any husband, either?"

"No. Mitch was a friend. I never even dated him. Like I told you, I just said it because I didn't know what else to say."

The Blazer bumped down the ruined road. "Okay. That's good, Peg. That's helpful. But here's the problem I've still got."

Overhead, thunder rumbled ominously. "See, I get that you didn't want Gemerle to stop helping your family. And you didn't want Tara to know her father was a monster, either, even if your eye-color change wasn't part of that."

Peg nodded again. "The kind of monster," Lizzie went on, "that you'd still have to hide from, even after you got away."

The kind of monster who kept a list: whom he'd victimized, where they were now. "But why'd you testify against him then? If you were still so scared?"

And with good reason, apparently. Peg stared straight ahead out the dark windshield.

"Henry always said that if he ever got in trouble, he'd play crazy. That he'd never get sent to jail if he was nuts enough, so he would fake it."

"So when his competency hearings started down in New Haven," Lizzie said, "you decided to do something about that?"

"Uh-huh." Softly, Peg took up her story again. "I remembered what Henry had said about it. And I knew that if he got sent to a mental hospital he might get out someday, but if he got tried and they convicted him then maybe he wouldn't."

"And then you wouldn't have to be terrified of him anymore. You'd be free of him, and so would Tara."

"It was my chance. So I called the police in New Haven. They set me up with the district attorney and I went there last week. On Friday. I told them he was faking being crazy, and I told them how I knew."

Outside, more rumbles of thunder rolled through the night. When Lizzie put down the window the air felt full of violence.

"Okay," Lizzie said. "But I still don't get it." The Blazer's high beams picked out fence posts crowned with bittersweet, the NO HUNTING signs on them peppered with rusty bullet holes.

"And what I can't get past is this," she added. "When Tara went missing and stayed that way, you refused help."

So there was something else; had to be. A crossroads appeared and Lizzie turned left. In the distance, fires burned jubilantly.

"And I don't care how you try to justify it, it just doesn't compute," she went on.

"See, I've met mothers of missing children before, and every one of them would've teamed up with the devil himself if she thought it would find her kid one damn minute sooner."

Up ahead, the swirly-cone shape of the Dairy Dream ice cream stand materialized. SEE YOU IN SPRING! the sign said.

"It doesn't matter, all right?" Peg burst out. "It can't be important, it doesn't have anything to do with . . ."

Lizzie's cell phone thweeped. EEKTARIMD, the display read; she swung into a U-turn.

"Where are we going?" Peg demanded, gripping the armrests.

"Hospital. Friend of mine." The surge of power from the big V-8 was instantaneous; acceleration-wise, the heavy Blazer was not at all like the nimble vehicles she'd driven back in the city.

Once it got going, though, the Blazer could *move*.

ELEVEN

THE WAY LIFE SHOULD BE! said the sign posted just inside the Maine state line.

It was not yet dawn on Tuesday morning, the sky to the east a pale, pearly gray and the stars dimming, winking out one by one. Beginning to feel tired after the long drive from New Haven, I pulled off the interstate into a rest area, took another couple of Cam's stimulant pills, then texted Finny Brill.

After that I went into the welcome center, which even at this early hour was being visited by a few bleary travelers, wrinkled and yawning. When I came out again Finny's reply was there.

He and Gemerle had left the night before, too, as soon as Gemerle got back to the forensic hospital and Finny could put his plan into motion. Now they were about two hours ahead of me, on their way to northern Maine. In his text message Finny gave the address they were headed for, suggesting that I meet them there.

But I wanted Gemerle to come to me; for my plan to work the way I intended it to, I would have to lure him to where I wanted him, then catch him by surprise.

An emailed photograph of the girl should do it, I thought. Cam's daughter . . . that's who he was here for; it had to be, or he wouldn't have come here to Maine. It's who he was obsessed with, for reasons I didn't yet understand.

But what I cared about now was that Cam had meant to join them here. Without me, even after all I'd done for her . . . she was the same vengeful girl I had known when we were children together. She had never forgiven me, and I'd have had to silence her sooner or later, I realized.

Now all I had to do was finish Gemerle off, too, and I'd be free. I could start a new life where no one knew what I'd done or what was done to me, because everyone who'd known was dead.

A few hours later I was forty miles north of Houlton, at a convenience store where I got a map. Next, bypassing two modern-looking motels on the main drag, I chose instead an old family-run place a few miles off the highway.

I just thought it would be better if my car wasn't visible from a well-traveled road. After I checked in I stowed my things in my room and washed down more pills with vending-machine coffee. Then I drove twenty more miles to the small town of Bearkill.

By then it was ten o'clock on Tuesday morning. It seemed like years since I'd left Cam's body in our apartment, but it wasn't even twelve hours. Already it all felt as if it had happened to someone else.

In town, I parked outside the red-brick public library, meaning to wait there until it opened at eleven. But instead, a stroke of good luck happened almost at once.

From where I sat I could see all the way down Main Street, past a double row of wooden storefront buildings and a Food King supermarket. What I needed was a way to identify Cam's child, so I could snatch her and use her to coax Gemerle into a trap.

It might not be easy, but I thought if I paged through high school yearbooks in the library I might spot a girl who resembled Cam. Then I'd have to find the girl herself, which of course would be another whole project. But one thing at a time, I told myself, and just as I was about to go into the library, to my amazement the woman I'd seen in the courtroom appeared. Blunt-cut blond hair, sturdy figure . . .

It was her, all right, getting out of a beat-up old Honda sedan in the

Food King parking lot. She was even wearing the same blue sweat-shirt.

Seeing her, it struck me: There had to be a reason she'd gone to the New Haven hearing at all, didn't there? A reason she cared? And now suddenly I had a hunch about what the reason might be.

After all, he must have given that baby of Cam's to someone. And meanwhile, I needed supplies for what I had planned. So when the blond woman had come out again and had driven away, I went in and bought coffee and snack food plus two stout wooden-handled mops, a small hacksaw, a barbecue lighter, and rolls of wire and silver duct tape. Then I told the clerk at the register that I thought I'd recognized the woman I'd just seen.

"Who, Peg Wylie?" answered the clerk.

And there it was, her name, just like that. They had a phone book in the library so getting her address was easy, too. And just as I had hoped, the library also had a high school yearbook with a picture in it: Tara Wylie.

Which meant I'd done it. I'd found her and now everything was in place, with Gemerle already settling in at a remote cottage nearby, where he thought Cam was coming to meet him. But instead I would get him to come to me, and then I would kill him.

I even had the tools now: the wire, the stout mop handles. I only wanted another look at him in person to be sure I could do it all the way I intended: that the wire would be long enough, for instance, and the mop handles strong enough.

So first I copied the yearbook picture, so I'd be sure to know the girl when I saw her in real life; I didn't think I would forget her face, but my mind had begun playing some funny tricks on me in the past couple of hours.

From those pills of Cam's, I supposed. Shimmery little halos kept forming around things I wanted to look at, and once I mistook the car's brake for the gas pedal, briefly but frighteningly. But after I'd eaten some packaged cookies—my mouth was so dry that I had to sop them in the coffee to swallow them—I felt better, and in the library I consulted Google Maps on the computer to find the cottage Finny had texted me about.

Finally I got back in my car and went looking for the place, feeling optimistic about finding it quickly. By now they'd have been there for a few hours; with any luck I could sneak up on them, get a closer look at Gemerle, and fine-tune my plan, if need be.

I hadn't decided what to do about Finny yet, but something would come to me. Popping another of Cam's pep pills, I drove out of town toward the cottage that he and Gemerle had rented.

And then everything went to hell.

There was one narrow road leading in to the lake area where the cottage was located, and the last thing I wanted was to meet Finny and Gemerle driving out. So I pulled into a gravel turnout and parked behind a bramble thicket.

The walk in was pleasant, a quarter mile or so on a packed-earth road between tall, fragrant evergreens. The air was warm, smelling of wood smoke and lake water; I kept my ears open for the sound of a car approaching in case I needed to duck out of sight.

But no car came. Soon I was at a cut in the undergrowth just wide enough to show the lake sparkling. I slipped down a woodsy path to where a gray van sat outside a shingled cabin with a stone chimney, a wisp of smoke curling from it.

The shades were drawn. No sound came from the cabin. I eased around to the lake side to try peeking in there. Then from behind me I heard the sound of a car moving slowly.

I stepped back into the greenery. It was a rental car, and as it went by I saw clearly who was driving. *Impossible* . . .

But it was Cam. Not dead as I'd thought, but only pale and tired appearing, with a gauze bandage wrapped around a dressing on her head. At the cottage she parked and got out, gazing around in the piney stillness. Then she went inside.

Stunned, I rushed up to her car and peered in. On the seat lay a rental agreement for the vehicle and two boarding passes, one for the airport in New Haven and one from Portland, Maine.

So she'd been faking it all. She'd let me think she was dead—or as good as—gurgling and gagging realistically enough to win an Academy Award. Then she'd cleaned herself up and rushed out to the airport as soon as I was gone, the traitorous little bitch.

At the rear of the cottage a small deck overlooked a wooden dock with a canoe pulled up to it. I tiptoed up onto the deck and crouched below one of the windows, which was open a crack.

Cam's voice came triumphantly from inside. ". . . but she forgot I've got that metal plate in my head. It bled a lot, but—"

But she'd survived. Or so she thought. *We'll just see about that,* I told myself. *We'll just see.*

I suppose I should've felt something. Remorse, maybe. Or a wish to be back with Cam. But seeing her with him showed me just how impossible that was. And anyway, when I'd killed the reporter something changed in me. It was as if a switch in my head had been on its way to flipping for a very long time, and finally it had.

And it wasn't going to go back. Then came Gemerle's voice, as low and gravelly as I recalled it. ". . . knew I could depend on you . . ."

Sure, like she'd done anything useful. I was the one who'd done it all, gotten him out of that loony bin he'd been stuck in and arranged for him to be here. Speaking of which, where was Finny Brill, anyway?

Cam again: ". . . together. The three of us . . . where is she?"

Of course she wanted to know about the baby. But it wasn't a baby anymore, was it? Tara Wylie was a teenager now.

". . . time for that foolishness," he responded harshly. Then the sound of a slap rang out suddenly in the still air, the smack of flesh striking flesh.

I raised up cautiously to peek in through the window. Cam looked shocked, holding her face, fighting back tears.

What did you expect? I thought angrily at her, *what did you think was going to happen?* But I guessed I knew. She'd spent years under his control. Now life felt strange without it, I imagined.

It didn't help how I felt, though, knowing she would rather get beaten up by him than be cared for by me. Knowing that all along she'd been despising me and hating me, and planning to leave.

Silence from inside; I peeked in cautiously once more. The cabin's interior was a single large room, all wood-paneled, with gas lamps hanging from wooden overhead beams. The furniture looked old but comfortable, bentwood rockers and upholstered settees in a half circle around a woodstove.

"Where is she?" he demanded, advancing threateningly on Cam. His back was to me. "Your little friend, where is she?"

Me, he meant. Finny must have said more than we'd agreed on. Or Gemerle had made him tell.

"I don't know!" Cam cried. "I thought you said we would be together, be a family again, I don't know!"

He spun her and shoved her down hard into a chair. "Oh, you thought, did you?" he snarled. "Let me tell you what I think."

Then he turned, and I saw him close up for the first time in fifteen years. His face, lightly freckled and nastily amused at Cam's misery, was not much changed. His wavy blond hair was only a little receded from his forehead.

And his eyes were the same, like dark blue stones, just as they'd been all those years ago when he told me to drink the juice or he would slit my throat for me.

"I got rid of the orderly," he told her. "I'll get rid of the stupid bitch who testified against me, and then I'll take care of that little fool nursemaid of yours."

He bent over her. "And if you don't do what I tell you I'll get rid of you, too. Got it?"

She dragged a hand across her bleeding lip. "All right," she whimpered. Then:

"I can help you find Jane, you know. I know what car she's driving and there aren't many motels around here, are there?"

Suddenly my ears rang, nausea rising insistently in me as wave after wave of dizziness hit me; *those pills,* I thought, and sank to the deck, wanting only to die there.

But his next words pricked my ears up again: "All right. When it's done, we'll go to Canada."

He was humoring her. But she couldn't hear it. "The baby, too?" she quavered.

"Yeah," Gemerle said after a moment. From his tone I could tell he was thinking the same as I was, that she wasn't right in the head.

That he could tell her anything, and she would believe it. Suddenly I wasn't so sure anymore that I hadn't killed her after all, back there in our apartment. Maybe her dying was just taking a while.

Or maybe on the inside she was already dead, and had been dead for a long time. "Sure, the baby," he said carelessly. "Whatever."

Just being near him made my skin crawl so hard, it nearly crept off my body. Or maybe that was from the pills, too. When I forced myself to peek in a final time, I spotted a gun sticking from his jeans pocket.

"But like I said, first we have to eliminate our problems," he told Cam.

He turned toward the window; I ducked down fast. "She knows I'm here," he added coldly. "She's been behind me getting out all along, the orderly said so. I got it out of him and then I got rid of him. But she knows."

Suspicions confirmed; poor Finny. I heard Cam sniffling. "All right," she replied faintly. "Whatever you say."

Then without warning she turned and threw up, barely making it to the sink, and I heard him cursing her.

I jumped off the deck and backed away, dry-mouthed, stumbling up the path as quietly as I could. But I must've made some sound; as I reached the clearing and plunged into the brambles along the driveway, the cottage's front door creaked open.

Footsteps clomped out onto the porch; glancing back, I saw him peering around suspiciously.

I froze. My legs felt watery, my lungs struggling to suck in enough air. The footsteps stomped nearer, sticks and dry leaves crunching as they approached me. I huddled, shivering, ducked down among the pine boughs, as he stopped, finally.

But he didn't come any farther. I waited, still nauseated and in terror, until he went back inside; then came more shouting, her shrieks of protest, and finally a dull smacking sound, again and again.

As I crept away toward my car I heard her sobbing. But there was nothing I could do about it. Anyway, she'd made her choice.

Nothing I could do about that, either, I told myself as I pushed through the brushy brambles. Scratched and filthy, horridly thirsty, and so scared I could barely breathe, I found my car and got in, not daring to slam the door or start the engine.

Luckily I'd backed up onto a slight hill, so I took the brake off and rolled silently out onto the road, then turned the key. As I sped away, I kept glancing in the rearview mirror, sure that at any moment he would be there, his face full of rage.

And Cam beside him, of course, urging him on. When I got to a crossroads I was crying so hard I couldn't see, and I must have taken a wrong turn. Soon I was in a forest, trees all around and no one to tell me where I'd gotten to, or how to get back.

No bars showed on my cell phone. I had no food or water with me, either; only the rest of the pills I'd poured into a secret compartment of my purse, not wanting to leave them in the motel room.

So I chewed two more, hoping the energy they gave would last me until I found my way to town again. The afternoon sun filtered weakly through the tall trees, then slid behind clouds. A drop of rain fell, then another, but as evening came on and the temperature plummeted the rain quickly changed to sleet.

A logging truck roared by, and then two more, but none of the drivers paid any attention to me. Finally, on a dirt road that was not much more than a rough track, I found a carved wooden sign with an arrow: BEARKILL, 2 MI.

Following it, I reached the town in a few minutes, and with it the realization that I'd been circling it for hours. Screwing up, in other words, and now here I was in a strange place, sick and tired and so scared I could barely think, all my courage shattered by what I had just seen and without an idea in the world of what I ought to do next.

Blinking to clear the spots swarming in my eyes, I parked in the Food King lot. By now it was past dusk, though the clock on the dashboard said only a little after four. Sleet slanted down in sheets, thundering across the lot's asphalt.

In the grocery store, people were buying food for dinner and chatting with acquaintances while I sat outside alone, hungry and tired and still so scared. I swallowed another pill, felt it hit my empty stomach and then the ugly rush it brought on, the harsh jagged-edged alertness like chewing on broken glass.

Then, fluttering in the icy gusts of wind on the wooden pole of a streetlamp not far away, I saw it: a paper poster with a photograph on it. Sick with premonition, I clambered from the car and staggered toward it, not wanting it to be true.

But it was. The heavy sleet had already soaked through the paper, but the photograph on the homemade poster was the same one I'd seen in the library. MISSING, the poster said, and then a description of the girl.

Tara Wylie was already missing. Which meant he must have her. What other explanation could there be?

Desperately I struggled back to my car; first sweating, then shivering, I fell into the front seat half conscious. Outside, the sky went light-dark, light-dark like a strobe light flickering while my brain sizzled hotly as if frying in its own fat, one despairing thought slamming the inside of my head:

The monster had won. Somehow he'd already snatched the girl. Maybe he'd even killed her, like he would kill Cam.

So it was over. I must have sat there for several hours just listening to the sleet pellets rattle wetly on the car's roof. I couldn't go home; my life there was over and I couldn't bear to see it again, to face what I'd lost.

But I couldn't go on, either; I didn't have the strength, and everything I'd lived for was gone, anyway. Maybe I should just kill myself, I thought. Swallow all the pills and end this misery that I'd brought on myself.

At last, though, through the sleet I saw people in an office across the street, behind the big front window. It was a sheriff's department office; I'd noticed it when I first got to town and now in my confusion I felt it might actually be my salvation.

I could tell the police everything and they might help me, I thought. After all, what did it matter if they put me in prison? My life was ruined anyway. So I did try telling them, but when I got into the office I couldn't even do that properly—

Fortunately, as it turned out. Because by the next morning all those pills had worn off and everything was different again.

Different, and better.

After the tranquilizers, the IV fluids, and sleep in the Bearkill hospital, by that Wednesday morning I felt like a new person. There were a dicey few moments when the woman sheriff's deputy took me back to the same motel where I'd already registered once and checked me in. But the desk clerk didn't notice, or at any rate he didn't mention it, and once Lizzie Snow left me I just moved my things.

My new room was next to a compressor clanking noisily in the hallway. But that might turn out to be useful, I thought, and so was the room's other flaw, a chronically running toilet. I had to take the lid off the tank to put the float up so it would stop. And that tank lid, I discovered, was heavy.

Once I could think clearly again I'd realized I didn't need Tara to lure Gemerle. After all, he wanted to find me, too, didn't he?

So I let him. I waited until late afternoon, then texted the name of my motel to Finny Brill's phone, figuring that if Gemerle had even half a brain, he'd have kept it. And it turned out he had, because later that Wednesday evening a van with Gemerle at the wheel pulled into the parking lot.

By then it was long past dark. I watched from the lobby as the dome light went on in the van and he got out. Cam was there, too, looking awful, her face bruised and swollen.

He came in the lobby's front door as I turned and scampered back to my room; I'd told the desk clerk it was all right to send him along, and soon I heard him out in the hall.

"Jane?" He tapped on the door quietly.

Like a normal person. But he wasn't. I stepped fast into the bathroom where he wouldn't see me. That noisy compressor in the hall clanked and rattled like a plane getting ready to take off.

"Jane?" I'd slipped a bit of paper into the latch so the door opened as soon as he touched it.

"Jane?" *Third time's the charm* ... As he took another step I raised that heavy ceramic toilet tank lid and brought it down on the back of his skull. He must have sensed something in the last instant, because he ducked a little. So I didn't quite hit him squarely.

He dropped, though, and I snapped the light back on. He lay between the dresser and the foot of the bed, one arm flung out. A gun lay fallen from his hand, and the back of his head pulsed red.

But he still breathed, his ribs heaving under his sweatshirt, and even now he was coming around a little. So my being slightly off-target with the tank lid was good luck, too, I realized; it meant I would still be able to do the rest of what I had planned.

Only I would have to hurry. I'd already prepared the chair, wedging it between the two beds, and readied the duct tape. Now I heaved him up into the chair and secured him there.

Finally I threw water in his face. Spluttering, he came to. "Wha?" he muttered, but then his eyes focused on me.

I flicked the switch on the barbecue lighter from the Food King. Blue flame shot from it, and that really got his attention; I could see him frantically trying to find something to say that would get him out of this.

The way I had, long ago. "Don't bother," I told him softly.

The barbecue lighter was tempting. But even that rattletrap old compressor out in the hall wasn't loud enough for some things. Besides, I wasn't here to hurt him.

Not yet, anyway. "Come on," he wheedled. "I'm not—"

The motel-room phone book was surprisingly thick. I smacked him with it.

His gaze darkened to a scowl; it had dawned on him now that this wasn't going to be so easy. He didn't have me tied up in a gloomy dungeon, did he?

I had him. But more to the point, he had Tara. "Tell me what you've done with that girl. Tell me now, or—"

He laughed, rearing forward, trying to break the duct tape. Putting a foot in his chest I shoved him back.

"Wrong answer." I touched flame to his earlobe; just briefly, enough to make him howl. "Next time it's your eye. Understand?"

He nodded. I suppose he thought that if he did what I asked, things might go better for him. After all, hope springs eternal.

It had for the girls, too. And for me. "Where's Tara?"

His eyes narrowed cunningly. "What makes you think—?"

I toasted the other ear. He screeched again briefly, eyeing the lighter wildly afterward.

"Another wrong answer, Henry. Seems to me you keep forgetting who the boss is here. Maybe I should refresh your memory."

This time I didn't even have to flick the lighter on. "All right, Jesus, how the hell do you know about that, anyway? I just found her last night, so how'd you—no, don't!"

I drew the lighter back. So I'd been wrong. He hadn't had her yesterday when I saw the MISSING poster. She'd been somewhere else. But the important thing was, he had her now.

"All right, I took her up the hill," he said grudgingly. "Last night."

He angled his head toward the window. "I put her up in the fire zone. I left her there, let her get a taste of what's coming to that dumb bitch cousin of mine, too."

"You mean Peg Wylie? You mean she's your—" A mental picture of the blond woman in the courtroom popped into my head.

"I warned her," Gemerle said, more to himself than me. "You say anything about me, I told her, I'll make your life hard. Like I did for the others. It won't matter how far you run."

I must have recoiled. Noticing, he grinned. "I kept a little list," he said proudly to me. "So I could find them again if ever I got lonesome."

He licked his lips as if relishing the thought. "That's how I knew she'd be here." Another idea seemed to strike him. "You, though. I never found you."

I'd been right to stay away from his neighborhood all those years, to keep my head down and stay out of sight as much as I could.

"Cam said she didn't even know you, that you two girls had just met in the park. And I believed her. Maybe," he added, "on account of what she was doing to me when she said it . . ."

His grin was lascivious. "Hey, what can I say? Thinkin' with the wrong head, I was, and I thought she was telling the truth."

It was all I could do not to burn that filthy tongue of his right out of his head. But I needed it.

I needed what it could reveal. "Where?" I said calmly. "Tell me exactly where Tara Wylie is and how to find her."

Because she might still be alive. And if she was, now I had a new reason to find her: Who knew what the monster might've told her? About me, maybe; about what I had done. Cam might've confided something to him about that, too, trying to humor him, get on his good side.

"You'll let me go, though, right?" Gemerle wheedled. "If I tell?"

I pretended to think about it. Then, "Sure. I want Tara. Once I have her, I won't need you anymore. So yeah, go ahead. I'm listening."

Make my day, I added silently. *You sick fuck.* And then he did tell: the road. A red bandanna marking the hole he'd buried her in. It was near some kind of a primitive shed, he added.

"Okay, so now I've told you." He worked his face into a fake smile. "So you keep your part of the bargain and—"

Right. My part. He was still talking, trying to weasel his way out of this as I slipped behind him, wrapped the heavy length of wire that I'd secured to the mop handles twice around his neck, and shoved the chair over frontwise. Then I climbed atop it, gripping the pair of mop handles and ignoring his wheezed pleas.

It was more difficult than I'd expected. Somehow he got the chair out from between the two beds; a lamp went over, then the TV on its metal stand. But as he squeaked and struggled, I hung on, fighting to keep my grip.

Until suddenly he went limp. Cautiously I let the wire go slack, ready for him to roar up again. But he lay motionless. In the struggle, his gun had gotten kicked away. Grabbing it up, I moved around to the front of the chair where his face lay mashed into the carpet, one eye goggling at me.

I still thought I might have to shoot him. But then I saw all the blood spreading across the carpet. I hadn't strangled him; instead the wire had been sharp.

So that's what did it, ended the monster at last. I stood staring at him for a long time until with a start I came back to myself and began trying to clean up the blood, wiping at it with towels and throwing them in a heap. While I worked, I thought about what I'd expected to feel once he was gone—triumph, satisfaction, relief—and what I did feel:

Nothing. Only the dull knowledge that he was eliminated at last, like smashing a bug that was poisonous and you knew if you didn't, it would sting you to death. It was too bad, really, that after all this time of hating him, and then finally slaughtering him, I didn't even get to enjoy it.

But it was like I was on autopilot. The room had a sliding glass door leading outside. When I'd used all the towels to mop up as well as I could, I opened it a crack so I could get back in that way, then slipped out the door leading to the hall past the clattering compressor. There was a side exit, so I was able to avoid the lobby.

Out in the dark parking lot, I jumped into his van where Cam sagged half conscious in the passenger seat. He'd beaten her very badly, her face bruised and fresh blood oozing from beneath the bandage on her head. Her breathing was irregular; for real this time, and in another life I'd have rushed her to the same hospital I'd been in earlier.

But that life was over. Instead I moved the van around to the motel's rear service area—the keys, luckily, were still in the ignition—and backed it right up to the sliding glass door of my own room. Inside, I rolled the chair with him in it to the door, cut the tape securing him to the chair, and shoved the chair hard, toppling him halfway into the van's rear cargo compartment.

Finally I hauled him all the way in so the doors would close. I flung the chair back into the room and slid the glass door shut. Behind it the heavy draperies swung gently and were still.

Now I just had to find Tara Wylie. Because now that Finny and Gemerle were dead—and Cam would be too, soon, I was sure of it this time—she was the only one Gemerle might have talked to about all this.

Not that he definitely had. And that was a chance I couldn't take; suspicion was one thing, but the girl's testimony would be another.

He might have repeated something Finny said about me, or told the girl something about Cam, for instance. Just some little thing.

But if some smart cop got to hear of it . . . well, maybe I was being too obsessive. I had to be sure, though—absolutely sure, or I'd never be able to sleep at night—that it wouldn't happen.

So, with Gemerle's body in the rear cargo compartment and Cam slumped alongside me in the van's passenger seat, I drove toward the fires flaring bright orange and yellow on the dark hillside just outside Bearkill.

I would dump Gemerle up there and sit beside Cam until she finally died, I decided, and afterward I would leave her there.

But then she spoke icily. "You didn't forget."

I jumped, nearly sending us careening off the road. It hadn't occurred to me that she might regain consciousness, she looked and sounded so awful. When I had the van back under control enough to glance over at her, though, she was smiling at me.

Bleeding, still. And her breathing was very terrible. But she was smiling unpleasantly and watching me from beneath half-lowered eyelids, one eye hideously swollen. "Hi, Janie," she said.

Before her surgery, the doctors explained to me that her waxing and waning consciousness—one day drowsy, the next bright as a penny—came from changing pressures in and around her brain.

That must be what was happening to her now, I thought, something leaking, blood pooling and pressing, then easing temporarily.

"Hi," I managed. Then I noticed she had the gun. Gemerle's gun, I realized with a burst of panic. I'd picked it up in the motel room, laid it on the van console, and Cam must have seen it and snatched it up without my noticing.

So now she had it. "You didn't *forget,*" she repeated, her face contorting in a lopsided snarl. "You lying little *bitch,* you *left* me there with him. All those *years* you left me down there. And even then I protected you. I could have told him where you were, you know."

So it was true, what Gemerle had said. Once that might have softened my heart, but now I didn't have one anymore. She was aiming that gun at me.

Ash swirled from the sky, sticking like gray snow to the windshield, smearing when I hit the wipers. We were nearly to the Ridge Road turnoff Gemerle had told me about, the one that led to where he'd left Tara Wylie. Uphill in the dark, flickers of orange flared warningly.

"I know how much you hated me," Cam slurred unevenly.

I glanced over at her again. In the dashboard's pale glow her face was swollen and misshapen, bruised and lumpy where he'd hit her.

Bleeding from where I had hit her, too, days earlier, a thin trickle now oozing from beneath the bandage on her head. When she turned to face me again, in just those few moments her right eye had bulged out to golf-ball size.

"Because I was pretty and I cared about being alive," she went on. "Because I had *fun.* And you couldn't. You just didn't know how."

We bumped off the paved part of the road. Gemerle had said it was another half mile or so from there and to look for a red rag tied to a branch stuck in the ground.

"You hated me," Cam said, "because you were jealous. Once I was gone, you wouldn't be getting compared with me all the time.

"Had you going for a while, though, didn't I?" Cam's words were barely understandable now but her grip on the gun still looked steady.

I swallowed hard. "Cam, I thought you were dead back in his cellar. I swear, I would never have left you there if I had any idea."

The road was rough and heavily rutted, the van jouncing in and out of deep holes and through soft, ground-up patches where the tires spun briefly before catching traction again.

"And then it's true, I did forget," I said. "What he did to me, everything about it, yes, I forgot it all as fast as I could, I admit it."

The gun was pointed at my head. "But afterward, when I found out the truth, when I found *you,* I was sorry. I took care of you, Cam, and . . . and I loved you. And doesn't that count for something?"

Had loved her. Now only the fear remained, so as I spoke I thrust my hand out very fast. And maybe her reflexes weren't so good after the beating she'd taken, or maybe she didn't really want to shoot me.

Maybe somewhere in that hard-as-nails little heart of hers, she'd loved me, too. But I knew she would never admit it and anyway, I didn't care. Not anymore. So I straight-armed her hard, hitting her in the throat, and her head slammed backward against the passenger-side window with a sick-sounding thud.

Then I saw the red rag like a danger flag in the headlights. Gemerle had said it marked the place he'd left Tara. I hit the van's brakes and Cam slid like a rag doll onto the dashboard, the gun falling from her hand. Scrabbling around in the darkness I found it. But by then she was on me, wide awake again, scratching and biting.

"You weren't taking care of me!" she shrieked. "You just wanted to shut me up so I wouldn't tell on you! Henry was the only one who ever—"

From down in the van's foot well I flung my head up and back hard and felt it connect with her jaw.

"The only one who ever what?" I demanded. "Raped you, beat you, locked you up and terrorized you?"

I hauled myself up, panting, and shoved the gun in my pocket. "He's the one who killed you, Cam. Or he as good as killed you. It wasn't me. I made a mistake, I admit that."

Fallen back against the window, she curled her split lip at me in revulsion. One side of her face was already puffing up from where she'd hit the dashboard.

"I made a lot of bad mistakes," I went on. "But if you still think Henry was anything but a monster, if your head's so twisted around that you believe *you* were ever anything but his *victim*—"

Her eyes widened. "Was?" she whispered.

She glanced toward the darkened rear of the van where Henry Gemerle lay on the other side of the metal divider screen behind the passenger seats. She hadn't known he was back there, but now she saw his shape and got it.

"Is that what we're doing here?" She glanced out at the smoky night. The fires seemed much closer, runnels of flame streaming up nearly to us and falling away again.

"He's dead? You killed him?" Before I could stop her she was out of the van, staggering through the headlight beams, her gait crablike and her face a misshapen horror as she struggled into the gloom beyond.

"Help!" she cried. "Help! Murder!" Not loud; she didn't have the breath to make much noise. But it was enough, if anyone heard her, to put me in prison, wasn't it?

Or it could be. She might say anything. So I went after her: out of the van, across the dusty soil, stumbling in the dark. Ahead I could hear her weeping, still gasping out cries for help.

"Cam!" I breathed. "Cam, wait!" But she didn't, and then it got very quiet. "Cam?"

No answer. In the distance, flames flared up and flattened again. It was as if they were teasing, creeping near, dancing away.

Then a breathy shriek sent me back toward the van. When I got there Cam stood bent at an awkward angle, one foot on the ground and the other plunged into it somehow, pinned in the headlights.

"Cam?" Squinting to try to make sense of what I was seeing, I ventured nearer. "Cam, are you okay?"

But she only bared her teeth at me like an animal, and as I got nearer I could see that her foot really had gone through the earth somehow. She had stepped into some kind of a hole, or . . .

"It's biting me!" she screamed, trying frantically to yank her foot out all of a sudden. But something held it.

"Cam!" I grabbed her calf in both my hands, pulling up with all my strength. Finally her foot emerged, shoeless and with fresh oozing bite marks around the heel.

Human bite marks. As soon as I'd freed her, Cam fell sobbing to the ground. I dropped beside her, hearing faint cries that I knew could mean only one thing. I dug frantically into the dry, loose soil with my fingers in the place she'd stepped through.

Almost at once I'd uncovered a box with one wooden top slat broken in, the splinters blood-streaked. Scrambling back to the van I found a tire iron by the spare tire in the cargo area, and in the next few moments I managed to pry the rest of the slats up and off the box. Inside, flat on her back and staring wildly up at me, lay a girl with a daggerlike shard of black plastic clutched in her two hands.

Blood smeared her lips, stretched into a feral expression as if in the next instant she might fly up at me and rip my throat out. Then Cam rose beside me, letting out a shuddery sigh as she peered down and glimpsed the girl in the box.

It was Tara Wylie.

TWELVE

Tara didn't recall when she'd found the sharp plastic piece.

She'd felt something digging into her leg and searched around with her hands as best she could, to try moving it where it wouldn't poke her.

The next thing she knew, she had the sharp thing in her hands, knew it for a tool, and began using it immediately on one of the box-top slats. Dragging the plastic shard's sharp point across the grain of the wooden slat nailed down inches from her face, she began digging a groove in it.

Don't give up, she thought, her mind echoing what her mother had always told her. Nagged her, actually: About homework. About cheerleading. Whatever. *Be lousy at it if you have to, Tara. But don't you ever, ever ...*

She wasn't hungry. She wasn't even thirsty, or if she was, she was not letting herself know about it. She was very, very scared, but as her mom always said, too, sometimes being scared just means you've got a brain in your head.

All Tara really knew, though, was that if she didn't find a way out of this box she was buried in, she was going to die.

And she did not fucking want to. She just didn't. Dig at that thing, she told herself. Dig, dammit: like her mom lifted weights and did pull-ups, and ran miles every morning before breakfast, so she could get in good enough shape to pass the firefighter test.

Just do it . . . Tara dragged the plastic shard yet again through the groove she'd already worn into one of the slats that imprisoned her in the box. Bits of dry wood flaked down itchily onto her lips; she blew them away and dragged the shard again.

And again. A while later, she thought she heard voices and then knew she did. Two women were arguing up there, practically on top of her. Elated, Tara opened her mouth to cry out to them for help. But only a whispery croak escaped her, and from above it seemed that the two women were actually fighting now, physically struggling with each other.

So they couldn't hear her weak thumping, which was all she could manage with her arms so restricted by the tight quarters she was in. All they cared about, Tara thought resentfully, was that stupid quarrel they were so involved in, and the more she thought about this the madder she got.

For God's sake, I'm going to die while you two bitch at each other, she thought. So when a foot suddenly came crashing into the box through the weak spot in the slat, Tara knew just what to do and by then she was pissed off enough to do it.

She grabbed it with both hands and bit into it. Hard, as hard as she could. The foot yanked away, leaving a satisfying amount of blood and tissue between her teeth. Then the broken slats were being torn away, dirt and ash cascading down onto her face.

Coughing and gagging, she felt herself lifted up by her arms, and screamed at the agony of moving her stiffened legs. Soon she was on her feet, wobbly and squinting in darkness at the two women whose faces, masklike in the glare of headlights from a vehicle not far away, peered astonishedly at her.

"It's her," one of the women whispered wonderingly, the one with the bandage on her head. But Tara didn't care.

"I want," she began, the words coming out a whisper. Where was she? Unsure, she scanned the darkness anxiously. And why was that van sitting there, the van *he* had been driving?

"I want . . ." At the sight of the van, terror hit her. She took a step, fell, and began scrabbling away on hands and knees as fast as she could, heedless of the stones bruising her hands.

Her fingers brushed something and closed onto it. The shovel lay there; the one he'd made her use to dig her own grave. She had forgotten it, but now her hands wrapped tightly around it.

She struggled to her knees, still gripping the shovel. One chance, just one, would she have to make use of it. Footsteps from behind her crunched softly in the dry earth.

Soon, whoever it was would be near enough. Tara took a deep breath and then hopped a little hop up onto the balls of her feet. Next, with the last of her strength she sprang up, swinging the shovel, letting its weight carry it out and away—

Hands seized her, knocking the shovel aside. Tara ducked fast and away from them, knowing she had to escape.

That her life depended on it. "No!" she cried desperately as she kicked out hard and felt the heel of her left foot hit flesh. Then she wriggled away once more, but the smoky night around her was now all at once hotly peppered with flying embers.

There was nowhere to go. Fire rose all around her, closed in smotheringly, and everything was in flames.

"Come on," someone gasped. "Come on, come on . . ."

Her shirt was on fire. One of the women was slapping at it, trying to put it out, but all Tara could do was sob.

"I want . . . my *mother*!" she wailed helplessly, and when the fire on her shirt was finally extinguished she didn't care about that, either. She was just so *thirsty,* just suddenly so thirsty and very tired, and after that she must have passed out.

Later she found herself being half dragged and half carried uphill in the dark. The fire was behind them but gaining hungrily, streamers of flame creeping out, falling back, nearer each time.

We have to get away from here, thought Tara. But they were heading in the wrong direction. The lights of Bearkill glowed hazily in the distance through a pall of heavily drifting smoke.

There, she thought yearningly. Ordinarily she could reach it no problem, even in the dark. But her legs felt as if they would dissolve beneath her; no way would she be able to run.

And that wasn't the worst of it. "He's coming," she whispered tremblingly. "You don't get it, he's out here."

"No, he's not." The bandaged woman spoke. She looked awful.

"He's not out there because he's *dead*. She *killed* him," the injured woman added nastily, slurring her words. "The way she'll kill *us*," the woman added.

The smoke smell was still gaggingly strong. When Tara's foot hit a rock and she stumbled, the woman gripping her arm jerked her roughly upright again.

"Please," said the injured woman. Pleading, her mood shifting like the smoke-billows that had begun rising and falling around them in the hot breeze. "Before you do it, please let me . . ."

Before she does what? Tara wondered, fright jabbing her, and then, *I need to get out of here,* she thought again, but the woman marching her along held on tight and she was too weak to struggle.

Then just ahead a low shed took shape in the gloom, with a dark rectangle suggesting a door. Tara balked, frowning at the structure. "No. No, I don't want to go in there."

"Sometimes we all have to do things we don't want to," said the woman who held Tara, before letting her go.

Tara stood swaying, gathering herself to run. But then she saw the gun. "Go on now," said the woman, waving it.

"Oh," murmured the other one suddenly, and fumbling at the bandage on her head she collapsed all at once like a puppet whose strings had been cut.

The woman with the gun dropped to her knees. "Cam?"

Tara backed carefully away toward some unburnt scrub trees. Beyond their whippy trunks, incongruous on the barren hillside, stood a bathtub, and suddenly she could see nothing else because maybe the tub had—

Yes! There was water in it. The tub was a makeshift trough, and the shed must be for a local farmer's grazing animals; goats or sheep, maybe, Tara realized, not caring how the young saplings cut her as she swept them aside, thirst urging her on.

Reaching the trough she fell gratefully against it, cupped cool, dripping handfuls and flung them greedily into her parched mouth. *Once more,* she thought each time she drank. *Then I'll run.*

But instead her body took over and she was still bent to the water when she felt what she knew must be the small, cold end of the gun barrel on her neck.

"Okay, honey, get inside."

Full of dread, Tara eyed the shed's dark door mistrustfully. But then having no other choice, she gave in and ducked through it.

"He hurt her," Cam managed when I returned from tying Tara up, using some twine I'd found in the shed. "He hurt my baby."

Even dying, Cam was no fool, and despite her delusions about Gemerle she still knew just exactly which sick son of a bitch would bury a girl in a box.

"Right," I said, crouched beside her outside the rough structure.

I saw no reason to tell her the truth, even though I knew it. Had known, actually, since the moment I read Tara's description on the MISSING poster. Brown hair, brown eyes . . .

Cam hadn't seen Tara Wylie clearly enough to know that the girl couldn't be her daughter.

And now she never would. "You hurt him back, though, didn't you?" she whispered through a grimace of pain. "That was good."

I found her hand and held it. My heart, thudding an awful drumbeat, suddenly felt as if it might burst in my chest; I'd felt blessedly numb but now as she squeezed my hand, in my memory Cam skipped down Whalley Avenue beside me again, singing about being free.

"I'm so sorry," she murmured. "You were right about him."

Something hot and stinging ran down my face, salty-tasting. A sob reached my throat but it wouldn't come the rest of the way.

"Never mind," I whispered. "Don't worry about anything now."

A smile touched her lips, and for an instant it was the old Cam there: funny and full of mischief, a girl who took dares and wore makeup and whose walk was a lovely, loose-limbed dance to music that I couldn't hear.

Except through her. And now I wouldn't ever hear it again. She reached up, childlike, wincing in anguish; I gathered her in my arms and while I held her and whispered to her, she took a shuddery final breath and died there on the dark hillside.

And then all I could think about was getting away. Looking up I saw fire roaring at me, hurling explosions of yellow-white sparks out ahead of itself. At me, at Cam's body, and at the girl tied up inside the shed.

Which was when I realized: I'd been dreading it, but I didn't have to kill Tara Wylie at all, did I? Not directly, anyway; all I had to do was arrange things so no trace of what had gone on here would ever be discovered.

And it wasn't as if the girl would burn alive. The smoke would get her first, surely. After all, I wasn't a monster.

"You let her *leave*?"

It was Thursday night. Jane Crimmins had been here in the emergency room again; here and gone, Emily Ektari had called Lizzie to say.

Clad in a blue scrub suit and lab coat, Emily shrugged impatiently, leaning down at the nursing desk to squint at something on the computer screen.

"Hey, I just got here. And you know we can't keep people who don't want to stay," said Emily. "But . . . okay, here it is."

The waiting area was full of worried-looking women and men, many of them with small children clinging to them. In the air hung a smell that Lizzie remembered from Boston emergency rooms, the sharp sweat of anxiety clinging to clothes flung on any which way.

Emily looked up. "I didn't take care of her this time, the nurse practitioner did."

"And no one recognized her?" Lizzie demanded impatiently.

Shrugging, Emily scanned the screen again. "Guess not. We've been jammed. But I called you as soon as I heard about it. Anyway it says here she came in with second-degree burns on her hands, a couple third-degree areas."

She squinted at the monitor again. "They got the burns cleaned up, applied a loose dressing, and then sent her out with a prescription for pain—they dispensed it here—plus instructions for self-care. She was okay to drive."

The blaze had somehow caught Bearkill's Fire One unawares, sent four men and a woman reeling through smoke and flame before their team finally located and evacuated them. Now Peg Wylie was out in the waiting area commiserating with the victims' loved ones while they paced through an agonizing wait for news.

Emily looked up, eyeing Lizzie. "You know, when you get a chance you might want to get some rest."

"Yeah, I should take up the fiddle, too, and play it while Rome burns," Lizzie responded. But then she relented; the young ER physician was right.

"Thanks, Em," she added as a commotion erupted in the waiting area. Hurrying out, she found Peg Wylie crouched over a fallen man, her expression grim and her index finger pressed to the side of his neck.

"Hey! Guy's in cardiac arrest here!" Peg shouted, and then before anyone could stop her she rolled the guy onto his back, tore his shirt open, raised a clenched fist and slammed it down very hard onto the man's exposed breastbone.

Somebody screamed; someone else yelled in protest. A crew of white-coated medical personnel swooped in, grabbed the man by his arms and legs, and swung him onto a gurney, speeding him away into the treatment area.

But as the gurney bumped through the doors an astonishing thing happened: He tried to sit up. He was already blinking. And breathing, Lizzie saw. He was looking around confusedly as if wondering what the hell had just happened to him.

"Whoa," said Lizzie when she reached Peg, who looked stunned.

"Yeah." Peg's shuddery breath came out in a small laugh. "I learned the chest thump in CPR training. Practiced it a hundred times. Never did it for real, though."

Lizzie had learned it, too, and seen it done. She'd just never seen it work until now. "Come on," she told Peg.

Outside, the flames on the hills danced orange against the oncoming night. As if summoned by Emily's words, a sudden wave of fatigue hit Lizzie, energy draining from her as if poured out of a pitcher, replaced by a bleak knowledge.

She'd been looking at this all wrong. When they reached the Blazer she headed for the passenger side and waved Peg the other way.

"Drive," she said.

THIRTEEN

Ten minutes after leaving the emergency room with Peg Wylie at the wheel, Lizzie looked up. They were already on the outskirts of Bearkill; stunned with fatigue, she'd barely noticed the trip.

Also, she'd been thinking. "That was some good work you did back there," she said.

Probably the ER team could have revived the stricken man. But you never knew, and anyway, because of Peg they hadn't needed to.

Peg gazed straight ahead. "Thanks. But all I did was slug the guy, you know? Anyone could've done it."

"Sure. Anyone who knew how. And where to hit him. And had the guts and the upper-body strength to do it."

All of which, Lizzie recalled, Peg had worked very hard to attain. Unlike some guys, she hadn't just fallen out of bed with the physical chops she needed for emergency response work.

Peg shrugged. They drove in silence a little longer. "Anyway, another thing. I'm sorry," Lizzie said quietly at last.

Peg pulled the Blazer to the curb in front of Lizzie's office and turned off the key. "Sorry? About what?"

The air here was thick with the stench of burning. The wooden buildings on Main Street no longer looked charmingly old-fashioned but like fuel for a coming inferno.

"For bullying you," said Lizzie. "Trying to make you tell."

Peg had driven well, with none of the tentativeness Lizzie might've expected from someone whose own car was the equivalent of a hamster wheel with seats. Which, along with the other traits Peg Wylie had shown, meant that she was a no-bullshit woman, not one who held information back for foolish or selfish reasons.

And *that* meant . . . "He kept you down there, didn't he? In his basement. Not with the other girls," Lizzie added, "but before. Alone. Before he had ever kidnapped anyone else."

She was guessing, but it was the only thing that made sense. Whatever Peg was still hiding, it had to be something she thought Tara mustn't ever know—that, if it were known, wouldn't help find the girl.

Otherwise she'd have revealed it by now. "But then you got pregnant and he let you go, maybe because with a baby you'd be too much trouble to have around?" said Lizzie.

Or just not attractive to him once she was pregnant, maybe. Later he'd probably found other ways of getting rid of women, ones that weren't so likely to get him caught.

The backyard of Gemerle's house, Lizzie still felt sure, would yield human bones when it got excavated.

Peg nodded brokenly. "That's it. And if Tara found out . . ."

She didn't need to finish. Tara was the product of rape and incest. Her father was a monster who had preyed upon women, trapped and caged them, brutalizing them in secret for years.

Women including Tara's own mother, who was probably his first victim. No child should have to cope with that knowledge. And you could tell a girl like Tara all you wanted that it didn't matter, that although she was the result of pain and shame, she herself was lovely and good.

Making her believe it, though. That might be a problem.

"He kicked me out," said Peg. "One day after I told him I was pregnant, he just brought me upstairs, dragged me out to the front door, and . . . bam. It was over."

"You went home? I mean, back to the rest of your family?"

Peg nodded. "They all just thought I'd run away. Nobody was look-ing for me, nobody . . ."

She stopped. "It wasn't even all that unusual. I mean, girls like me end up on the streets all the time. When I showed up home again, even pregnant, no one even made that big a deal about it."

"And you never knew about the other girls."

Peg shook her head. "It never occurred to me. I guess it should have—that once I was gone he'd try to find some other, I don't know . . . outlet. For his urges."

She turned to Lizzie. "But I just wanted to put it all behind me. So I did."

And a hell of a job she'd done with the project, too, Lizzie thought. Raising a child alone, keeping it clothed and fed, making a good life for herself and her daughter come hell or high water—against all odds, Peg Wylie had accomplished it, meanwhile taking on one of the hardest volunteer jobs that a civilian could have, as a volunteer fire-fighter in a little town way the hell out here in the hinterlands.

And she'd made it work. "Okay," said Lizzie. "I get it. And you were right. Knowing the whole thing wouldn't have helped me."

It happened. You chased down the wrong lead, it didn't pan out. It went with the territory.

You had to accept it. "But now," Lizzie went on, "we still have to find Tara."

She summarized what they knew: "We think Gemerle grabbed her Tuesday night and buried her in that box up in the fire zone to punish you, because you testified against him."

Peg bit her lip. "Okay. What else?"

"I think Jane Crimmins was here looking for him, wanting to get revenge, maybe, for that girl she took care of, Cam Petry. And when she found him she turned the tables on him, killed Gemerle in the motel and then dumped him in the fire zone. That would've been last night."

If it was Jane Crimmins. Emily Ektari's results still said otherwise. But maybe there'd been a mistake.

Peg caught on fast. "And when she took his body up there, she found Tara? She was the one who dug Tara up and moved her, maybe, sometime last night? So maybe she's still alive?"

Lizzie paused. There was such a thing as too much hope. "I don't know. I don't understand that part yet. But we know Crimmins burned her hands pretty badly doing something recently, and the fires were all over the place up there, so—"

Peg nodded slowly. "So it could be that's what happened. But even if it was, where's Tara now?"

"I don't know that, either." Not far from the original burial site, maybe; moving Tara any great distance, against her will and with people around fighting the fires, would've been problematic.

So the girl really could still be there. Whether she was dead or alive, though, was another question. Through the front window of her office, Lizzie could see Missy Brantwell with her blond head bent over a map as she talked on the phone.

Missy should've been with her family, somewhere safe. But probably she'd come back for some small thing she'd forgotten and gotten caught up in helping someone.

Behind her Trey Washburn stood with Missy's toddler in his arms; together, they looked like a family. Lizzie swallowed a pang of envy, turning from the pretty interior scene to the smoke drifting like fog under the streetlights, yellowish in the gloom.

"I'm sorry about all this," she said. "All that's happened."

The lights in the office went off and the trio inside came out into the street, heads down, squinting in the smoke. With the little boy now clasped in her arms, Missy followed Trey through the murk to his truck and he helped them in; then his headlights flared in the acrid gloom and they were gone.

Peg rested her hands on the Blazer's steering wheel, her face desolate. "I never should have gone to court. If I'd just kept my fool mouth shut, he never would have—"

"Yeah, maybe." *Don't poke a stick at it* was a fine rule for dealing with psychopaths, in Lizzie's experience. But there were exceptions.

This one, for instance. "I knew if I didn't, though," Peg went on, "it would be just a matter of time until it was some other woman's daughters. He'd be after them the same way he went after those new girls, once he was done with me."

She sighed heavily. "But I never thought helping someone else would mean sacrificing my own child."

"No. Of course you didn't. But . . . listen, do you want to tell me the rest of it? I mean," Lizzie said, feeling inadequate, "just so you can. Tell it, I mean, to someone. Anyone at all."

Secrets like Peg's were like acid; they ate through you. If you kept them, they ate right through your soul.

Besides, Lizzie still did need to know all of it, just in case. She might have the luxury of kindness without any ulterior motives, someday.

But not now. Peg spoke softly. "He drugged me, like I told you, and when I woke up I was at his house, in the cellar. I was thirteen, I was naked, and he'd already. . . ."

Lizzie waited, saying nothing. "It went on for two years," Peg said when she could speak again.

"And you didn't tell because your family depended on him."

Peg nodded. "Yes. And because he said he'd kill me if I did." Her next breath came out in a sob.

"Besides, I was so ashamed. I thought it was my fault, what he'd done to me. He *said* so. He told me I *made* him do it. Lizzie, if he's had Tara all this time, what if he—"

Peg got control of herself again. "Anyway. Finally he just . . . kept me. A couple of weeks, then it was a month. He kept promising I could go home. But it never happened until I said I thought there was going to be a baby. And then suddenly I was free."

She took a shaky breath. "So like I said, I went home. Just another knocked-up girl in the neighborhood."

An old pickup truck rattled by in the smoky gloom, its bed loaded with hastily gathered belongings, mattresses and toys.

"So," said Lizzie, "when Tara disappeared you figured it couldn't be him. He was confined, and he wasn't supposed to know you'd testified against him. That's why you thought it was okay to wait, let her come home on her own like she'd done before?"

Peg nodded again. "Uh-huh. And later even if he did have her, you knowing all this wouldn't have done anything to find her."

She took a hitching breath. "If she was alive, it would only shame her. If . . . if she survived."

Lizzie hesitated. Finally: "You're right, it wouldn't have," she repeated. Hell, it wasn't even helping anything now.

Because sometimes the truth set you free. But other times it just hurt. "Well, the good news is that he probably had her but he doesn't anymore. The bad news—"

The bad news was that it looked as if Jane Crimmins did have Tara, or at least that Jane might know where the girl was now.

Lizzie explained this. "And unfortunately," she added, "it's starting to look as if, in her own way, Jane Crimmins might be almost as bad as Henry Gemerle ever was."

"I don't get it," said Dylan half an hour later in Lizzie's office. "You're saying you want to go up to the fire zone again tonight? Like, now?"

"Right," said Lizzie. Minutes after Missy Brantwell switched the lights out and departed, Lizzie had gone in, turned all the lights back on again, and summoned Dylan Hudson and Cody Chevrier to meet her there.

"I don't know," said Chevrier, passing a hand back over his brush-cut silvery hair. "Pretty wild up there. There's hot spots sparking up all over the place."

It was long past midnight, well into the small hours of Friday morning, and the blaze raging in the hills beyond town had crept perilously near; helicopters whap-whapped overhead and tanker trucks rumbled in the distance, trying to get more water to the firefighters still battling to hold off the flames.

"I think Jane might've killed Gemerle in the motel and hauled his body there," she said as the siren atop the firehouse went off again. "And if I'm right there's a chance we might find Tara alive there, too, near where she was buried."

"Because?" Dylan asked. They'd been partners long enough back in Boston to respect each other's wild theories. But what Lizzie was suggesting now meant walking into a firestorm, and even Dylan Hudson wasn't that ballsy.

Not, anyway, without persuasion. "The only reason Jane would have dumped Gemerle there at all is if he told her about the spot," Lizzie said. "About Tara being there, I mean, before Jane killed Gemerle. Otherwise, why would Jane even think of it?"

Lizzie sucked in a breath. "So what I'm saying is that maybe Jane found Tara and moved her somewhere else."

Chevrier made a skeptical face. "So she didn't save her? Didn't bring her home, just stuck her in a different spot?"

"Yeah, I don't get that yet, either," Lizzie admitted. "The why of it all."

Which was a problem, a big one, when it came to getting these guys on board. But Dylan had been thinking.

"The important thing," he told Chevrier, "is that maybe Tara Wylie really is somehow still alive. Out there," he added, "alone, just hoping and praying that somebody cares enough to try one more time."

Lizzie glanced gratefully at him as the sirens sounded again. "Before it really is too late," Dylan finished.

Chevrier's lips pursed doubtfully, but the rest of his face said he was coming around to Lizzie's way of thinking, even if it was against his better judgment. "Peg's back home?"

Lizzie nodded. "I took her there, dropped her off, and told her she needed to stay put in case I need to call her. Or in case Tara shows up."

Cruel, but they couldn't have Peg Wylie getting in the way.

"The last thing we need is her going off half-cocked so that she ends up having to get rescued herself," Lizzie added.

What they needed, actually, was a miracle. But as a pair of boxy white ambulances screamed by outside, their cherry beacons stabbing the night, Lizzie knew they weren't going to get one.

And Chevrier still didn't look completely convinced. "Look," she said, "if it's bad we won't stay. But we can say we tried."

He sighed heavily. "I don't know, Lizzie. If you ask me, the whole idea's just flat-out nuts."

And that did it. "Fine," she snapped. Calling these guys had been a mistake, and wasting any more time trying to convince them was a worse one.

"I'm going. Don't like it, you can fire me when I get back."

"Lizzie," Dylan began, but she put a hand up at him.

"Just don't, okay? I appreciate what you've done so far. Stay here if you're staying, is all. Or get your stuff together."

"Hey." Chevrier spoke mildly. But his posture and expression were anything but. "Aren't you forgetting something?" He took a step toward her.

"What, that you give the orders around here?" Not backing away an inch, she pulled out her badge wallet, slammed it on the desk. None of this was working out. Not the job, not the place or her situation in it, not even the reason she'd come here, which was to find Nicki, about whom there'd been not one solid piece of information. "Well, that's something I can fix right now, too."

"What, you're quitting?" Chevrier demanded in a voice like razor wire. "Things get rough and you jump ship?" He grimaced disappointedly. "Funny, that's not the woman I thought I'd hired. Not the one this fella here told me I'd be getting, either."

His snort was dismissive. "A quitter. And here I thought I'd found the woman for the job, a real stone bitch."

Another thought struck him. "And what about Rascal. Huh? You thought about that?"

She hadn't, she realized, stricken. The dog . . . her building in Boston didn't allow them.

The phone rang. Chevrier thrust a hand past her to answer. "Yeah, I hear you," he said after a few moments. Then: "Where?"

He listened some more, then hung up. "Guys on the fire line say they saw a woman up there a little while ago. Caught sight of her, then they lost her in the dark."

He looked at Lizzie. "Short dark hair. Bandaged hands. That sound familiar?"

"Yes. Yes, it does." Slowly, Lizzie picked up the badge once more, then turned to face the two men.

"So, are you coming with me or not?"

FOURTEEN

utside, Dylan hurried to keep pace with her. "Hey, listen, the Bangor PD got back to me with the autopsy on Aaron DeWilde."

"And?"

The thick, warm air smelled like a house fire, wood and tar-paper, shingles and plastic siding, mingled with the sour stench of steaming embers.

"Kid OD'd," said Dylan.

He shook his head ruefully. "Needle must've fallen out of his arm and rolled under the dumpster, syringe and all."

A disparaging snort escaped her. "Funny, last time I looked a set of works wouldn't roll. Spoon, lighter . . ."

In the street, the last few diehards who'd been sticking it out had begun getting out of Dodge, cars and trucks packed with people, belongings, and pets. One guy had four snowmobiles piled like cord-wood in his pickup bed, a child's tricycle tied to the top.

Dylan shrugged. "Hey, maybe he cooked the heroin back at the place he got it from."

More likely the uniforms had missed the needle the first time around; nobody liked crawling through rotting garbage in the dark.

They piled into Chevrier's vehicle; he knew the way better, and anyway, he insisted on driving. On the dark country highway he sped toward the fire zone, its glow painting clouds that were themselves flickering with lightning.

Lizzie stared out the window. "Where'd they say they'd seen her? The woman with bandaged hands?"

What had smelled like a house fire turned out to be three of them, all burning unattended as stretched-thin crews turned their attention to unlost causes.

"Up the Ridge Road." Chevrier snapped on the lights and siren and hit the gas harder. "Where we found Gemerle."

"You've relayed all the info? About Gemerle's body, the hole in the ground and all, to the team looking for Tara?"

The state and federal people, she meant. "I told them," he confirmed. "They already got Gemerle's body down."

He swerved around a cardboard box stuffed full of clothes that had probably fallen from someone's trailer. "But before they could go back and do a thorough search or even process the scene properly, that whole area was in flames again," he added.

"No one's been there since? Not even looking for Tara?" She fell back against the passenger seat. "Jesus. So all along, you mean we've been the only ones who've—"

"Lizzie, it's an active fire zone," said Dylan. "What're they supposed to do, pull on their asbestos suits?"

"Can it, you two." The Blazer sped up the paved part of the Ridge Road, then hit the dirt section, bouncing over rocks and through deep ruts. Drizzle turned the windshield's thin coating of ash to muddy smears, while thunder boomed overhead.

"Big rain headed this way on radar," Chevrier said, flipping on the windshield washer. "Whether we get it in time to help us, though, or whether it misses us entirely is still anyone's guess."

The gear heaped in Chevrier's rear passenger area left barely enough room for Dylan to hunker back there: a fire extinguisher, some respirator masks and goggles, heavy gloves, and a rugged pair of high leather boots, their laces flopping.

"Hudson, hand up one of those fire blankets," Chevrier said. "Silvery packages, they've got black nylon straps on 'em. Deputy Snow, you put one on, and you too, Hudson. And grab that go-bag that's back there."

Dylan rummaged in the gear heap. "What about you?"

"Each fire blanket's big enough for a couple of people," the sheriff replied. "Probably we won't need 'em at all."

He steered abruptly around an especially murderous-looking rut. "But if we do, remember this was all your idea. We run into trouble looking for this girl, one of you two heroes is gonna save the boss, okay?"

He braked the Blazer to a halt amid the skeletal remains of trees, low ash heaps that had been brush thickets, and a line of black charcoal sticks that were all that remained of fence posts.

As they got out, Dylan's cell phone thweeped. "Yeah. Yeah, I understand," he said, then noticed her watching and looked away.

Avoiding eye contact. Which was weird. Dylan could look you in the eye and make you believe night was day. "But listen, we've got kind of a situation here," he said, then listened some more.

"Okay. Yeah, do that, will you? Not until we get there. Okay, man. Hey, thanks a lot." He thumbed the phone off.

"What?" she demanded. He still wouldn't look at her.

"Bangor PD's got an unidentified body. One of those found-in-a-wooded-area deals."

"And?" Her heart thumped. "Dylan, what *kind* of a—"

Chevrier led them toward a cleared patch where a burn barrel brimming with fast-food wrappers and drink cups stood surrounded by tire tracks in the dust, a staging area for the fire crews.

Dylan met her gaze finally. "Lizzie, it's a little girl. Blond hair, blue eyes . . . and there are no current missing persons reports for a child like that. Not anywhere in New England."

She wondered if not being surprised by that meant she was getting too calloused, even for a cop. But she knew what he meant; that the dead girl might be Nicki, her murdered sister's lost child. The one she'd been searching for.

The one she'd given up her whole life for. Dylan took a deep breath, let it out. "Lizzie, when we get done with this here, they want you to come and look. Because . . ."

"Yeah," she heard herself say dully. "Yeah, I understand."

"Okay, both of you, listen." Chevrier stood backlit by the Blazer's headlights. "We walk from here."

The rough, unpaved road had deteriorated with the passage of volunteers and fire vehicles; there was no point trying to drive on. Besides, this kind of search needed boots on the ground.

"We'll start by the hole where we think the girl was buried," he said. "From there, it's half a mile to the top of the hill."

Lightning flashed so close by that they could hear its deadly crackle. The glare turned the burnt, ruined landscape to a black-and-white disaster scene, as barren looking as the moon.

Then came the thunderclap, so huge it seemed to suck all the air out of the Lizzie's lungs. Chevrier's face set itself into a bleak expression as they started off.

But after a few minutes: "I've shot deer back here," he said.

Lizzie stepped into another rut, her ankle turning painfully. She bit back a yelp and trudged on, strafing the burnt grass and low bushes with her flashlight but seeing nothing.

"Yeah?" Dylan asked interestedly. "What, with a rifle?"

"Nope. Bow hunting." Chevrier held a flashlight, too, and she noticed that the safety strap on his duty weapon was unfastened.

"Birds, I'll use a shotgun." They reached the place where the road ran out. Ahead, charred trees steamed in the mist.

Chevrier had called in their location before leaving the Blazer, a precaution she'd thought was overkill at the time, but now she was glad for it.

"But for the big game I figure I should give the animal a sporting chance," Chevrier said.

Then he stopped. "Okay, here's the hole." The coffinlike box they'd seen earlier had been reduced to blackened bits; as Dylan had said, sometime on Thursday the fire had been through here.

"'Course," Chevrier said, moving on, "with bow hunting, you might have to track the animal a way after you hit it, if you miss your kill shot."

It was why he was so familiar with this land, she realized: He'd walked it. The hunting chatter was his attempt to put her and Dylan at ease in what he knew was a foreign environment to them.

I just hope we're not the ones being hunted now, she thought suddenly, and where had that idea come from? The prickling on the back of her neck was her imagination, surely.

"Rifle shot'll bring 'em down by the shock of its impact," Chevrier mused aloud, "but your arrow might not. Animal's got to bleed out before it falls and while it does, it's running."

He stopped again, aiming the flashlight around. Behind them and downhill, the long, pale cones of the Blazer's headlights stabbed the night. The smoke-billows drifting on the uneven ground were like ghosts, creeping furtively along.

Dylan stopped suddenly. "You hear that?"

They stood silent. Below in the distance a huge fire still burned, flames licking toward the sky.

"I didn't hear anything," said Lizzie finally.

But Chevrier had already turned away to follow his flashlight toward something she couldn't see.

"I did," Dylan insisted stubbornly. "It sounded like . . ."

A stick snapped, and then another. She turned toward where Chevrier had been heading just as he vanished among some charred birch saplings, their trunks falling to ash as he passed.

She hurried to follow. The crackling from somewhere out ahead was probably just him stepping on burnt stuff, she told herself.

Probably. Dylan's voice made her jump. "Somebody's out here."

"Uh-huh." There were other explanations, though: burnt-crisp branches whickering, or animals disturbed by the fire, trying to find some safe place to rest.

An explosion of sparks lit the night, then a flash. Finally came the dull boom that meant a propane tank had gone off like a bomb somewhere.

"Pretty close to town," Dylan observed. In the darkness they could just make out the lights of Bearkill, gauzy in the smoke. No fire showed there yet.

"Dylan . . ." The mental picture of a small body in the Bangor morgue kept assailing her.

He understood. "I don't know, Lizzie. It might be Nicki. But then again it might not."

"Hey!" Chevrier called out of the darkness, and when they found him again they fell into line behind him; he at least seemed to have some idea of where they were going.

They walked through the remains of scrub trees, now puddles of dust. Burnt thickets spread out flat, whitish gray. Then:

"Here." Chevrier's voice came from beyond a miraculously un-torched stand of undergrowth. In the distance, explosions went off like firecrackers popping, but bigger, as they pushed through the brambles to where he stood.

"This way," said Chevrier. "There's a shed up ahead, as long as we're here we'd better look. But then it's time to leave."

The rank air thickened, each breath full of a gritty stench. Either the wind had turned or the fire was getting too close for comfort again.

The latter, it turned out; Chevrier cursed as yellow flames jumped up in front of him, snap-crackling suddenly.

"Damn," said Dylan, "let's just cut this short, okay? This is getting way too—"

A sound sent her hand to her duty weapon—*damn, I should've brought both guns*—before she knew what she'd heard. But in the same instant something slammed into her head; her vision blurred, her knees weakened, and she went down.

Then came the hard, concussive crack of a gunshot. When her sight cleared, a figure loomed over her. She struggled to get up but before she could, the figure aimed a gun at her.

Her own gun. She grabbed at her duty holster, its safety strap un-snapped in imitation of Chevrier, and found it empty.

"Lie down." The butt of another weapon stuck out from their at-tacker's waistband. The figure's sooty clothes and ash-smeared face nearly obscured her identity. "Do it now."

Nearly but not quite. Jane Crimmins's hands were bandaged, only her fingers poking through the white gauze wrappings. But the injury didn't seem to be slowing her down much.

"Lie down," she repeated, waving the gun briefly at Dylan and Chevrier, on his knees in the ash-strewn dust, before targeting Lizzie again.

"That's right," Jane said. The rock she'd hit Lizzie with lay by her feet, blood-smeared.

"Now, don't any of you move a goddamn inch."

Tell us where she is, Jane. Just tell us, and we can sort everything else out later."

But the woman who'd ambushed them had no intention of telling anyone anything. Lizzie caught Dylan's eye.

His answering glance confirmed her own assessment. They'd seen that same expression on other people: desperate, deranged. This woman was ready to fire the weapon she held.

Ready and able. They knelt, then lay facedown. "Now put your hands up behind you where I can get at them," Jane said.

She looped some kind of plastic material around Lizzie's wrists and slip-knotted it; a plastic bag, maybe, Lizzie thought.

Whatever. It was an effective restraint. Then Jane seized the rest of the guns and phones. "All right, on your feet again."

Jane waved her weapon, lit by the glow of Chevrier's fallen flashlight. She'd tossed the rest of the guns out into the night along with the comm gear; at her urging, Dylan and Lizzie sat up, then made it to their knees and onto their feet.

Only Chevrier stayed prone, and after a moment Lizzie saw the dark stain spreading on his jacket. "He's hit."

She moved toward him but stopped short when Jane jerked the gun at her. "Get him up," Jane said.

She angled her head at Chevrier. "And turn off that damn flashlight of his."

Dylan half turned with a cooperative smile. "You bet, just get these ties off my wrists, and . . ."

"Yeah, right, because I'm so stupid. Stomp on it if you have to, but get over there and put that light out or I'll blow this bitch's head right off her . . ."

"What's this all about, Jane?" Lizzie crouched and clumsily kneed Chevrier's flashlight switch to the off position, hoping he would have sense enough to go on playing dead.

The trouble was, she wasn't sure he was playing. "Don't ask questions," Jane snarled as the wind shifted, the ash drifting out of the sky changing from feathery fragments to—

Hot. Those ashes are . . .

They were embers blowing from the wildfire now burning very nearby. Pinpricks of heat peppered Lizzie's neck; bright flames munched the underbrush only a few yards away.

She glanced at Dylan again as fire's hot breath gusted in her face. "Is Tara still alive?"

A kick to the thigh rewarded her question; she stumbled and nearly fell. But it was worth it; while Jane focused on Lizzie, Dylan crouched swiftly, managing to snatch something up in his fingers even with his hands still tied behind him.

Whatever it was, he'd been lying atop it to hide it, Lizzie realized as a nearby cedar tree went up with a dazzling whoosh.

Lizzie hesitated. "What about him?" Chevrier lay motionless.

"Leave him." Down on the main road, the whirl of a dashboard beacon mingled confusingly with the fire's glow.

That backup call Chevrier had made, Lizzie realized. She bent to Chevrier. A cold touch of metal on her neck froze her.

"Alive? Or is he . . . ?"

"No. He's dead," Lizzie said flatly. A rush of fury fueled her sudden spring upward, her weight automatically shifting onto her left foot and her right kicking back hard.

She spun to deliver a head-butt but Jane danced away. Dylan lunged but she avoided him too, and she had that damn gun.

Soon this whole area would be ablaze, all the remaining unburnt fuel fully primed by heat to go up in another, even more annihilating wave of flames. And the squad's headlights were still only halfway up the ridge.

Jane's gun thrust hard into Lizzie's ribs. Another cedar tree flamed up like a torch and for an instant it seemed that all the oxygen had been sucked out of the world; then came the new rush of heat.

"Walk," ordered Jane. "Or stay here if you want." She jammed the gun into Lizzie's side again. "*Is* that what you want?"

But Lizzie couldn't answer. A sharp, unexpected pain knocked the breath out of her suddenly. The squad car topped the hill, the driver raking the area with his vehicle's spotlight but unable to see the Blazer from his position.

Slowly, the car turned. A trickle of panic went through Lizzie as it moved away. She sucked in a breath. With the air came another thrilling jolt of pain, as if that last hard shove with the gun had cracked a rib.

"Like I said, you can stay," Jane repeated unpleasantly. "But I'll have to shoot you first."

"Come on, Lizzie," said Dylan resignedly, and if she hadn't known him so well she'd have thought he'd given up.

But Dylan never gave up, and now she glimpsed what was hidden behind his back. The gun stabbed Lizzie's ribs again, and this time through the agony she could feel the tension in Jane's hand, the way just one extra twitch would jerk the trigger through its pressure point, discharging the weapon.

"Now *walk*." Another shove, bringing with it another crashing thunderbolt of pain, nearly dropped Lizzie to her knees.

"Don't you get any dumb ideas, either," Jane added to Dylan. "You rush me, I'll shoot her. Get it?"

Dylan nodded slowly as the flames cavorted nearer, sucking in oxygen, exhaling fiery death. The cop car that Lizzie had set her hopes on was now stopped entirely, maybe while the driver called in for help on the location.

No point, Lizzie decided, in trying to yell to the cop, even if she could draw enough breath to do it. Just getting any air in at all was a struggle.

Pierced my lung, she realized with dawning horror, *a broken rib has a sharp end on it and when she jabbed me—*

And when a lung got pierced, it didn't heal up by itself. It collapsed, and if you didn't get quick medical help . . . But with that gun suddenly in her side again, she had no options left.

"Come on, Lizzie," said Dylan again. "We'd better just do as she says."

In the glow of the relentlessly approaching flames, his gaze met hers. It was a look she'd seen before, perhaps over a couple of wineglasses late at night.

Or in her bed. And he'd been lying then, too. Only this time it wasn't Lizzie that he was lying to.

The thought got Lizzie moving, her breath coming in short, agonized gulps. The squad car reversed and slowly turned back toward them.

"Hurry up," Jane ordered. They reached a narrow trail, well used and seemingly without tripping hazards.

Still, almost at once Dylan stumbled.

Jane spun toward him. "I'll shoot her, I swear—"

She would, too. It was in Jane's voice, strained nearly to the breaking point. No matter that a gunshot would alert that cop down there; Jane wasn't making clear decisions now, only reacting to her own distress.

As Lizzie thought this, the emergency flare that Dylan had been clutching behind his back—from the go-bag that Chevrier had told Dylan to take, Lizzie recalled suddenly—erupted with a yellow-white sizzle of brilliance. At once the distant squad car's lights glared on, static from its radio crackling through the night. *"All units . . ."*

"Bastard," Jane snarled, letting go of Lizzie long enough to get off a single shot.

Dylan's low grunt of pain said he'd been hit; in the flare's Day-Glo brightness—*Careful, you'll start a forest fire,* Lizzie thought, woozy and in terror—he staggered and fell.

No! she thought, not realizing she'd sobbed it aloud until the gun savaged her ribs again. She felt a sharp pain and a terrifying popping sensation, and her shortness of breath got worse.

Much worse. "I can't," she managed as the brightness flaring around her faded blessedly to black, velvety and welcoming . . .

She felt herself being hauled to her feet.

Around her the world burst into flame.

———

"What do you want?" Lizzie gasped it out. Only a few minutes had gone by since Jane Crimmins had appeared out of the darkness.

Now at Jane's grim order Lizzie trudged forward, her eyes streaming with smoke, her chest heaving as she sucked in gulps of air that seemed suddenly to be in desperately short supply.

The trail curved sharply between cedar trees and up a steep slope. Jane switched on a flashlight she'd taken from Dylan, which gave Lizzie hope until she realized the beam was weakening, so dim that it wouldn't be spotted through the smoke from the blazes now blowing up patchily all around them.

"Stop," Jane uttered flatly. The flashlight's yellowish beam picked out the rough boards of a small shed with a slanted roof and a dark, rectangular door opening. A few feet in front of it stood an old claw-footed bathtub, the water in it reflecting the orange-tinted sky.

At Jane's gesture Lizzie ducked through the shed's doorway. The interior smelled of hay and of something less pleasant.

"Why?" She dropped to the wooden floor, thickly covered with straw. "What's this all about?"

Her back found the shed's rough wall and she sighed in relief until it occurred to her what the other smell was: fear-sweat, not her own. She peered into the shed's far corners.

In one of them lay Tara Wylie, her eyes wide with terror in the reflected glow of Jane Crimmins's flashlight. Lizzie crept toward the girl. "Hey."

The girl shrank back. Her thin wrists were bound by multiple wrappings of twine tethered to an old iron loop driven into the wooden floor. Her lips were bloody and swollen, the skin on the backs of her hands torn and purple with bruises. By the look of it, she'd tried pulling her wrists out of their restraints and when that hadn't worked she'd tried chewing through the twine.

But she hadn't been able to do either; now her wavering gaze lit briefly on Lizzie before her eyes drifted shut.

"What do you want?" Lizzie asked again. But Jane didn't reply as beyond the shed's low opening the night filled with smoke and flame. Then Lizzie saw what else was happening out there:

The fire's sudden resurgence had apparently summoned fresh emergency crews, just now arriving; lights flared and faded in the billows of steam rising from half-doused blazes. Down on the main road a red flashing beacon sped away, its siren a thin whine. *Dylan* . . . Lizzie yanked her thoughts back with an effort of will as fiery light seeped threateningly between the boards at the rear of the structure, outlining the girl's shape.

"Hot," Tara moaned fretfully.

Lizzie struggled up, then jumped forward at a sharp stabbing pain in her arm, followed by a trickle of blood.

Interesting, she thought, then leaned back again cautiously, edging her bound wrists up toward where the sharp thing had been: broken glass, perhaps, or the tip of a nail poking through one of the old boards.

Lit by the glow of the fires creeping nearer, Jane's eyes were pools of misery hollowed by rage. Lizzie stretched on tiptoe, ignoring the jolt of pain it cost her.

Her rib's broken end was probably raking through some new, even more vital bit of tissue inside her. But she had to keep Jane talking, keep her preoccupied. *Don't let her see* . . .

"Well," Lizzie managed, tasting blood and shoving aside the new jolt of fright it caused, "if I'm going to die here . . ."

A cough, deep and agonizing, cut her words off; she spat and went on. "I'd like to know why," she finished.

"Oh, you would, huh?" Jane laughed unpleasantly, sounding as if what she really wanted to do was weep. But the gun in her hand was steady.

She shook her head as if in regret. "Well, if you must know, it's because of a girl named Cam and a creep named Henry Gemerle."

She began to weep quietly. "I thought she got free, but Cam was never really free."

"I see," said Lizzie, not seeing at all. But that wasn't the point.

The point was keeping Jane Crimmins distracted. "That must have been disappointing. Where's Cam now?"

As she spoke, Lizzie lifted her bound wrists up behind her yet again, hooking the plastic bags tied around them over the nail's sharp end. Finally the nail end, or whatever it was, caught on the plastic and tore it . . . but only a little.

Not enough. "She never came back to me! It was always *him,*" Jane sobbed. "Even after he took her baby away from her. She still forgave him. But she never forgave *me.*"

Fifty yards distant, a flaming tree crashed to the earth in an explosion of fire.

"She chose him," Jane said bitterly, "not me. Right up until the end, and then . . ."

Lizzie stopped working her bound wrists against the nail. "Oh," she said, understanding. Not all the details, maybe, but the reason; the heart of the matter.

"You loved her. And she betrayed you. Is that it?"

Jane nodded mutely. "All she really wanted was to get back to him. She just used me. But—"

She stopped, biting her lip anxiously. But in the end she couldn't resist saying it aloud:

"But at the end, she knew I was the one who cared about her. The only one."

"The end?" Lizzie inquired, more to keep Jane talking than anything else. After all, the New Haven apartment had been a slaughterhouse according to the cops reporting from there; Cam's body would no doubt be found sooner or later.

She jerked her wrists upward again, more blood running warmly over her hand. She hoped it was washing the nail wounds clean, at least. Tetanus, blood poisoning . . . the list of stuff you could get from a rusty nail was long and terrifying. But none was as bad as burning to death, and now the flames outside leapt eagerly, ever nearer.

"Never mind about Cam." Jane evaded Lizzie's question. "Now all I've got to do is get away from here."

Lizzie hooked the plastic-bag wrist restraint over the nail again and it held there this time. "So how will you do that?" she asked, very short of breath again suddenly.

But before Jane could answer a cedar torch outside ignited with a vicious roar. A shred of the plastic around Lizzie's wrists gave way just as a shower of orange sparks erupted only a few feet from the shed's low doorway.

"I'm waiting until I know the fire will burn everything," Jane said as the roar faded to a steady crackle. "You, both your buddies down there, this place . . ."

So there'd be no evidence, Lizzie figured, an assumption she thought was incorrect despite the fire's fury. It took a lot to incinerate teeth, for instance. And it seemed the emergency crews might've found Dylan; she prayed they had.

But despite her struggles the plastic around her wrists hung on stubbornly. And now not only were the bindings that held her refusing to tear any farther, they were stuck on that damn nail.

Around her, the air thickened like poisoned syrup. Pain-sweat prickled her armpits, blackness creeping at the edges of her vision. She couldn't even tell if Tara was still breathing.

And any minute now I won't be, either. Yanking against the nail only rocketed another thrilling jolt of torment through her, so intense this time she felt her eyes roll back for an instant.

"So you killed Gemerle," she gritted out, sawing desperately back and forth with no result. "You got him out, got him to come here, somehow."

The wind swept the flames sideways, whipping them up for a final assault. "And then you killed him?"

As she'd hoped, Jane couldn't resist. "Of course I did," she declared proudly. "Someone had to," she added, and seemed about to go on.

But Lizzie wasn't listening anymore, all thought suddenly dissolved in a vat of pain. One whole side of her chest felt like an animal was in there, chewing its way out, as she went on sawing desperately at the ties still restraining her.

A wind gust sucked the smoke from the shed briefly. In the blessedly clear interval she breathed shallowly through her own blood, the salt taste sickening her. Then:

"What's that?" Jane demanded, and stepped outside just as Lizzie's wrist wraps gave way abruptly, one last ferocious yank bringing on a jackhammer of agony.

Jane's dark shape loomed in the doorway, silhouetted by fire, as Lizzie hit the floor hard and rolled away from the acrid smoke gushing in at the shed's opposite corner. The blaze *screamed* . . . but it wasn't the fire this time.

It was a voice. *"Tara!"* someone screamed hoarsely, the sound as wildly ragged as the fire's crazed howl. *"Tara, are you here?"*

Lizzie bent swiftly to the unconscious girl as the inferno shrieked. But the knots in the twine on Tara's arms were pulled rock-hard by her earlier struggles.

"Tara!" The scream came again as Jane turned, fully exposed in the doorway, her weapon raised and her face flat with sudden, unwelcome knowledge: that someone really was out there.

She must still have been realizing it when in the next moment a sharp pop sounded from outside and a chunk the size of a silver dollar flew out of her head, sailing through the smoky gloom in an explosion of bright-red blood.

"Tara?" Scrambling over Jane's body, Peg Wylie half fell into the shed, her face soot-smeared and her yellow hair a fire-crazed frizzle. She fell weeping by her daughter's unconscious body.

A slough of burnt skin sagged from her jaw, and her eyebrows were gone. But she'd found her lost child and the tears streaming down her face weren't from the searing smoke.

"Oh, honey," she breathed. "Mommy's here now, it's okay . . ."

But it wasn't. Flames munched one corner of the shed and an ominous creaking sounded from above. The roof's far end sagged abruptly, releasing a sparkling shower of glowing embers.

"Tara," Peg cried brokenly, trying to lift the girl. But the strands of twine that bound Tara's arms, still tied to a ringed iron spike set into the floor, were too short to stretch any more.

When Peg tried again, though, a bit of the floor moved, too. Lizzie shoved Peg aside, gritting her teeth against the misery of each labored breath.

"Try once more," she gasped while her fingers scrabbled on the splintery wood for what must be there: a trapdoor.

Because why else would the floor move, why would a shed like this even have a wooden floor, unless—

Finally she found the edge, hooked her fingertips onto it, and pried upward. As the trapdoor rose at last, dank air gushed up from below like a blessing, smelling of cool earth.

"Go," she told Peg just as the roof overhead sagged again with a sharp, splintering *crack!*

Peg dropped her legs through the opening, shimmied down the rest of the way, and held her arms up for Tara. "You've got to cut that twine somehow, please!" she cried. "Hurry . . ."

Glancing around wildly, Lizzie saw no tools at all. And Jane had taken the jackknife she always carried from her duty belt. But then she spied her own weapon fallen beside Jane's body. And it was a crazy idea but maybe, just maybe, it would work.

Seizing the weapon she laid the barrel end at an angle against the twine, now stretched taut across the floor. Then she let her finger tighten on the trigger, felt the firing mechanism slip past the pressure point until . . .

The weapon's report was like a bomb going off, deafening her. But the rope's strands parted and Lizzie half dragged, half rolled Tara down through the trapdoor into her mother's arms.

Then as the roof dropped warningly with an agonized groan of burnt timbers, Lizzie looked back a last time at Jane Crimmins's motionless body. Sparks flared in her hair and a tide of dark blood spread around her.

"Hurry," Peg cried again from below.

FIFTEEN

Above them in the burning shed, a row of beams let go with a sound like big bones snapping. Lizzie rushed to the open trapdoor Peg held up for her.

A rafter slammed down. A splinter daggered her arm. "Come *on*," Peg urged as a wall ignited with a *whoosh*.

Fire poured through the roof as Lizzie slung her legs hastily down into the hole and fell through it. The trapdoor dropped shut with a dull, final-sounding *thud*. Hitting the floor, she felt her teeth click together and her head snap forward with the impact.

"Ugh." The agony in her chest was nauseating. She managed to haul herself up on her elbow, opening her eyes just as Peg's flashlight snapped on.

Then as she turned her head woozily she came suddenly face-to-face with the other occupant of the crawl space:

Short, dark hair, wide-open eyes, mouth sagging sideways in a life-less yawn . . .

"Gah." Lizzie scrambled back. Dead bodies were one thing . . .

"Who's that?" Peg Wylie stared.

. . . but *sudden* dead bodies were something else again.

"I'm not sure. But I'm guessing it's Cam Petry." From above came a cascading crash: the rest of the roof falling in, Lizzie thought. Which meant . . .

"You know what, though?" she said as a new wave of dizziness swirled through her. "Never mind who that is. We've got—"

Other things to worry about, she'd meant to say, but instead she passed out. When she came to again, Peg was bent over a blue plastic jerrican in the cellar's corner.

"What are you doing?" Lizzie whispered, the words coming out in little gusts on the tiny sips of air she could get.

"Opening up the stored water." Peg had pushed the dead body into a far corner, laid burlap sacks over its face. Tara lay propped against the opposite wall.

Lizzie licked her parched lips. "I didn't know you had a gun." She rose up on one elbow, felt a gritty crunch of something grating deep inside her, and coughed up a wad of blood.

"There's a lot you don't know about me," said Peg. "But I've been waiting a long time for Henry to show up. Worrying, being afraid. So I took a few lessons. Gun safety and target shooting at the VFW range."

The .22 pistol stuck out of her jeans pocket. "I never really believed I'd shoot anyone, though. Until I did."

"Yeah. I felt that way the first time, too." Lizzie squinted around, trying not to think about the pain in her chest and her shortness of breath. "What is this place, anyway?"

Above them, the shed went on thudding and shuddering as the rampaging fire devoured it like a ravenous beast that howled and stomped as it ate.

"Shepherd's hut," Peg said. "That bathtub outside is a trough. Hauled water for the animals, someone got it up here in a pickup truck. This crawl space is to stash supplies in, animal feed and supplies for people, too, so no wild critters can get at it."

A metal cup hung from the jerrican. Peg unscrewed the can's spout, removed a plastic plug from it, then reattached the spout and poured liquid into the cup.

"Up here in Maine, if a blizzard blows in and catches you by surprise you still have to take care of your livestock. You need shelters like this one."

She brought the cup to Tara's side, lifted the girl's head tenderly, and dribbled a little water onto her lips.

"That's probably why it hasn't burned," she went on calmly, "because sheep graze right down to the ground around these things, eat the roots and everything."

She pushed the moisture into Tara's mouth with a finger. "Wrecks the grass, that's why cattlemen and sheep people always butt heads. Makes a kind of natural firebreak, though."

She carried some water to Lizzie. "But now stuff is blowing, the fire doesn't need tinder on the ground to spread. Sparks fly through the air, and—"

Something large fell somewhere above. "Anyway, in bad weather the shepherd might have to hole up here awhile," Peg said. "Get the animals under cover, then come down here and wait it out. So that's what the supplies are for."

She put the cup to Lizzie's lips. "Drink if you can."

The water tasted like blood; Lizzie repressed a gag while above the fire bellowed, crackling and snapping. At the time, coming down here had seemed like the right move.

The only one, in fact. But now they were trapped. A glowing crumb fell from between the floorboards over their heads, blazed for an instant, and went out.

Another bright invader fell. Struggling up, Lizzie got her feet underneath her. "Take my jacket off me."

Peg looked disapproving. "You should keep still. You'll lose a lot less blood if you'll just—"

"Get over here and get this jacket off. There's a backpack underneath it, with a fire blanket in it."

More embers sifted down, and the crackling sound they'd been hearing all along was much louder suddenly.

"Hurry." The shed's floorboards were ablaze. Lizzie's knees sagged as Peg hauled the jacket off her shoulders; swaying, she spat another mess of dark red.

"Sorry," she said, "but I think I'm—"

Bleeding. Suffocating. Dying. Cold fright pierced her.

Peg bent and draped one of Lizzie's arms over her shoulder. The next moments were a blur of agony as Peg straightened with a sudden surge Lizzie recognized from her gym-rat days in Boston.

When the anguish cleared she was resting against the packed-earth wall. Peg pulled the fire blanket, like a gigantic sleeping bag made of shiny, silvery stuff, from its pouch.

"How come they issued you a big one?" Peg yanked the handles on the tightly folded item.

"Didn't. Got it from Chevrier." Panic hit her as her air-hunger worsened.

No comment from Peg as she maneuvered the bag open, wrapped one side around Tara, then pulled it all over the three of them.

Suddenly they were in the dark. Lizzie felt the cool earthen wall through her hair. "We forgot the flashlight."

"No we didn't." Peg's voice seemed to come from a distance. "I don't want the batteries in here with us if it gets hot."

Really hot, she meant. Battery-exploding hot. Lizzie nodded, not having the heart to comment on this possibility.

Above them all hell was breaking loose; she pressed her face into the cool earthen wall, letting it draw the heat that seemed to be boiling out of her skin.

"How'd you find us, anyway?" She felt Peg shrug beside her.

"Scanner. I've got one, remember? I heard the dispatch call to send someone out here. Just cops at first, not fire equipment. And when I heard it I had to come, in case . . ."

"Sure," Lizzie said.

Then another bad thought hit her. "Peg, once the fire gets down here why won't it suck all the air out of the blanket?"

Peg shrugged again. "I don't know, maybe it will. I've never been in a situation like this before."

Lizzie closed her eyes tiredly. "Yeah, me neither."

Then without warning the fire-tent material was very hot. The gaggingly sweet smell, she knew suddenly, was the skin of her own forearm cooking where it touched the tent.

The air thickened further; she choked, then spat out a large volume of what she realized must be blood. A wave of nothingness went through her, a helpless feeling of everything flowing, of it all just . . .

Going away. Her life jumped up before her in bright freeze-frames, like flash cards: *Who's this? Where's that?*

She knew the answers and then didn't, tried to cry out and couldn't, the breath stopped in her throat, torn raw by her own screams, and her ears full of Peg's shouts.

The fire tent disappeared, and Tara and Peg, too. Every voice Lizzie had ever heard was all at once in her head and gone.

Then, though she had never believed—*never could have*—the angels came, lifting her, and she felt the slow, deliberate beat of their heavy wings as they carried her.

Carried her away.

*B*eat. Beat. Beat.

That's not right. That's not what . . .

"How are the others?" someone said. *Someone . . .*

She lay on her back, white light all around, shining from above so brightly that it penetrated her closed eyelids.

Beat . . . beat . . .

"—okay. Not like this one, anyway. I'd have triaged her to Boston, but she's nowhere near stable enough for the trip."

Something heavy pinned her. Heavy and cold, like a concrete block weighing down her rib cage.

I have a rib cage. How odd. And that rhythmic sound was not the beating of rough wings at all, was it? But instead—

Beat. Beat. A heart monitor. She was in a hospital, and the voices she heard belonged to . . .

She opened her eyes, forcing apart her lashes, which were sticky with something jelly-like. *Chevrier . . .*

The stocky, silver-haired sheriff sat in a wheelchair with an IV pole attached, the needle taped to the back of his big hand running something into his vein. He wore a blue cotton hospital gown and a white woven hospital blanket was draped around his broad shoulders like a shawl.

"She going to be okay?" he asked.

There was a heavily padded bandage around the sheriff's left shoulder and his rugged face looked sunburnt, irregular patches of his short hair heat-frizzled and one of his eyebrows taped.

But he was alive. "Well, is she?" he demanded.

She peered sideways, not raising her head since doing so felt approximately as possible as lifting a ten-story building using only her pinkie finger. Clear fluid dripped from an IV bag on one side; dark-red liquid flowed from a plastic pouch on the other.

"I think so," Emily Ektari replied judiciously. "Another few minutes, different story. But she never lost her blood pressure entirely. Good thing that helicopter showed up when it did."

Fabulous, Lizzie thought with an irreverence she realized was probably inappropriate for the seriousness of her situation.

On the other hand, she was almost surely stuffed with very strong painkillers so she should cut herself a little slack, she thought, repressing a giggle.

Then the first voice spoke again, hoarse sounding as if its owner had been shouting, and this time she recognized it. *Dylan . . .*

The memory flapped up out of a nightmare: first the shots fired, then Dylan grunting with pain, falling.

But now she recalled the new body armor he'd told her he was trying, with the space-age nanoparticles and the . . .

Ouch. Thinking made her head hurt. Also, not thinking. Then as she moved her neck slightly to try to ease the pain slamming through her skull with every heartbeat, she glimpsed the thick plastic tube sticking from between her ribs, running down to a—

Nope. Not gonna look. But then she did look, curiosity overwhelming a lurch of nausea at the sight of her own blood bubbling into some kind of collecting system hanging off the bottom bed rail.

"Fortunately the broken bone end that pierced her lung also stuck in it like a plug," said Emily Ektari. "If it had dislodged before we got her to the OR, she'd have—"

But the rest was way more information than even Lizzie's curiosity needed. Fortunately, Emily's beeper went off and she hurried away.

"All right," said Chevrier when she had gone. "I'm getting out of here right now, one night in this joint is plenty."

A night? I've been here a whole—

"Hudson, I want to see you this afternoon in my office," Chevrier went on. "I still don't know what the hell all that was about, and you're going to—"

"Forget it." Dylan sounded defiant. "You know as well as I do what happened. Those two New Haven women had some kind of a wacko revenge plot going, and it went even more haywire than it was when they first came up with it."

How's he know that? she wondered. The scrape of a metal chair being pulled up to Lizzie's bed was followed by his next comment.

"And I'm staying right here until further notice, so if you want to know more," Dylan added to Chevrier, "you can just put the footrests up on that wheelchair of yours . . ."

A figure in a blue scrub suit appeared by the bed. Lizzie glimpsed a syringe of something being shot into her IV. Almost at once her pain eased, then floated away.

The beep of her heart rate slowed; she felt her neck muscles relax. Even the tube in her side no longer troubled her—or at any rate not much.

And I'm not afraid. It was as if a sharp metal clamp around her heart had been removed.

Emily Ektari approached Lizzie's bed again, eyeing Lizzie's monitors judiciously.

"So what was the story with the dead woman from the shack?" Chevrier asked the ER physician.

"The medical examiner says she'd had big-time head surgery within the past couple of months," Emily replied. "They put a shunt in her brain. Among other things, it was supposed to drain excess fluid."

Emily adjusted Lizzie's IV, then made a note on a clipboard. "Then sometime within the past few days, she had another injury that started a slow brain bleed."

She laid the clipboard down. "The shunt drained the blood for a while, but it wasn't meant for that, so it clotted off. And when it did—"

She snapped her fingers softly. "Lights out."

Dylan nodded as if this was no more than he'd been expecting to hear. "Our girl Jane knew how to do people in, all right."

"Bunch of damn goofballs." Chevrier sounded fed up, as if he might just spin around and wheel right on out of there.

Wish I could. Lizzie opened her eyes but the funhouse effect this brought on made her close them again, dizzily. She tried reaching for Dylan's hand, but didn't seem to have one of her own to do it with, her body dissolved somehow to a vaporous substance that was blessedly pain-free. But she could still hear.

"How'd Gemerle get hold of a box and shovel, anyway?" Chevrier wondered aloud.

"Forest service," Dylan replied. "The box had had a dozen shovels crated up in it." His hand found Lizzie's and gripped it.

"I'll say one thing about Jane, though," he added. "She may be nutty but she's got nine lives."

Say what? Lizzie thought, fully alert suddenly.

She'd been floating along on the two men's conversation, happy as a little clam on a tide of the IV morphine or whatever it was that they'd given her. But now the blissful no-worries effect of the drug faded away fast.

". . . alive," said Dylan. "I got to talk to her when she first came into the hospital, before they started working on her. She'd lost a big chunk of her scalp and bled like hell, but she came to. Rolled out of that shed and into the water trough outside just in time."

At his words, another sharp stab of anxiety pierced Lizzie's opiate cocoon.

"Saved herself," Dylan said. "But she's not going anywhere." His head jerked toward a stretcher just now rolling by the foot of Lizzie's bed. "Not under her own power, anyway."

Strapped to the stretcher by thick leather restraints, the figure was near unrecognizable with its bandage-swathed head and thickly gauze-wrapped arms, its face heavily painted with white ointment and scalp mottled with patchy burnt areas.

But I'd know her anywhere . . . They'd have wanted her medically stable before the cops took her into custody, of course; that was why Jane Crimmins was still here.

"Hey," Dylan said, frowning abruptly.

Following his gaze, she blinked in amazement at how much blood she'd just suddenly produced. Then came shouts, hurrying nurses, and Emily Ektari's dark eyes peering from behind a hastily donned surgical mask.

Finally came a feeling of speeding along way too fast, as her injured body—*I have a body,* she thought wonderingly—was rolled out of the treatment cubicle.

"Prep the OR stat," someone said.

Seated outside the eye clinic, Tara watched the stretcher rolling by with eyes that still felt raw and scratchy. Her throat hurt, too, from screaming to get out of the box she'd been buried in, and from crying pretty much nonstop since she'd been rescued.

"That's her, isn't it?" she murmured. "She's the one who was with me in the shed when you came and saved me?"

She felt her mother's arm tighten around her. "Yes. But it wasn't only me. We did it together, all three of us."

She squeezed Tara's arm again. "You by hanging in there and never giving up, me by being prepared . . ."

Pushed by two nurses, the stretcher rolled away fast through a door marked SURGERY. In its wake a housekeeping aide mopped a trail of bright blood drops.

"And Lizzie Snow," Tara's mother finished. "By not giving up on me."

Tara bit her lip. "Is she going to die?"

"No, honey. Deputy Snow is going to be fine."

Her mom's arm tightened again. Ever since they'd been home, her mom had been saying that everything bad was all over, and from now on life was going to be good.

But Tara didn't believe it. Aaron was dead, for one thing, and she still felt guilty about it. If she hadn't gone off with him, if she hadn't been hitchhiking; if, if, if.

And somehow the worst of it was that her mom seemed to think *she* knew what Tara was going through. But she didn't. Being *taken,* sure she was going to die . . . no one could understand.

No one. "Honey?" Her mom peered at her in concern. "Honey, I know what you're—"

"No you *don't,*" Tara spat. "You *don't* know, stop *saying* you do." Screaming now and not caring. "No one understands *any* of it! You're all just *stupid* and ugly and . . . and *bad*!"

She was on her feet, sobbing, the fear coming back again and the shame along with it because it was *all her fault* . . .

"Tara." Her mother's arms were around her suddenly. "Tara, listen. You don't think I get it?"

And here it all came again, it's all going to be all right, blah-di-blah. But what she heard next was not what Tara expected:

"You're right. Nothing will ever be the same."

Tara glanced up. "How . . . how do you know?"

Her mother looked weary. "I never meant to tell you. Now I have to. But first, you have to promise that afterward . . . that you'll still love me."

Tara's throat ached with tears. "Okay," she said, meaning it.

The clinic nurse beckoned. Peg stood. "Come on, then, let's get this appointment over with."

Tara got up, too. "And then I have a story to tell you," said her mother. "I don't think you're going to like it."

She sighed, guiding Tara forward. "But it's a story you need to know. So you'll believe you're okay."

"Okay," Tara repeated, thinking *one step. Then another.* Not that hard if you just took them one at a time. So maybe—

"Hello, Tara." The nurse smiled kindly at them.

So maybe her mother really did know best.

SIXTEEN

FIVE DAYS LATER

Unidentified white female, age approximately ten years, hair blond, eyes blue . . .

"Those space-age polymers worked."

Saying this, Dylan glanced over at Lizzie from behind the wheel of his own car, a beautifully kept old red Saab 900. He'd insisted on driving her to the medical examiner's office in Augusta to view the body.

Nicki. It might be . . .

"In the vest?" she replied. He'd kept up a line of chatter all the way from Bearkill, on country roads to Houlton and then on I-95.

"Yeah," he said. "Frickin' bullet packed a helluva punch and I've still got a bruise the size of Texas on my chest. But since the rescuers didn't have to pick me up in pieces and stuff them in a body bag, I'd call it a success."

Engaging her in small talk was his attempt to keep her mind occupied, she supposed. That way maybe she wouldn't dwell on the small body awaiting her identification.

But it wasn't working. *Cause of death, blunt-force trauma.*

"You never asked how come they found us there," Dylan said.

"And I wouldn't bring it up, but you owe that office assistant of yours a big vote of thanks."

That got her full attention at last. "Missy Brantwell? But I thought—"

"Right, that she'd hightailed it out of town for the last time along with everyone else. Which she had. Got her mom and her kid situated. But then she came back."

Oh, for pete's sake. But of course; that was Missy.

"Couldn't raise you on the phone or the radio, or find me or Chevrier, either, so she called Trey Washburn," Dylan said. "He started phoning around, and once he heard about Chevrier calling for backup, he had some creative suggestions about where to look for you."

Now they were south of Bangor, speeding through flat, empty territory with nothing but a thin scrim of evergreen trees on either side: each exit miles from the previous one, gas stations and convenience stores sited directly at the ends of the ramps, signs visible from the interstate.

"Trey knew about the sheep hut," she said.

A state cop flew by with his lights on, no siren. When they caught up, the trooper had a car pulled over and was approaching. Dylan lifted an index finger in salute as he drove past, and the trooper nodded sideways in reply without taking his eyes off the targeted vehicle.

"Right," said Dylan. "Trey called the forest service and the 'copter pilot said she thought she could probably beat the flames back enough with the rotors, 'cause it was raining by then."

The storm, when it finally came, had been historic; two-plus inches of rain overnight and more the next day, dousing the fires decisively. Not that Lizzie had noticed any of it; she'd been busy learning to breathe again after surgery for a punctured lung.

The first exit sign for Augusta appeared. He pulled out and passed a small sedan, then got over to the slow lane once more.

"And Trey was right," Dylan said. "About his hunch. So here you are now."

"So here I am," she repeated shakily. Once the chest tube was out there'd been little reason to keep her in the hospital.

Or so she had insisted, and at last Emily Ektari had given in. They rode in silence awhile. Then: "What about the cars?"

Dylan laughed humorlessly. "Turns out Cam Petry flew here. Bangor to Portland, there to Houlton. Then she rented a car."

He pulled out and passed a fuel truck. "And Jane had a Lexus she'd bought back in New Haven. Both vehicles in the impound lot now."

He returned to the right-hand lane. "Plus the stolen van, that's all of 'em."

The Saab still handled as neatly as ever, she noted, trying not to think about how much she had missed it.

And him. "Snow tonight," she said, looking out at the iron-gray sky.

He glanced at her again. He had been, since the events of a few days ago, unceasingly kind. "Yeah. Lots, they say."

In the heavy rain's aftermath it had turned very cold. Back in Bearkill, people were wearing parkas and boots and mounting plow blades on their pickup trucks.

"Here we are." Dylan took the downtown exit with the ease of long familiarity, wound through back streets along the river, and pulled into a gated parking lot.

Inside the low brick building, the walls were institutional green, the overhead light buzzing fluorescent. He led the way down linoleum-tiled corridors to an office anteroom, then into a large cool open area like a surgical suite.

The clock on the only wall that was not lined with morgue drawers read two o'clock; they were right on time. A young man came in, wearing a lab jacket, corduroy slacks, and Hush Puppies.

He had an ID badge, too, but she didn't bother reading it. Her mouth was dry, her heart hammering. Dylan's hand cupped her elbow.

"Will you know?" he asked.

She nodded. Half the toe tag was in the slot on the drawer's end plate. The other half would be on the body.

The technician grasped the drawer's handle and pulled, and the drawer slid out soundlessly. Inside, the small, defenseless-looking bundle lay wrapped in a white sheet.

The smell of bleach rose from the sheet. "Are you ready?" he asked gently, and she nodded again.

He drew the sheet back, revealing the small, still face with its lavender eyelids, its bluish pinched nostrils and marine-blue lips. A bruise mottled the forehead and one cheek.

Lizzie dug her nails into her palms, bent closer to be sure. Nausea rose up, but as the room swam tiltingly she felt Dylan's hand still gripping her arm.

She stepped back, steadying herself. This child had a broad, flat nose, a dimple in her chin like a vertical knife mark, and curly hair.

And no tiny birthmark. "It's not her."

The technician glanced up questioningly. "You're sure?"

"Quite certain, thank you. This isn't my niece."

Turning away sharply from the body lying before her, she felt nothing but a moment of pride as she realized she'd gotten through it all right. After all the worry over how she might react, what she would do if it turned out—

But it didn't. Because it wasn't Nicki, I came and saw that poor little girl for myself, but it wasn't her it wasn't—

"Lizzie?" said Dylan worriedly when they got back out into the corridor. But she didn't answer, pulling roughly away from him. She made it all the way down the hall into the ladies' room and then into the stall before she began to weep.

"So all that time you spent with Peg wasn't really a waste after all," said Dylan a few hours later.

They were in Area 51's familiar barroom, decorated with North Woods memorabilia: yellowing photos of beast-drawn carts, a cross-cut saw blade as tall as a man, bills of sale for the lumber camp's provisions—salt, sugar, lard.

"Yeah, you think?" A small laugh made Lizzie's chest hurt.

But it was true. If she hadn't kept Peg in the loop, then Peg wouldn't have shown up with a gun.

And that would've been bad. Meanwhile Lizzie's own weapon had been returned to her; her hand went reflexively to it just to make sure.

"Hey," she added, "you never know when persistence will pay off. Although in this case it was just my own personal brand of damn-fool stubbornness, I guess."

Chevrier looked up. "Don't bust your own stones, Lizzie, all right? That's my job."

"Yeah, okay, boss," she shot back at him. But she was still glad to hear it.

Leaning back, she looked around at what remained of dinner: burgers for everyone but herself. She'd managed a scrambled egg. Dylan and Chevrier were there, and beside Missy, Trey Washburn was returned from a farm where he'd been moving the animals back in.

Any thoughts Lizzie might've had about Missy and Trey being a couple were banished by the way Trey looked at Lizzie now: like a dessert he'd thought had been snatched away from him but now here it was again, as delicious as ever.

"Anyway, if you ask me," said Chevrier, "I think all Jane Crimmins's I'm-so-unstable act has always been fake, and now it's just another plank in the cockamamie insanity defense the legal hotshots're trying to build for her."

The attorneys who'd petitioned the court to be allowed to represent Jane Crimmins pro bono, he meant, since the county was not exactly swarming with lawyers who were experienced in murder cases, their request had been granted.

He drank some beer. "I still want to know how this Gemerle guy picked the spot he did, though. To bury the girl, I mean."

Trey Washburn looked up. "Well. I've been doing some research about that. What?" he added at Chevrier's look. "There's plenty on the Internet, you know, you don't have to be a cop."

Chevrier nodded skeptically. "Okay, Doc, let's hear it."

"Well," Trey began, "from what I've read it seems the only decent thing the guy ever did was volunteer firefighting. Those big fires in Vermont, remember? Gemerle was seventeen that year."

Chevrier's look changed to one of interest as Trey went on: "Gemerle went up there, joined a crew."

"No kidding. So he'd have known . . ."

Trey looked vindicated. "Yup. Same kind of rural area we've got here. And wasn't that Rusty Harris's van he stole, from up in Allagash?"

Now Chevrier got it. "Sure was. Rusty was retired from firefighting per se, but he still had a scanner in the van's dash."

"Right again," said Trey. "So he'd have heard where the fires were, what he'd find up there, too. Tools, maybe the crates they came in . . ."

"Everything he'd need," Chevrier agreed.

Listening, Lizzie winced at the misery in her ribs. She'd skipped the pain pills to keep her mind clear for the morgue visit, and afterward had forgotten them.

When I get home, she promised herself as Chevrier finished his beer and turned to her.

"You get your applications sent? Better do it soon, Lizzie, if you want to get out of here before winter really settles in."

For the Boston PD, he meant. Her old job, catching homicide cases in the metro area; bright lights, big city.

She frowned at her Coke glass, took another painful breath, and said: "Yeah, well. Change of plan. I'm not going."

She looked up. "I'm staying here." She felt their astonished eyes on her. "I just . . ."

Trey Washburn's face lit up. Missy looked pleased, too, and Dylan worked unsuccessfully to hide a smile of surprised relief.

Only Chevrier remained expressionless. "How come?"

Which was the question she'd been asking herself, too. When she'd talked to her old lieutenant again, he'd made it clear that her vacated spot would be available to her once more, no problem.

Even the high-rise condo overlooking the river, still full of the rugs and furnishings she'd lovingly collected for it, had not yet sold; in a week she could be sleeping in her old bed.

She closed her eyes, imagining it, then opened them to find Area 51's enormous clear glass jar of pickled eggs still looming beside the antique cash register on the polished mahogany bar. A rerun of *The Andy Griffith Show* was on the big-screen TV, the sound turned down low so the scanner on the shelf behind the bar was audible.

The scanner was always on when she was in here now, just as the bartenders knew she drank single malt when it wasn't Coke; they kept a fifth of Battlehill under the counter for her. Then there was Rascal, waiting patiently for her out in the Blazer right now.

But the dog wasn't the reason, either. "I don't know, boss. Guess maybe I just don't want to be a quitter."

She got up, the bandage over her ribs pulling annoyingly, and dropped some money on the table.

"Anyway, I guess if I'm still welcome here I'll come to work tomorrow, and for the foreseeable future."

Nobody replied, but nobody had to. Chevrier's silent nod of agreement was all she needed. Flipping the collar of her leather jacket up against the chill, she stepped outside where half-frozen rain dripped steadily from the AREA 51 sign.

The fires on the ridge had come very near to burning Bearkill to the ground; partly melted, the big-eyed alien with the cocktail glass in his hand looked as if he'd been hit by a science-fiction ray gun, his glowing head smooshed sideways by heat.

But you survived, too, didn't you, buddy? As she walked down the gleaming wet sidewalk to where the Blazer waited, the doused-campfire scent of drenched embers drifted in the night air. But behind that floated the crisp smell of snow, from the mountains where the ski lifts had at last begun operating.

"Hey." The voice came from behind her.

"Hey, yourself." It was Dylan, hands in pockets, shoulders under his black topcoat hunched up against the cold. He caught up and walked alongside her.

"I heard from the New Haven cops. They dug up Gemerle's yard like you wanted. Found bones in it. An infant's. And some others. Adult women, one young girl."

So she'd been right. She wondered how many of them would be identified and how many consigned to unmarked graves; even dental records worked only if you had some idea of which dentist to ask.

"So that's where Cam Petry's child got to," she said.

Dylan nodded slowly. "Yeah. D'you suppose she ever found out? There at the end, do you think he told her?"

"That he'd killed the baby?" She gazed down the empty street. "I don't know. I hope not. Jane might've told her, though."

She took a deep breath. "But the big question, when it comes to whether or not Jane told the truth in the end, was . . ."

"Yeah. Did she love Cam?" Dylan put in. "Or did she hate her?"

". . . was could they forgive each other," Lizzie finished.

He nodded, purse-lipped. Then: "I'm glad you're staying."

Behind them Trey Washburn came out of the bar alone, headed for Lizzie, but then saw Dylan and turned away toward his truck. In his puffy down jacket he looked even larger and more bearlike than usual.

But just as good, as genuine and well intentioned as ever. She would have to have a talk soon with Trey, to explain . . . what?

Even she didn't know. "As far as staying goes, I've still got some unfinished business here," she told Dylan.

Meaning Nicki; it was going to take more than a few weeks or months to find a little girl who'd been missing for years, if she was here at all.

If she was even alive. Dylan poked the curb with the toe of his shoe, then spoke quietly.

"I miss you, Lizzie. I know you don't want to hear it, but I do. And I could be wrong but I think you feel the same."

He looked up at her. "I know you do, in fact."

"What about your new girlfriend?"

Trey got into his truck, the interior light showing his kind, honest face for an instant before he slammed the heavy door. Then after a few seconds the light went out.

"That's not going to work." Dylan shook his head ruefully. "I was kidding myself. No sense kidding her, too."

He waited until Trey pulled a U-turn and drove off, then went on: "I'm going back to Bangor tonight. Or I could . . ."

He stopped, started again. "Or I could come home with you. If you want."

She was tempted. But that way lay disaster.

He spread his hands in appeal. "It's never going to work with anyone else, Lizzie. I know that now. I'm in it for the long haul with you, pretty much whether I like it or not."

That made her smile. "How flattering."

His answering grin, darkly handsome as ever, nearly trashed her resolve. "Yeah. Well. Anyway, see you around."

Turning, he strode through the icy rain to his car and got in. As he pulled away from the curb, the light in the AREA 51 sign went out, leaving her in darkness.

She got into the Blazer, where Rascal's slobbery kisses didn't substitute for the ones she could have had. But it would be too ungrateful to let the dog know that, so she smoothed his long satiny ears, praising him in a way that would have been excessive if he hadn't been such a noble beast.

The Blazer started with a roar. She snapped the headlights on and set the wipers to sweeping smearily across the windshield. By now the rain was an icy torrent, sheeting down the glass.

At home, a fast trip around the cold, dark yard satisfied Rascal; once inside, she fixed herself a toddy of whiskey and hot lemonade, passing up the pain pills yet again, and took her mug with her to bed.

Flannel pajamas, clean cotton socks, and the patchwork quilt that Missy Brantwell's mother had made for her all conspired with the soft lamplight in her pine-paneled bedroom to make her feel, if not much less lonely, then at least warm and safe.

Hey, it ain't Boston. And I still hate knotty pine. But it'll do. She pulled the quilt up snugly and settled against the pillows with Rascal sprawled by her side.

It'll do just fine for now. She'd opened her book, a history of the French people in Maine's St. John Valley, and had taken the first soothing swallow of her hot drink when the high-low signal tone from the scanner unit on the kitchen counter alerted her.

"All units . . ." Springing out of bed, she was dressed, had her boots on, and was tightening her duty belt when she realized:

No pain. Not much, anyway. Certainly not more than she could handle. "Rascal, you hold down the fort here for me, okay?"

The dog looked up wisely, then slowly lowered himself, his huge paws crossed in an attitude of patience. Lizzie grabbed her badge, keys, and duty weapon, not bothering to turn on the outside light; she knew her own front walk by heart.

Outside, she breathed in the ice-washed night air. *Alive,* she thought, savoring it.

Something cold kissed her cheek. It was snow, swirling down unseen like a blessing in disguise.

ABOUT THE AUTHOR

SARAH GRAVES lives with her husband in Eastport, Maine, one remote rural road away from the Allagash wilderness territory and the Great North Woods.

sarahgraves.net
Facebook.com/SarahGraves2011
@SarahGraves2011

ABOUT THE TYPE

This book was set in Garamond, a typeface originally designed by the Parisian type cutter Claude Garamond (c. 1500–61). This version of Garamond was modeled on a 1592 specimen sheet from the Egenolff-Berner foundry, which was produced from types assumed to have been brought to Frankfurt by the punch cutter Jacques Sabon (c. 1520–80).

Claude Garamond's distinguished romans and italics first appeared in *Opera Ciceronis* in 1543–44. The Garamond types are clear, open, and elegant.